WIZARD for Hire

WIZARD for Hire

SHADOW
MOUNTAIN

TO KRISTA

the girl who works magic at every turn
and makes this world a place worth being.

Interior illustrations by Brandon Dorman

Visit us at ShadowMountain.com

Library of Congress Cataloging-in-Publication Data

Names: Skye, Obert, author.
Title: Wizard for hire / Obert Skye.
Description: Salt Lake City, Utah : Shadow Mountain, [2018] | Summary: After fourteen-year-old Ozzy's scientist parents have been kidnapped, Ozzy's only help may be a classified ad that says, "Wizard for hire."
Identifiers: LCCN 2017040909 | ISBN 9781629724126 (hardbound : alk. paper)
Subjects: | CYAC: Friendship—Fiction. | Wizards—Fiction | Parents—Fiction. | Missing persons—Fiction. | Brainwashing—Fiction. | LCGFT: Action and adventure fiction.
Classification: LCC PZ7.S62877 Wk 2018 | DDC [Fic]—dc23
LC record available at https://lccn.loc.gov/2017040909

Printed in the United States of America
LSC Communications, Crawfordsville, IN

10 9 8 7 6 5

It is a fact that all who have lived have lived through some loss and heartache. Yes, there is happiness, but everyone alive experiences sadness at one time or another. If you ache you are not unusual—friends disappoint, betrayal is real, and there is always the possibility of losing someone dear. It is worrisome to begin a story beneath shades of shadow and gloom but it is wise to remember that despite all the worry there is magic afoot.

CHAPTER ONE

SUCH A SHAME TO RUIN THIS BRIGHT, LAZY SUNNY DAY

In the dense Oregon woods, there was a small cabin, a little wooden home with a crooked green roof and round windows. The cabin was surrounded by aspens and oaks and topped off with clouds that loved to huddle above it. Behind the home was a thin stream that ran parallel to a tall wall of black mossy stone.

As the noon hour arrived, a small hole opened in the clouds, allowing a loose rope of sunlight to drop down. The light coiled up into a mound of warmth, flopping against the ground and lighting up the front steps of the cabin. A man with a dark mustache and thick brown hair sat on the steps. He lifted his right hand above his eyes to look up at the light. Next to the man was a woman with glowing skin and hair the color of milk chocolate. The man was Dr. Emmitt Toffy—the woman, his wife, was also a doctor, but her name was Mia.

Two charming people sitting in front of an interesting cabin in the middle of a lush forest.

Make that three.

Because, next to Mia was Ozzy, their seven-year-old boy with wide, grey eyes. His complexion was dark and his hair was thick and black, like a night with no stars. At seven he was already tall for his age, but thin. He had a deep purple birthmark that covered the pointer finger on his left hand like a single-finger sheath.

Despite the dark complexion, hair, and finger, Ozzy's face was giving the sunlight some competition.

The boy smiled at his parents as he played with a plastic dragon on the steps near his mother.

"I never get tired of this sunshine," Ozzy's father said, still looking up. "I have an affection for light."

"It *is* wonderful," his mother observed. "The forest is perfect, Emmitt. I'm afraid I don't miss the East at all."

Two months before, they had moved with Ozzy into the isolated Oregon forest. Emmitt was a neuroscientist. He was also an inventor. Mia was a brilliant theoretical psychologist, studying how people thought and acted and dreamed. They had lived successfully back East for many years, but they had recently sold everything and, under the cloak of darkness, taken Ozzy across the country to Oregon.

The cabin they had purchased was hidden from the world. There were no roads leading up to it or even trails. They received no mail, had no visitors, and since they had arrived, Ozzy had seen no one other than his parents. The inside of their wooden home was filled from floor to ceiling with boxes that had yet to be opened or organized. The only place that had any semblance of composure was Ozzy's space. His room was in the attic, which was accessible by climbing twenty thin wooden stairs. Engraved on the front of each stair were dozens of small black stars that made it look like Ozzy was traveling the cosmos to reach his room. Other than that, the inside of the house looked like a convention of cardboard and chaos and it didn't seem as if the doctors were in any hurry to remedy that. They had unpacked only the essentials for the moment.

"The boxes can wait," Dr. Emmitt always said. "Today is about what's already unpacked."

The family had spent their first few weeks walking through the trees and planting a garden back by the stream. Ozzy's parents taught him how to do things for himself and let the boy read to them to improve his mind. At night he would be tucked into bed in his small attic room, where a single round window let in moonbeams and lit the space in a magical light. While Ozzy slept, his father would work in the basement and his mother would put pen to paper in the ground-floor office, both laboring over things that Ozzy knew nothing about. But today there was no laboring, just sunshine and a bit of resting on the steps after a small hike.

The image was idyllic—a mother and father and their small child on the porch steps of a quaint mountain cabin.

There were city families that would have paid good money to have their pictures taken in such a scene—a family portrait they could show their friends as proof of how close they were to nature and each other. For the Toffys, however, it wasn't an act—it was their life. They were safe and hidden away from something of which Ozzy was completely unaware.

The grey-eyed child moved his plastic dragon into the soil of a potted flower on the porch. He pillaged the bright azaleas.

"Ozzy," his mother said with a warm smile, "your dragon might enjoy running through the stream more than dirtying its talons here in the mud. And you're old enough to play behind the house by yourself."

"Just don't go beyond sight of the cabin," his father said.

Ozzy grinned. He collected his dragon and, like a small, independent adult, walked around the house and behind the cabin.

The stream wasn't more than a couple of feet wide and a few inches deep, but it ran all year and filled the air with the constant burble of tumbling water. It originated from a spring near a dark stone wall and wove through the nearby trees and down away from the cabin. The dark wall was covered in moss and the stain of a million years of wet skies. Animals of all kinds gathered often near the water to drink. A skinny brown fox who had been doing just that saw the boy and darted off.

Ozzy knelt and set his dragon in the water.

A cold trickle of liquid washed around his small fingers and he shivered. The toy stomped through the water and over the slick rocks.

Ozzy missed his home in New York, but memories of it were already beginning to fade—the few friends he'd had, the store on the corner that sold cheese and bread, Jonathan the doorman who always gave him sweets.

The dragon splashed through the water as Ozzy created new and mossier memories.

"Attack, ambush . . ."

Ozzy heard his mother scream from the front of the cabin.

The young boy dropped his toy and kneeled tall.

His mother screamed again.

He could hear his father shouting and unknown voices shouting back.

Ozzy stood up and ran. His steps were uneven as he bolted forward in what looked like a prolonged stumble. He reached the front of the house and saw several men in green clothing. Some were in the cabin. Two of them were pulling his parents into the trees and away from the scene.

"Mom!" Ozzy screamed.

"Ozzy!" she yelled.

Ozzy froze; fear made it impossible for him to move. He was too scared to help his parents, but there was no way he could turn and run away. His feet felt like roots planted deep in the ground and hardened from age.

"Ozzy!" his dad screamed. "Ozzy—"

One of the men put a rag over Emmitt's mouth. Another did the same to Mia. Ozzy's parents thrashed and kicked, but their mouths were covered and they were no match for the hulking men who had them bound. Ozzy's father was struck behind the head and collapsed. Mia saw the strike and lost consciousness from the horror of it all.

The men picked up the two Toffys and threw them over their shoulders like rolled-up rugs. Then, as if they were subtle brushstrokes on the edge of a painted forest, they faded into the trees and were no longer discernible.

Two of the green men stepped out onto the porch and spotted Ozzy.

"Hey!" one of them yelled. "Stay right there!"

The man yelling was thin, with a black beard and a hooked nose. Ozzy stared as the man slowly began to move closer. The look on Blackbeard Hooknose's face was sinister. The other man was short, with red hair and an uneasy look.

"We're not going to hurt you," Hooknose said calmly. "Don't move."

Ozzy shivered violently and his feet broke free from the soil. The two men lunged forward as Ozzy spun around and took off running. He ran back behind the cabin, across the stream, and scurried up over the black wall. Once there, Ozzy jumped down under a fallen tree and hid himself beneath the branches of a feathery bush.

He could hear Hooknose stomping around nearby.

"Come out, boy! We won't hurt you."

Ozzy stayed perfectly still.

The red-haired man moved closer.

Through one of the cracks in the bush Ozzy watched the men searching for him. He closed his eyes and clamped his teeth, wishing he could disappear and reappear someplace safe.

He opened his eyes to discover that his wish hadn't come true.

The men yelled a few more times before Blackbeard hollered out, "Forget it, Eric. Let's search the home."

"What about the kid?" the short man asked.

The hole in the clouds above cinched up and took every bit of sunlight and warmth with it.

"Leave him. We've got the doctors."

Ozzy didn't dare even quiver.

Tears dropped from his eyes like wet coins. They plunked softly into the pool of water collecting in the dirt around him, creating a hopeless wishing well.

The men climbed over the stone wall and returned to the cabin to do some pillaging of their own. Ozzy stayed where he was, too frightened to move. Eventually the sun went down and all sounds of anyone in or around the cabin ceased.

The world was silent.

The boy worked his way out of his hiding place and, slowly and cautiously, snuck back to the front of the cabin.

What he found was sickening. There were boxes and

papers tossed all over the front porch. The door was open and he could see that inside the home had been ransacked as well. His parents were nowhere to be seen.

Ozzy stood like a small broken tree. He hung his head and cried.

If anyone had been there to witness the scene, their hearts would have broken for him. But no one was there. In fact, Ozzy was very much alone, and he would remain that way for quite some time.

It's terrible to be lonely.

It's even worse to be lonely, seven, and on your own.

CHAPTER TWO

YOU'VE JUST NEVER BEEN OUT IN THE WOODS ALONE

Ozzy was left for dead. He was a seven-year-old child in a thick, lonely forest with no real knowledge of where he was or what he should do. His only desire was to see his parents again and that desire was not going to be fulfilled anytime soon. He would have buried his head in the rich brown soil and given up, but his will to survive kicked in just enough for him to drink a little water and eat a little food.

The cabin had been properly torn apart by the men who had taken Ozzy's parents. All the boxes on the main floor and the basement had been rifled through. And his small attic room at the top of the starry staircase had been turned inside out.

It was a rustic home with no electricity and because of that the nights were cold and dark, and fear like Ozzy's seven-year old brain couldn't even imagine would take over until, exhausted, he would fall into a sleep that offered no comfort.

Each day, however, the pain lessened in tiny, unfelt increments. As months slipped by, the relief became more measurable. The nights weren't as frightening—in fact, they became somewhat familiar. And his slumber offered dreams that would replay memories of his parents' faces and give him reason to smile in his sleep.

In the light of day, Ozzy would sit on the porch steps waiting for his parents to return. When that grew too painful he would search through the boxes he was strong enough to move and open. In the basement, he found crate after crate of dried and canned food. His parents, it seemed, had been planning to stay hidden and fed for a very long time.

On the main floor, he pushed and shoved the boxes to make a maze of sorts.

Outside of the house, the bushes grew lush and wild. They began to consume and cloak the exterior. By the time Ozzy was ten, the small cabin resembled more a large leafy knoll than an abode. The trees and bushes around the home had begun to work their roots and branches through the walls and windows. The invading growth made the place look like a home that a wizard—or a talking beaver—might live in, and camouflaged it nicely. A stranger walking by wouldn't notice there was even a home there. Of course, due to the remote location, no strangers ever walked by—or even near.

By the time Ozzy turned twelve, the cloaked house was just that.

Now, as night began to fall, Ozzy stood up on the porch stairs and looked into the sky. He was wearing a white T-shirt that had belonged to his father and shorts that he had made from a pair of his father's pants. He wore no shoes. Because of that, his feet were tough. He could easily walk barefoot on the stones around his home. His black hair was long and his grey eyes had darkened a bit over time.

Ozzy felt at home by himself and almost content. He had lived off of stockpiled food and what he had grown in the garden. He had no way of knowing how unusual it was for someone to have a basement full of canned food. He thought perhaps every boy had their parents taken from them, that it was par for the course to live alone in a vegetation-cloaked cabin without any influence from the outside world. He figured he would grow old, meet a girl, have a son, and then one day be taken away from that child.

The circle of life.

Ozzy turned and walked into the cloaked house. Like most nights, he planned to read by candlelight until he was tired. It was no small miracle that Ozzy was a voracious reader when his parents were taken. Because of that, he had gone through all the books that were on bookshelves and any he'd found in boxes. His vocabulary and understanding had grown in leaps and bounds. His parents had been obsessed with the mind; many of the books they owned were medical or philosophical in nature. Recently, however, Ozzy had discovered a few large boxes filled with titles he hadn't seen before. Many of them dealt with science and invention and psychology, but in one of the heaviest boxes he found books of adventure and fantasy—Lord of the Rings, Harry Potter, *The Hitchhiker's Guide to the Galaxy*. The words were all more imaginative and fun than the books he had been reading. And the stories took him away from the cloaked house and into castles and caves and spaceships that were exciting, magical, and improbable.

The books had also given Ozzy something to hope for. Reading them made it seem entirely possible that he, too, had a gift of some sort, a power or wondrous ability. He just needed to figure it out. He had begun writing a short list of gifts he could eliminate since he had already tried and failed. So far the list consisted of flight, super speed, and whistling.

Ozzy gathered some food and walked through the maze of boxes on the main floor, making his way to the starry stairs. He could see the small black stars engraved into the fronts of all twenty steps. Climbing to his attic room always made him feel like he was ascending to the heavens. He grabbed the wooden ball on the top of the newel post and pulled himself forward. As he did, his foot slipped on the edge of the stair and he fell forward. He landed on his stomach and hit his head against the fifth stair.

His eyes saw additional stars.

He turned and sat up on the third stair. Glancing down to assess his condition, he noticed that he was holding the round wooden ball from the top of the newel post.

Ozzy looked at the wooden knob. It was about the size of a tennis ball, with a base like the bottom of a lightbulb. At the end of the base, however, there was a two-inch metal rod sticking out. The end of the rod was shaped like an eight-pointed star. Ozzy turned his head as he sat on the third step and looked at the stars on the stairs.

"I wonder . . . ," he said.

He turned further and pressed the end of the metal star up against one of the shapes engraved on the first step. The size and design matched the painted stars.

He studied the object in his hand.

Ozzy felt the stars stamped on the front of the first and second stairs. They were all solid and simple. He felt the stars on the front of the third step. Two stars over from the right edge, his fingers detected a slight difference. This star felt different than the others, and when he pushed on it there was a very slight give.

Ozzy placed the tip of the metal key over the star; it lined up perfectly. He carefully pushed the rod right into the stair.

With almost no effort, the strange key slid in.

Ozzy let go and took a moment to collect himself. He grabbed the wooden ball and turned it. There was a soft clicking noise followed by the top of the third step popping open. It rose to reveal a hidden storage area as large as the step itself.

"Whoa."

Inside the stair there was a carton about the size of a shoe box. He pulled it out and saw that the lid was taped shut. He set the box on the second stair. The boy felt around on the rest of the stairs but he could find no other stars that felt any different.

Gathering the box under his arm, he quickly climbed up to his room.

The small attic space was cozy and tucked away. Some tree branches had begun to grow into the walls and curl through the wood, and like other parts of the house, it seemed to only add to the general enchantment of the place. Ozzy's bed was soft; there was a small wooden night-stand next to it. In one corner of the room was a cloth-covered chair; books were scattered everywhere. Any book he had read had been brought up and stacked onto one of the many piles. His bed was cocooned by all of them. The room had one single round window that squeaked mightily whenever it was opened.

Ozzy set the box on his bed and lit a candle. The small flame illuminated his room nicely. He sat on his bed and put the container on his lap.

Moving it around, he studied each side. It was made of a hard, dark material—not rubber, not metal, but some-thing in between. The lid was like a shoebox and was sealed with thick grey tape. Written in marker on top of the box was the word *Clark*.

Ozzy grabbed a small pocketknife he kept on his nightstand and carefully sliced the tape open. Then, with more excitement than he had felt in a while, he grasped the edge of the lid and pulled it open.

Ozzy smiled.

Inside the box was an old cassette player. It was wide and long and had a cassette tape already in it. There were six buttons and a six-inch square of silver painted on the top of it. *Toffy* was written in gold marker across the bottom of it. Having no idea what a cassette tape was, much less a cassette player, Ozzy pulled the machine out of the box and stared at it in awe. Beneath it in the box there were a dozen carefully stacked cassette tapes.

As interesting as the small machine was, the box held something Ozzy thought was far more intriguing. Lying there on top of the cassette tapes was what looked to be a black bird. Ozzy reached in and gently lifted the creature. It was lighter than he'd expected; its wings were an odd sort of plastic fitted between thin wires. It had a tail of tin and a golden beak. Its feet were sculpted and each talon was tipped with copper. Its two eyes were shut and attached to its round head. Wire-like feathers stuck out the top. The body of the bird was about five inches long and cylindrical.

Ozzy studied every inch of it, looking for a button to push or a switch to turn on. There were nonc. Like the cassette machine, the bird had a wide line of silver painted along its back.

"Brilliant."

Ozzy had no idea what it really might be, but he was happy he had found it. Something with a face to keep inside and near him. Clinging to the bird with one hand, he played with the cassette player with the other. Even after figuring out how to get the tapes in and out, pressing play, and shaking it a little, nothing happened. Still, he kept trying to make either the bird or the machine do something.

A couple of hours later, Ozzy blew out the candle and lay back in his bed.

It had been over five years since his parents had disappeared into the trees and this was the happiest he had been since. Sure, the things he'd found didn't seem to *do* anything, but they had belonged to his parents, they had been important enough to hide, and one of them had a name. *Clark.*

CHAPTER THREE

EVIDENCE OF WHAT HE WAS LIKE

The next day the sun came out in full force. Like a skilled pugilist it pounded light through the branches and into shadows it had never broken up before. Water from the stream tasted better. The dried carrots from the basement seemed almost fresh—and Ozzy had Clark.

All morning he had studied the cassette player and the bird. At noon he had taken them outside to observe them under the bright light.

Ozzy set Clark on the porch step right next to him and focused on the machine.

"There has to be a way to start this," Ozzy told the lifeless bird.

Clark didn't reply.

The cassette player was ten inches wide, twelve and a half inches long, and two inches tall. Ozzy knew this because he had measured it with a ruler. There was a square of silver paint on the top that matched the strip of silver on Clark's back, and a plastic insert that popped up so you could slide tapes into it. It had six buttons—one for play, one for stop, one for record, one for fast-forward, one for reverse, and one for eject.

Ozzy pressed eject and the tape popped up again. He pulled it out of the machine and twisted the two sprockets with his fingers. One side of the tape was labeled *Approximations*; a word Ozzy didn't totally understand. The other side was labeled *Results*. Ozzy didn't care what the tape contained; his only thought was that it might have the sound of his parents' voices, and that to him seemed like a magical possibility.

"I know machines need electricity to power them," Ozzy said to Clark. "We used to have power when we lived in New York. It was a big place. The buildings there were taller than trees, and they had all kind of foods. Not just dried and canned things. I remember a man who sold huge pretzels from a cart in the park."

Ozzy put the cassette tape back into the player and looked up at the sunlight coming through the trees. He let the warmth soak into his skin and stayed still as it worked its way into his bones and being.

The last place he had been with his parents was here on the now-overgrown steps. The plastic dragon he had been playing with was still in the stream behind the house, buried by years of dirt and leaves and sadness.

"I don't like thinking about them," Ozzy said to

himself. “I know I should, but every thought makes me feel horrible.”

“I feel the same way—maybe worse.”

Ozzy froze.

Something beside him had spoken. He wanted to turn his head and look, but, like the moment his parents had been snatched away, he was paralyzed.

“It’s okay to feel bad,” the voice said. “And you shouldn’t be afraid to think of them.”

“Who’s saying that?” Ozzy asked, still too scared to turn his head.

“Me.”

Ozzy felt a small prick on his left arm. He screamed and scurried backward up onto the porch and against the house.

“Easy,” the voice said. “Panic isn’t a good look on you.”

Something black hopped towards Ozzy—and he saw it was Clark. Except now the bird was standing on his feet, his wide dark eyes and wings open. He hopped closer to Ozzy and the boy howled again.

“That scream isn’t going to make us any friends,” Clark said. “I mean, it shows you’re vulnerable, but is that a trait people like? You should be glad you’re in a forest and nobody can hear you.”

“You’re . . . talking,” Ozzy said needlessly.

“I think communication is important,” the bird reported. “And the sunlight seems to have restored my spirits. I have to admit it feels pretty good to be alive again.”

Ozzy just stared.

"Sorry . . . I should tell you that I feed off the light. Any light, really, but I guess it took some real sunshine to kick me back into gear."

Ozzy's expression did not change.

"I can tell you're confused, so let me explain. The sun is a mass of incandescent gas, a giantic nuclear furnace. It sends its rays billions of miles through outer space and when they hit the silver strip on my back, they sort of juice me up."

"I know how the sun works," Ozzy managed to say.

"You do look smart. What happened to your finger?"

Ozzy held up his hand and looked at his red finger. "It's a birthmark."

"It's cool looking," Clark said. "The color reminds me of a bird I once knew. She was beautiful."

"Thanks, I guess. So you've been in that box the whole time?"

"I remember being created, pieced together, and brought to life by a man who, judging by appearance, was your . . . father?"

"My dad built you?"

"Was Dr. Emmitt your dad?"

"Yes—so you know him?"

"I do. He built me to be a sounding board for his ideas. He would talk to me as he worked. We're pretty close."

"What about my mom?"

"The woman? I remember moments with her. She would come around while he was working. She was smart."

"Why did my dad pack you away? I mean, I never saw you."

"I don't know. One day, he took me out of the light and my will faded. From there things are nothing but dark."

"Will you stay with me here?"

Clark tilted his tiny metal head and gazed at Ozzy.

"I mean . . . you won't leave, right?"

"Not unless you pack me away," Clark said.

"I won't."

"Good, because I prefer the light. And I'm no trouble. I don't even need food. Although I do enjoy the texture of chewing certain things. Oh yeah—I'm attracted to stuff made of metal. That's not weird, is it? No, that can't be weird. Do you mind if I take a short flight up into the sunshine?"

"You'll come back?"

"Wow, you've got a real fear of abandonment. That's sad. But don't worry—I'll always come back."

Clark flew up off the porch and straight up into the blue sky. He twisted and dove down, letting the wind catch his wings.

True to his word, after a few minutes he turned and glided back down to the porch. He landed near Ozzy and then hopped up and perched himself on his right knee.

Ozzy studied the bird in awe.

"Are there any other birds around here?" Clark asked.

"None like you. But there are lots of regular ones."

Clark brushed back the wiry feathers on his head with his wings. "I don't mind regular. There was this sparrow I kind of liked outside of your dad's work. We sort of had a thing, but we were divided by glass."

"Sorry."

"That's okay. There are plenty of birds in the sky. At least that's what your dad used to tell me before he shut me down. Besides, my real love is metal."

Clark cocked his head and looked Ozzy in the eyes.

"Why are you named Clark?"

"I'm not sure. Probably because it's a strong name?"

"Right, but does it mean something? Like . . . Computerized Living Animal Research Bird?"

"Then my name would be Clarb."

Ozzy continued to stare at Clark.

"I bet I know what you're thinking," the bird said. "I'm actually good at assessing people's thoughts. Your father built me to be observant. Besides, your grey eyes are an open book."

"Okay, then what am I thinking?"

"You're curious about how I work. You're excited thinking about the silver paint on my back and how the sunlight brought me to life. I bet you're also wondering if the light that brought me to life could do the same for the cassette machine."

Ozzy's expression was one of amazement.

"Go ahead and try it," Clark said, pointing his wing

toward the small machine sitting on the steps. "It's been in the sun for a few minutes. It probably works now."

Ozzy scooted over to the machine and touched it. It *was* warm from the sun. He looked at Clark and then reached out and pressed *play*. There was a slight whirring, followed by the sound of Ozzy's father's voice.

"In times of suspicion and ignorance, people turn to superstition to answer their problems. We must help those who do so see the error of their ways."

Ozzy didn't want to, but he began to cry. Clark, being both observant and compassionate, tried to do the same. Unfortunately, it's difficult for birds to shed a tear, and trying to move his shoulders like Ozzy made him look like he'd been accidentally electrocuted.

"I'll just look sad," Clark offered.

Ozzy played tape after tape. Most of them were filled with his father talking about the human brain and experiments he was doing at the university where he taught. He listed different test and failures. Some of the tapes were boring, but Ozzy's favorite was the one labeled *WC SUBJECTS*; it contained the stories of five different people who had done remarkably stupid things. Another tape was labeled *BEN FOLDS FIVE*. When he played that tape, he was surprised by the sound of music. It was exhilarating and filled his head with emotions he had never felt before.

"What is this stuff?" Ozzy asked.

"Um, music. You humans are always trying to sing

things, but it's us birds that do it best. Your father used to play this tape constantly."

I wanna be lonely. When seconds pass slowly, and years go flying by.

The music filled the forest and caused Ozzy's heart to simultaneously sink and soar. He listened to the entire cassette and then switched tapes and listened to his dad's voice until the machine finally stopped, a few hours after the sun went down.

CHAPTER FOUR

WONDERING WHO I AM

The cloaked house became a much different place with Clark around. The bird needed light to live, but he could gather strength from the weak glow of a cloudy day. He also had the ability to store enough energy to keep himself active through most of the night. At times, he would need the assistance of candlelight to recharge. Or he would shut down for a few hours until the sun rose again. But as soon as he was placed in any light, he would always come alive once more.

On sunny days Clark would fly off on long excursions and bring back news of birds he had seen and been rejected by. He would travel to the ocean and return with seashells. He would fly to the mountains and come back with pebbles and leaves. He would scout the forest and return to tell tales that Ozzy listened to carefully and with great interest.

As much as Ozzy loved having Clark around, Ozzy was equally taken with the new wonder of hearing his father's voice. Most days he would spend hours listening to his dad talk about boring things like particle decay and brain peptides. Ozzy didn't mind the topic because it was as if his father was there with him.

He had listened to all the tapes. As he listened to the last one, he was thrilled to find that there was a brief instance of his mother's voice. She said only a few words, but it was magic. She had come in as Ozzy's father was recording, and before he shut off the machine, she said, "Do you think you might like to take a break? Ozzy's awake and asking for you."

The recording stopped after that.

"I'm guessing he took a break," Clark said.

"Yeah, I like to think he took a break to be with me."

"You know what *I* think you've been thinking?" the bird asked.

"What?" Ozzy said.

"That most parents don't just get taken. I mean, I bet you think it's unusual that your parents would move out here where there's no electricity and no other people and then just be snatched up. They must have had to hike to even get here. How did they transport all of these boxes? No offense, but your house looks like a storage unit on the inside."

"I don't know," Ozzy replied.

"Don't you think that maybe we should figure out a few things? Are we just going to stay here forever?"

"No. Someday I'll have to leave to find my parents."

"What day is 'someday'?"

"I don't know," Ozzy answered honestly. "I've just always thought that I'd need to be older. I'm not ever sure what's beyond the next mile of forest. I've seen pictures and read books, of course. J. K. Rowling does a pretty good job of describing Harry's part of the world. But here? You keep finding shells at the ocean and you talk about seeing cars and people, but I don't know what's real and what's not. For example—are dragons real?"

"I think so, but I haven't seen one yet."

"I think they can't be, but then here I am, having a conversation with a metal bird."

Clark hopped onto the porch and looked Ozzy in the eyes. He tilted his head. "So—are you going to do something about it? Do you think someday your parents will just walk up and say, 'Sorry, we got a little distracted. We're back now—how about some soup?'"

"Soup?"

"It's a comfort food," Clark informed him.

"Not the dehydrated kind from the basement."

"Forget the soup; think big picture. What if your parents never return? You have water, but at some point you're going to run out of food. There are fewer boxes of it in the basement every month. You have your garden, but you're still hungry. How often do you think about roasting something meaty over a fire?"

"I wouldn't mind that."

"Just make sure it's not a raven."

"Is that what you are?" Ozzy asked.

"I think so."

"Well, what if the world is only filled with horrible people like the ones who roast ravens and took my parents?" Ozzy asked.

"Wouldn't you like to find that out? Some people are mean and some are nice. You just met some of the bad ones first. You said there were nice people in New York."

"I was little and I can barely remember. Besides, Oregon is so far away from there. I read in a book yesterday that New York is almost twenty-five hundred miles to the east. Twenty-five hundred miles."

"Yeah," Clark said. "But who really knows how long a mile is?"

"Five thousand, two hundred and eighty feet."

"Well, what if you started out walking that way?" Clark pointed east with his right wing. "And you counted each foot? Eventually you'd get there. We could do a little each day. Or at least explore the world around you a bit more. The cloaked house isn't going anywhere."

"I can't lose sight of home."

"Yes you can. Come on." It was a plea that Clark had given to Ozzy many times. He'd begged the boy to move farther into the trees, to find a world outside of the cloaked house, to go to the beach. But Ozzy had always refused. His heart felt certain that if he left, worse things would happen. "Seriously, Oz. It's time to push farther."

Ozzy looked at Clark.

"I'll be right with you," Clark promised.

Ozzy steeled himself and stood up. He turned and faced west. "Okay, but let's go this way, towards the ocean."

"Really?" Clark chirped. "It's the opposite direction of New York, but I like that you finally made the decision. They have some terrific seashells that way."

Clark tweeted happily. Since he was made of metal, his chirping sounded more like hot wires sparking together than a bird. Still, his enthusiasm was contagious. The bird flew up to Ozzy's head and did a sort of dance in his hair.

"By the way, your hair has all the makings of a terrific nest."

"Thanks."

"Seriously, give me an hour, a few twigs, and some sap and I could make something amazing."

"Please don't."

"I can't promise I won't. Let's go!"

Ozzy reached down and grabbed two handfuls of dark dirt. With soil in hand he began to walk west.

"One, two, three, four, five . . ." he said as he walked.

Each time he said ten, he would drop a little soil and then begin to count to ten again. When he ran out of dirt he would reach down and get more. With his heart pumping wildly he moved farther and farther away from home. He contemplated turning around countless times, but Clark was always there to make sure he didn't.

Ozzy continued picking up soil and marking his path for almost an hour before he came to some stony ground where he couldn't find dirt to pick up. Where the stony ground began, the trees ended, the land dropped away, and past that Ozzy could see nothing but sand and ocean.

"Wow!" Ozzy was mesmerized by the sight—his tight secluded world unfolded in a way that made him shiver. "I should have done this sooner."

"Yeah, you should have."

Ozzy climbed down the stone cliffs and ran to the water.

CHAPTER FIVE

A SMALL FIRST GLIMPSE

The sun set slowly, like stubborn butter refusing to melt. The last rays hit the front of the castle and lit up the two beings standing at the door, one a wizard, the other unimportant. The wizard pushed back the sleeves of his oddly short, bathrobe-like robe and knocked three times. He looked over at his trollish companion.

"Pay close attention and you'll see how things work."

His companion only sniffed.

With a loud whine, the doors were pulled open and the wizard and his companion were escorted in. They were led quickly down a hall by a man with very little chin and too much forehead.

"Tell me the need?" the wizard asked the man as they walked.

"She needs sleep," little chin said. "It's been days and her livelihood suffers because of it."

The three of them entered a small sleeping chamber.

Near the end of the bed there was a woman sitting in a soft chair. In the low light, she looked dark and troubled.

"You seek sleep?" the wizard asked.

"I require it," she whispered fiercely. "Give me slumber and I'll reward you. Fail and you will pay."

"Sharp words from such a desperate soul," he replied. "But your terms are more than fair."

The wizard pushed back his sleeves, pulled out his wand, and went to work.

CHAPTER SIX

BEING AWAKE NEVER FELT LIKE THIS BEFORE

Almost every day for the next few months, Ozzy and Clark would run through the forest and make their way to the beach. That particular stretch of shore was always empty, but every once in a while there were footprints on the sand from someone who had walked through at another time.

But those footprints always faded.

To Ozzy, Oregon seemed like a place with no inhabitants and miles and miles of lonely forest and sand.

A few times they saw boats miles out on the water, but they all eventually disappeared into the distance. Ozzy wanted Clark to fly out and see what the boats were hauling, but Clark had an irrational fear of water, so flying over the ocean was a no go.

"Say I break a wing and fall into the deep water. I'm all metal and plastic, and I don't have lungs. I'll sink like a stone or, in my case, a metal bird."

The lonely beach area was cut off on both sides by rocky cliffs and boulder-strewn shores. Ozzy would swim in the water and play his music as the sun beat down. The melodies sounded even better when accompanied by the ocean.

Did Mother Nature tell you, boy
You come and go as you please?
That's what she said to me.

Ozzy would also build sandcastles in the shape of buildings he had read about in books. Then Clark would hop around them until gravity or the waves caused them to break up and fall apart. When darkness came they would walk back to the cloaked house through the forest and fall asleep dreaming of the next day.

The hike to the beach became a routine, and before Ozzy knew it he was thirteen and almost four inches taller. His father's shirts he wore were no longer dress-length, they were shirt-length. So to cover his bottom half, Ozzy would wear his mother's pants. Having no idea what society deemed appropriate, Ozzy didn't mind borrowing from his mother's wardrobe at all.

The ocean was bright and sunnier than usual. The brown sand along the shore was warm and begged Ozzy's toes and fingers to bury themselves in it. He set the cassette recorder down on a large, flat rock and pressed play. The air filled with songs that were overly familiar to him now.

"Do you ever wish you had more music?"

"I think I'm lucky to have this," Ozzy said.

"I can set my beak to auto-play and we could listen to me for a while."

"No thanks—I like this song."

Ozzy played in the waves and collected some shells. When that was done he built a large sandcastle in the shape of Hogwarts. Clark hopped around the outside pretending to be a dementor as Ozzy perfected the edges.

"Is that supposed to be Hogwarts?" a strange voice asked.

Both Ozzy and Clark froze.

"I mean, it's not bad."

Ozzy looked up from the castle and saw what could only be described as a human. She looked female and close to his age. She had long, black, curly hair and smiled even though she wasn't trying to. Her skin was light brown and more interesting than the entire sea.

Ozzy didn't know whether to throw up or pass out.

"Are you all right?" she asked. "And is that your toy?"

She was pointing at Clark, who was standing completely still near the front entrance of Hogwarts.

"Are you okay?" she asked again. "I like the music you're playing."

"It's good," Ozzy awkwardly managed to say.

A tall woman in the distance yelled, "Sigi! Come on. Let's go!"

The girl turned and yelled back, "Coming!"

Sigi looked at Ozzy.

"Well, I guess I'll see you later. Or maybe not. Either way, nice Hogwarts."

The girl took off running down the shore toward the tall lady. Sigi's exit didn't do anything to put Ozzy at ease. He stayed in the same hunched-over position until Clark finally spoke up.

"Wow, you are *not* good around other humans. Not good at all."

"I . . . well, I . . . you . . ."

"See what I mean? You should probably find a book in your house that explains how to interact with others."

"I've never seen anything so amazing or strange."

"I'm sure whoever that was would love to hear you describe her as strange."

"I mean, she looked like the sun."

"Ugh—do I sound that bad when I talk about metal or birds?" Clark's gold beak sparkled under the sunlight as he spoke. "She's a girl and she tried to talk to you and you said nothing. She ran off, and now you're free to be alone again."

"She might come back."

"You think that about everything."

"Do you think she lives around here?"

"I've seen a few homes and other buildings on my flights."

"Maybe it's time to start exploring other directions."

"A girl named Sigi compliments you on your sandcastle and suddenly you're Magellan."

"The explorer?" Ozzy said. "Still, that's not a bad idea. We should map out our surroundings. You could fly and report things and I'll draw them."

Clark clapped his wings. "Great, with my wings and your hands we can't fail."

"And I think we should start with that direction." Ozzy pointed down the beach in the direction Sigi had run off.

"Even if I wasn't observant, you would still be easier to read than a book. You want me to follow her?"

"Just to find out if she's a visitor or if she lives around here."

"Right."

"I'll head back to the cloaked house to sharpen some map-drawing pencils."

Clark took to the air and Ozzy stood up and shook sand from his clothes. He turned off the music and picked up the cassette player. He put it in his backpack and then started the run back home.

Existence is so much more enjoyable when you have a purpose for moving.

FROM THE TAPES OF DR. EMMITT TOFFY: SUBJECT #1

Lisa

It was the middle of the last act of an off-Broadway musical titled *Lament.* The theater was small but sold out. As the story built and the music swelled, the audience could feel the rise of emotion and the climax approaching.

Lisa stood up from her seat and walked down the aisle. Wrapped up in the story, nobody paid much attention to her. She got to the front of the stage and turned left as if to exit out the side door. Instead she pushed through a heavy velvet curtain and climbed three steps up the side of the stage. Without pausing she walked into the middle of the performance and began to sing and dance in place.

I saw the sign and it opened up my eyes
and I am happy now!

The shock of it caused the entire cast to momentarily stop what they were doing and stare at the strange woman.

Two stagehands raced in from opposite sides of the stage and hauled her off. The actors, ever professionals, picked up where they had been interrupted and continued to act.

Lisa was taken to the nearest police station and questioned.

She had no idea why she had done it.

She also had no police record, no history of mental

illness, no prior moments of impropriety. She was a well-to-do New York socialite who had never done anything remotely out of place. She also didn't care for the song she had been singing.

Lisa was released and instructed to check in with her doctor.

When she did visit her physician, he found no signs of any illness. He also couldn't explain why she had done what she did.

CHAPTER SEVEN

GET THE JOB DONE

Ozzy was fourteen. He had no way of knowing this because despite his desire for learning and inquisitive mind, he had never begun to keep track of the days. The weather grew slightly colder and then warmed up a bit. Summer followed and fall stomped in behind that. His parents' books made him aware of time and dates, but he'd never made the effort to keep track. There were no clocks or phones or TVs to yell out the time and date. He had grown from a child to a boy who stood over six feet tall and looked considerably older than he was.

During the last year he had gone to the beach often, hoping to see Sigi again. But he never had. In fact, he'd not seen another single soul on the shore.

But things were different in his other directions of exploration.

Ozzy and Clark had mapped out an ever-widening circle from the cloaked house. Ozzy no longer thought he was alone in the world. He and Clark had found countless homes and roads and even a small town, Otter Rock, about five miles to the north. Ozzy had walked on paved roads, peered through store windows, and lived to draw about it.

"That's looking amazing," Clark said as he watched Ozzy sketch another tree on the master map. "You must have cartography in your blood."

"I just like knowing where things are in relation to home."

Clark hopped around the map. It was spread out on the kitchen table, drawn on thick white sheets of paper taped together in a giant square. The map detailed the shore and about five miles in all other directions. It didn't show every tree and puddle, but if there was an unusual landmark or oddity, Ozzy had drawn it, like a tree that grew sideways, a rock the shape of a lounging hippo, bushes growing in a perfect circle, and of course the cloaked house, sitting in the middle of the map like the sun, sketched out to the last bushy detail.

Ozzy and Clark had spent a lot of time exploring Otter Rock. Careful not to be noticed, they had walked each street and drawn every building. There was a main street with stores and restaurants. There was a McDonald's on one end of town and a Jack-in-the-Box on the other. There was a drive-in movie theater that Ozzy and Clark had watched from a distance. There were a few motels and some houses, but the building that interested Ozzy most was Otter Rock High School. He had watched children coming in and out and marveled at how many people his age existed in the world. He'd seen long yellow buses picking kids up from the side of the road and dropping them off at the school, and also observed those same buses shuttling kids home when the day was done.

"Who drives those things?" Ozzy asked Clark.

"Someone important, I bet."

Ozzy thought about his parents, his life, and his surroundings, but most of all he thought about school. It seemed like a breeding ground of possibility and acceptance.

"I mean . . . shouldn't I be going?" Ozzy said. "I could hike to the road every morning. The closest is Mule Pole Highway—it's only two miles away." Ozzy pointed to the map on the table. "I'll stand next to the road and wait for the bus. When it picks me up, I'll ride it into town, and then see what happens when I get to school."

"It does seem like a lot of kids your height or shorter stream into that place."

"I think I have to do this. Don't get me wrong—I love hanging out with you, but if I'm ever going to find my parents, I need to understand the world better."

"You really just want to see if Sigi's there, don't you?"

"Yes."

"So take the bus. Do you think they allow birds?"

"Probably not."

Ozzy set his pencil down on the map and sat down.

"Hey, Clark, do you remember those movies we watched?"

"At the drive-in?" the bird asked.

Ozzy nodded. "I know we couldn't hear what they were saying, but everyone looked so . . ."

"Large and two-dimensional?" Clark guessed.

"No. They looked cleaned up."

"Oh . . . right," Clark said. "And you're the not-cleaned-up type. It might help if you took the leaves out of your hair and didn't wear your mom's shirts."

Ozzy pulled a leaf from his hair and looked down at the T-shirt he was wearing, which was light purple and covered with a dozen butterflies in flight.

"I read a book once where a fairy changed a young woman from a poor, uneducated person to a dressed-up one," Ozzy said.

"Well, then, let's do the same to you," Clark suggested. "Your dad's clothes will fit you better now you're so tall. And you can cut your hair and wash your teeth and put on some shoes. Go get the scissors so you can chop off your hair!"

"You think that's a good first step?"

Clark nodded his tiny bird head.

Ozzy went to get the scissors, and, without his parents around to tell him differently, ran back to the kitchen with them.

It wasn't quite the magical night that Cinderella experienced. No one turned a vegetable into a vehicle or rodents into horses, but Ozzy did take off several inches of hair and the butterfly shirt and put on shoes for the first time in years.

There was excitement in the air. The cloaked house felt warm, like an oven cooking something wonderful. Tomorrow was the first day of school.

It was actually the first of March, so it wasn't everyone's first day. But it was for Ozzy—and because of that, he could hardly sleep.

CHAPTER EIGHT

NOW WHAT A PERFECT WORLD THIS WOULD BE

Charles Plankdorf stroked his beard as he sat behind his mahogany desk at Harken Corp. He was attempting to control his breathing. Attempting. The project he cared about most was on the brink of falling apart. The science team were still not producing. The latest test results had come back and they weren't good. After so many years of bitter disappointment, he was sick of it. Charles wasn't accustomed to losing. His father had taught him many hard lessons about the importance of finishing what he began.

The intercom on his phone buzzed. He pressed a button and shouted at the phone. "What is it?"

A bored voice said, "Eric's here to see you, sir."

Charles's breathing exercises collapsed and, red-faced, he yelled, "Send him in!"

Eric entered the office and approached the desk.

"I'm sorry to bother you," Eric apologized. "But as you know, the results are still negative. The board is recommending that we no longer pursue this course. They want—"

"'*No longer pursue*'?" Charles shouted. "Throw away years and years of work on an idea that could give us all unlimited power? The board are cowards."

"Nonetheless, it's a failure. I've been sent to tell you that we—"

Charles slammed his fists down, making both the desk and Eric shake.

"Tell the board I need more time. I *will* make this work. I'll put everything I have into it. We're close; I know it. Remind them that once we have a working formula, we'll have the ability to stop all hunger, anger, and misguided will. We'll be bathing in money and we'll change the course of mankind."

"They're aware of your goals," Eric said. "They need you to stop."

Charles gave Eric a look that indicated the conversation was over.

Eric had grown to hate Harken Corporation. The things they had done and were doing strangled his soul. The place was destroying him—and Charles was the worst part of it.

"Go! Just go," Charles insisted.

Eric was happy to oblige.

CHAPTER NINE

STOP THE BUS

Ozzy stood on the side of the highway looking like a tourist who was not only lost but in no condition to be out of bed. He'd woken up early and hiked more than two miles, arriving at the Mule Pole Highway a little after dawn.

His chopped black hair was slicked back and combed into a style Clark swore he'd seen before. He wore one of his father's dress shirts, blue paisley with pearl buttons. His pants were a shade of purple that older folks might have found trendy when disco was popular, but that anyone under fifty would find embarrassing. The dress shoes he had chosen pinched his toes, making it hard not to wince anytime he took a step. Ozzy didn't know what he might need at school, so he held a pencil in one hand and his pocketknife in the other.

"Are you ready?" Clark asked.

"I think so."

"If you wonder what to do or say, just be quiet. People will think you're mysterious."

"I can do that."

"I hope they come," Clark said.

"The bus stops for some kids a little up the highway. So when it sees me it should stop."

"Okay," Clark tweeted. "Once you get on, I'll fly behind and find a spot near the school to hide while you're there. There are some really interesting metal things I can hang out with. Remember that flagpole?"

"The one in front of the school?"

"Yeah, that's the one. She seems sort of tall and standoffish, but I think if we spent some time together we'd get along."

The yellow bus appeared around the curve. Instantly Ozzy's heart began racing. He waved Clark away and the bird flew into the trees. Standing up straight, Ozzy tried to look brave. The bus got closer, its engine thundering.

Clenching his fists around his pencil and knife, Ozzy tried to calm his breathing. He looked expectantly as the bus approached, but it didn't even slow down, whizzing right on by. A blast of air pushed Ozzy backward, and he rocked slightly on his heels. He watched the yellow vehicle disappear into the distance and sighed a sigh of both relief and disappointment. Clark flitted back from the trees and landed on his head.

"So, what happened?" the bird asked.

"Well, it didn't stop."

"I saw that. Should we hike into town?"

"No way," Ozzy said. "These shoes are killing me. Besides, it's more than four miles from here. By the time we got there, school would be half over."

"Should we try again tomorrow?"

"I guess. Maybe I'll wave at the bus driver next time."

Ozzy took off his shoes and crossed the highway, stepping off the asphalt into the trees.

~

About twenty-three hours and fifty minutes later he was back in the same spot, wearing the same clothes, standing the same way. Clark was in the trees when the yellow bus popped up on the horizon and sped closer.

Ozzy leaned forward and waved.

The bus blew by without stopping.

Clark glided in from the trees. "You probably should work on your wave. I've seen other people do it and they look much less pathetic."

Ozzy waved to see what it looked like.

"Oh, boy," Clark said. "That's not going to make anyone stop."

"So what do we do?"

"First we work on your wave."

"And I'll stand *in* the road so the bus has to stop," Ozzy suggested.

"Perfect."

Ozzy and Clark went back to the cloaked house to practice.

~

Another twenty-four hours later, Ozzy stood on the highway. He was just as nervous as before, but now there was an added element of fear—if the bus decided not to stop, it could easily be the end of his quest.

Ozzy stayed planted for ten minutes in the middle of the road before *any* vehicle appeared. It wasn't the bus, though, so he stepped off the road. Once the car had passed, he returned to his spot.

Half an hour later, only two more cars had passed by, and neither one was a bus.

"Maybe the bus driver hated your wave so much that he went a different way."

"Let's go home so I can change. We need to hike into town to figure this out."

Ozzy returned to the cloaked house and changed into something more comfortable. Then, as he had done more often lately than he could count, he ran through the forest to Otter Rock. By the time he and Clark arrived, it was past noon.

They hid in the trees on a ridge just east of the high school. The moment they arrived they saw instantly that something was wrong.

"Where is everyone?"

The school was deserted; there were no cars in the parking lot or buses parked to the side.

"Don't they have school every day?" Ozzy asked.

"I don't know. The flagpole's still there."

"Maybe it's like Harry Potter. He had weekends and holidays off. I'm going into one of the shops on Main Street and ask them what day it is."

"Good for you. I'll stay right here and chat up the flagpole."

Ozzy made it to Main Street with no problem and, before he could talk himself out of what he was doing, dashed into the first business he saw, a jewelry store called Sparkles. A woman was standing inside behind a glass counter.

Ozzy pushed on the door a little too hard and found himself half stumbling in. He stood up, trying to catch his breath, and noticed the woman was staring at his shoeless feet.

"Um, what day is it?" Ozzy asked.

"Excuse me?" the woman said, more confused than bothered.

"Is it a holiday today?"

The woman smiled. "Not that I know of. It's Saturday, March 5th."

"And there's no school on Saturday?"

"No."

It was more information than Ozzy could have hoped for.

"Thank you." Ozzy paused. "That is what people say, right?"

The woman smiled again. "If they're being polite."

"Well, then, thank you," Ozzy said.

As Ozzy left the shop, not looking where he was going, he ran into someone, falling backward onto his rear. He looked up and saw, backlit by the sun, a strange silhouette of a man wearing a pointed floppy hat. The sun made it hard to see the man clearly.

"You okay?" the man asked, reaching out to pull Ozzy up. Reluctantly Ozzy reached out.

"I think so," he said as the man pulled him to his feet.

"Nice to know people still think," the man replied. "Now, if you'll excuse me, I need to move. I hate to think what the consequences might be if I'm not home by sunset."

The strange man seemed to be wearing some sort of bathrobe and shivered as he said "sunset." He took off, striding away purposefully. Ozzy rubbed his eyes and watched as he disappeared, then he ran back to where Clark was supposed to be hiding. After a brief search, he found him sitting in a tree about a block away.

"How's your flagpole?" Ozzy asked.

"I tried talking to her, but she was really pretty stiff, personality-wise. Just a tall stick. What about you?" Clark asked. "Did you find someone to ask?"

"Yes. She kept staring at my feet."

"You do have nice feet, but I think most people wear shoes when they're outside."

"They also told me that it's Saturday. And there's no school on Saturday."

"Just like your wizard books said."

"And if there's no school on Saturday, then there's none on Sunday. So . . . I think we should return to the cloaked house and regroup. That way I'll be ready for Monday."

The mechanical raven hopped down from the tree and sat on Ozzy's head.

"Oh, I bumped into someone while I was coming out of the store. He was blocking the sidewalk and I fell to the ground."

"People are so bulky."

"He was wearing a pointed hat. Like a wizard. And he had on a robe of some sort."

"The way some of you humans dress yourselves is embarrassing."

They hiked back to the cloaked house. When they got there Ozzy ate the last pouch of dried apples and a seven-year-old can of creamed corn.

CHAPTER TEN

I'LL GET OFF HERE

Monday morning took far more courage than Ozzy had thought he would need to leave the cloaked house and hike to the highway.

"You can do this," Clark kept encouraging him. "Just think—you'll get on the bus, go to school, find Sigi, and she'll help you find your parents. Boy meets bus meets girl meets parents."

"I hope so," Ozzy replied.

This time, the boy and the bird exited the trees farther up the road, near the spot where train tracks crossed the Mule Pole Highway. Ozzy had a plan. He had never seen a train there, but he had heard some from a distance on more than one occasion.

Where the tracks crossed the road, the shoulders of the highway were long mounds of dirt that looked like giant fat snakes running parallel to the asphalt. Next to the tracks there was a tall, yellow tree and two railroad crossing signs that looked like big Xs against the sky. The crossing signs were familiar because Clark had been sort of sweet on them for a while. Ozzy had made the trek out to the signs once or twice when it was nearly dark and Clark was still trying to get the signs to talk to him.

Clark tried not to make eye contact with them as Ozzy stood on the right side of the road next to the tracks.

"And you really think this will work?" Clark asked.

"I'm pretty sure buses have to stop before they cross the tracks, remember? We saw it happen with that one when you came to visit the signs. They even opened the door. I have no idea why. Maybe . . ."

Ozzy heard the bus coming.

"Get into the trees!"

"I'll be in that tall yellow-leafed one. I think I just saw a dove fly in there."

The bird flew off and the boy stood there with his pencil in one hand and his knife in the other.

The bus drew nearer. The sound of its engine gave Ozzy's heart fits and made him doubt every aspect and piece of the plan. It drew closer still. Ozzy wondered if there was enough time for him to throw up before it arrived.

It got closer, and he heard it downshift and watched it decrease its speed. Ozzy discovered he hadn't breathed in a while and sucked in a lungful of air.

The bus came to a complete stop just before the tracks. It snorted like a giant yellow beast and then the driver opened the door to check for trains. Not waiting for permission, Ozzy stepped onto the bus and climbed up the metal stairs.

The driver stared at the boy in disbelief. He leaned back in his seat and looked at Ozzy as if he were a new responsibility that he didn't want.

"You can't bring that knife," was all he said.

Ozzy looked at the knife in his hand and tossed it back out the door before it closed. The bus driver motioned with his thumb for Ozzy to move back into the bus and the vehicle began to move slowly.

Ozzy Toffy had never thought his plan would work. Now he was on the bus and wasn't sure what to do next. There were rows and rows of empty seats; only a handful of students were already on board. One student stared at him, one didn't even look up, one had headphones over his ears, and another was working on homework she should have completed over the weekend. A boy with dark blue eyes and the left side of his head shaved looked at Ozzy and what he was wearing.

"Nice clothes," the boy said, laughing.

"Thanks."

"Who are you, anyway?"

"Ozzy."

"You live by the train tracks?" he asked.

"We just moved here."

"Whatever," the boy said. "I wasn't looking for a conversation."

Ozzy moved two rows down the aisle and took a seat on the right side of the bus. He looked out the window and saw a small black dot flying behind them.

Nobody else talked to him the rest of the ride, and the bus filled up almost completely before it finally reached Otter Rock High.

It took everything Ozzy had not to leap from the bus and run back home, but he knew if he ever wanted things to change in his life, he needed to go forward. The books he'd read told him that things happened when people acted on their own. So he shuffled into the school with everyone else and picked a random classroom to enter.

He sat down at one of the desks and waited.

Boys and girls, both louder than wolves and as interesting as spring, filed into the room and sat down where they wanted. The desks around Ozzy stayed empty.

A bell rang and a man with more stomach than butt came into the room carrying a stack of folders and looking as bothered as most people did at the end of a hard day.

"Quiet! No talking."

He set the folders on his desk and began to write on the whiteboard at the front of the room. He talked as he scribbled.

"Now, there's no time to hear all the wonderful things you did to improve the world this weekend. I'm sure all of you stepped outside of yourselves and did something of value."

He finished writing and turned around to face the class.

"Oh, wait, you're teenagers. You probably spent the weekend staring at your phones."

None of the students made a noise.

"Regardless, you were to put down your phones and read the fourth and fifth chapter of *Animal Farm*. Who'd like to give us their thoughts?"

Nobody raised their hands so Ozzy decided he'd give it a go. *Animal Farm* had been in one of his parents' boxes, and he'd read it a couple of times so far.

The teacher saw Ozzy and stared sternly at him.

"Who are you?"

A few of the other students laughed, happy to have their teacher talking about something else.

"I'm Ozzy Toffy."

"And you're new here?"

Ozzy nodded.

"Fine. The office never tells me anything. So, you're new and the only one who's read the assignment? Perfect. Well . . . tell me what you thought."

"I think the book believes it's more important than it really is."

The teacher looked stunned. "Really?"

"It had a few words I didn't understand, which was good, but the rest of the writing was sort of unpleasant."

"Yes, well, that's because it's a classic. Who else has something to say?"

And just like that, Ozzy was a student at Otter Rock High School. The teacher didn't seem to be interested enough to find out who he was or why he was there. When class was over, he followed a couple students to another room. The next class was almost the same as the first, and the third was worse; the teacher just asked him his name, wrote it down, and never addressed him again.

Ozzy was tall enough that no boys wanted to mess with him and quiet enough that the girls were left to imagine what he was really like. The way he was dressed made him odd enough to be ignored. Regardless, he loved what was happening. People were doing things and interacting. A girl lent another girl a pencil. Two boys argued over the score of a sporting event. A couple of kids stared at him and one girl asked him if he was an exchange student.

"Exchanged for what?"

"You know, a different country."

"No."

"Then why are you dressed like that?"

At lunchtime, Ozzy followed the herd to the cafeteria, where he mimicked them by getting in line and grabbing a tray for food. He saw three women putting delicious, warm-looking things on plates and handing the plates to the students. One handed a plate of hot mashed potatoes and turkey to Ozzy.

"This is mine?" he asked.

"Unless you don't want it," the woman replied.

"Oh, I want it." Ozzy was gleeful about having a full plate of real food.

"That's great," she said, thinking his enthusiasm was sarcasm. "Happy to hear it meets your needs. Give the attendant your number."

Down the line there was a row of plates with cake, cups of Jell-O, and corn in little round dishes, then cartons of milk and juice.

He took one of each as he slid his orange tray towards the cashier. He listened as student after student told the cashier a number and then walked off with their food. The boy in front of him said, "2527."

"Thank you," the woman said. "Next."

"2528?" Ozzy asked.

"Thank you. Next."

Ozzy picked up his tray in disbelief. What he didn't know was that three weeks before, a student named Emily Reardon had moved to Idaho, and when she'd left Otter Rock High she'd also left a balance of $31 in her lunch account. It was by luck alone that Ozzy had said her number.

He found a long table half-filled with students and sat down at the empty end. The table was next to the back wall of the cafeteria near the windows. As much as he might have enjoyed the company of friends, he was too enthralled with the food in front of him to care. He'd never had food before that wasn't canned or freeze-dried or straight from his garden. He had eaten a lot of fish, but the school turkey tasted like something out of a celebration at Hogwarts. And the warm potatoes and gravy seemed like spoils that only the wealthiest in the world could ever afford. By the time he got to the fruit punch, his mind was properly blown.

He drank every drop and upon completion let out a terrific and grateful "Ahhhh."

The kids at the other half of the table stared at him.

"What's your problem?" a red-headed boy asked.

"Have you *tasted* this stuff?" Ozzy asked.

Everyone laughed.

Ozzy didn't know enough to be embarrassed. He cracked open a chocolate milk and, after a small sample sip, downed that as well. It was so much more enjoyable than the powdered milk he'd mixed with water all these years. He laughed after finishing it off.

"Dude, you're messed up," a boy sitting near the redhead said.

"Am I drinking it wrong?"

"And what's up with your finger?"

Ozzy held up his hand and looked at his birthmark.

"That's wrecked," the redhead said.

Everyone laughed again and then they got up and left.

"I don't think they like you . . . yet."

Ozzy looked down. Clark was standing next to him on the edge of his bench.

"What are you doing here?" Ozzy whispered.

"It's boring out there. The flagpole's a bust, and I was perched up in that window and saw you blowing it.

I thought I could help, seeing as how I'm pretty good with the opposite sex . . . or alloy."

Ozzy scooped up Clark and hid him under the table.

"I'm doing just fine on my own," Ozzy said defensively.

"Well, everyone just got up to get away from you."

"It doesn't matter—they give you food here. All I had to do was say a number."

"Well, the food looks too soft and there's no texture, but your fork isn't unattractive. Maybe you could bring it home."

"I'm pretty sure it belongs to the school."

"That's too bad. Have you found your parents?"

"Did you think it would be that easy? I can't just go around asking people if they happen to know about two grownups who were abducted years ago. That would be weird."

"Are you talking to yourself?" someone asked.

Ozzy shoved Clark under the table and looked up. There, standing across the table from him looking every bit as mystifying as she had the day at the beach over a year ago, was Sigi. Her dark, curly hair was longer, and she was older in the way that a person should be. Her brown skin stood out against the dull walls and she had a smile that didn't match the mood of the room. Sigi's eyes were so deep Ozzy needed new words to properly describe them.

"I mean, if this table is reserved for you and your invisible friends," Sigi said, "I can always go away."

"No, no," Ozzy stammered, still not believing his eyes. "I don't have any friends."

"Interesting. Not really something most people admit. I'm Sigi, by the way."

Sigi took a seat on the long bench right next to Ozzy. It appeared that she didn't remember Ozzy from their beach encounter. As she sat down, Clark crawled inside Ozzy's pants pocket. Hoping to motivate him, he bit down hard on his leg with the tip of his metal beak.

"Ahhhhhh!"

Sigi slid back a few inches and stared for a moment.

"Again," she said, "not a normal reaction to someone sitting down by you. What's your name?"

Ozzy swallowed as if there were food in his mouth.

"Ozzy."

"That's all right. What's your last name?"

"That's the last one I had. Actually, it's the only one I've had."

Sigi smiled, showing more patience and compassion than most high schoolers.

"Right," she said. "I mean . . . do you have a name that comes after it?"

"Oh, yeah. Toffy."

Ozzy executed the kind of nervous smile someone might display if they were holding a bomb but still trying to be polite.

"Should I leave?" she asked.

"No!"

"Good. Then I'll eat my food right here."

"Thanks."

Sigi smiled again.

"You know, your name sounds like an eighties dance move or a cooking technique. 'Ozzy Toffy.'"

"I don't really know how to dance *or* cook."

Sigi took a bite of the small sandwich on her tray.

"You're new here, aren't you?"

Ozzy nodded.

"I'm always glad when new students come. I've lived my whole life in Otter Rock and, to be honest with you, I find most people around here played-out and boring. Are you a sophomore?"

"They said I was."

"That's an odd way to say that." Sigi smiled. "But I'm a sophomore too. How long have you been here?"

"I moved here recently, but my family has vacationed on and off here in the summers," Ozzy answered, reciting the story he and Clark had planned. "We're going to be here for a while now."

Sigi looked okay with his answer.

"Hopefully we move before I'm played-out," Ozzy said, making his first real attempt at a joke with another human being.

"Yes, hopefully. There's nothing more dreadful than running your course to the point where no one cares any-more."

"I'll use my words sparingly."

Sigi actually laughed.

"Can I ask you something, Ozzy?"

"Of course."

"Of course? I like that. Why you are so dressed up?"

Ozzy looked down at himself. He glanced at his sleeves and his pants and then finally at his shoes.

"I wasn't sure how people dressed here."

"Well, they don't dress like that," Sigi said. "You're lucky you're tall and good looking, because even I'm tempted to make fun of what you're wearing."

"This is wrong?" Ozzy asked while trying to stare at himself.

"It's not a totally bad thing, it's just . . . different. I mean, it's not like I always fit in, but you don't seem to want to match at all."

"Okay, tomorrow I'll wear a T-shirt and shorts."

"There's a cool clothing shop off Main Street. They sell all kinds of cool clothes that most people here wouldn't bother with. I think you'd like it."

Ozzy kept quiet.

"What's it called?" Clark said from the pocket and mimicking Ozzy's voice as best as he could.

Sigi looked up from her sandwich.

"Are you okay?"

"Yeah." Ozzy cleared his throat. "What's it called?"

"Zell's. Not that you have to go there, but you seem interesting enough to shop there. Is that a birthmark on your finger?"

Ozzy nodded.

"Very cool; it makes my hands look boring."

Ozzy thought her hands looked just fine, but he liked the compliment.

Sigi finished her sandwich.

"So what's your next class?" she asked.

Having no idea, Ozzy asked her. "What's yours?"

"Chemistry, with Ball."

"I have the same."

Sigi took a drink of her white milk.

"You know, they have that in brown," Ozzy told her. "And it's *amazing*."

"You're an interesting guy, Ozzy."

A tall boy with spiky hair in a group of friends called out to Sigi from across the cafeteria.

"I gotta go, Ozzy," she said. "See you in Chem."

"Okay, that's okay. You go and I'll stay . . . and then I'll see you in that thing you just said . . ." Ozzy wanted to stop, but the words just kept coming out. "You know . . . that ball class where I guess we'll learn . . . and listen . . . and whatever."

Sigi was standing now.

"You're quite a poet, Ozzy."

She smiled one last time and walked off.

"That could have gone better," Clark whispered from Ozzy's pocket. "In fact, I'm not sure if it could have gone worse. Maybe she'll feel sorry for you and fall in love with you that way."

"I've never talked to people before," Ozzy said defensively.

"Well, I hope you improve quickly."

Ozzy gathered his tray and dumped the garbage, then took the rest of the lunch period to randomly ask kids what room Chemistry with Ball was in.

By the time he figured it out, the bell had rung and he was five minutes late. He took the only vacant desk left—four rows back and five rows over from Sigi.

FROM THE TAPES OF DR. EMMITT TOFFY: SUBJECT #2

Tom

Paris was unseasonably warm. Tom stopped at the souvenir store with his family and questioned the shopkeeper about a snow globe.

"Is this the best one you have?"

"The very best."

"What about that one?" Tom asked, pointing to a large snow globe on the shelf behind the man. A detailed sculpture of the Eiffel Tower was inside the globe, surrounded by ornately carved flowers.

"That's even better."

"Better than the best," Tom said happily. "And how much?"

The snow globe cost more than a night in their hotel, but it was a piece of art. And as a collector of globes, Tom had to have it. It took a little bit of haggling with his wife, but then she consented and happily watched him purchase it.

Tom held the snow globe so his family could admire it.

"Just beautiful," his wife said.

Tom had a vast collection of snow globes back home. He had collected them since he was a child, and this globe was by far the finest.

"You need to wrap it up," his wife said. "We'll take it back to the hotel and put it in the safe."

Tom smiled at his family and then walked across the

street, where two policemen were standing. Without warning, he threw the globe down at their feet, shattering it in a tremendous burst of water and glass. The two officers threw Tom to the ground immediately and handcuffed him as everyone around screamed and ran for cover.

Tom was taken to the police station and questioned for hours. He had no history of mania or vandalism. He was the president of a small company in Florida and, aside from one parking ticket he'd paid at age sixteen, his record was clean.

The strange thing was that he had no idea why he'd done it. In fact, he couldn't remember a thing about it.

He was given a ticket, charged a fine, and asked to leave the country.

CHAPTER ELEVEN

FORTUNATE LIKE YOU

For the next week and a half Ozzy got up, hiked two miles to the Mule Pole Highway, and stood by the railroad tracks every weekday. When the bus stopped and Mr. Goote, the driver, opened its doors to check for oncoming trains, he'd hop on. At the end of the day he would get on bus number 1015 and hop off when it stopped at the tracks again.

He went to the same classes he had attended the first day and turned in homework and took tests. Teachers treated him just like they treated everyone else. Nobody bothered him because he was tall, strong, and kept to himself. And nobody talked to him because he was tall, strong, and kept to himself.

Some days Clark would wait for Ozzy near the train tracks. But most days he would stow away in the front pocket of Ozzy's pants and attend school with him.

Today was a stowaway day.

Ozzy had spent as much time as he could in the school library using the computers. At first the machines had blown his mind, but now he knew what they could do and how they could help him find his parents.

There was very little information online about Emmitt and Mia Toffy, just a few newspaper articles about his father and mother teaching in New York. One link took him to a picture of both of them at a banquet where they were given an award for achievement in scientific studies.

The lack of information made Ozzy uneasy.

Ozzy also didn't enjoy the lack of Sigi. Since their first conversation they hadn't talked much at all—a couple waves in the hall, a half dozen nods, and five or six smiles.

The lunch bell rang while Ozzy was in the library. He logged out of the computer and headed to his locker. The school hadn't actually assigned him one, but he'd taken over an empty locker in a corner by the stairs. He'd even found a padlock at home and brought it to use.

"Anything else on your parents?" Clark asked from Ozzy's pocket.

"Nothing. I think we need help."

"I'm pretty sure we do."

Ozzy opened his locker, put his stuff in, then made his way to the cafeteria. Once there he grabbed a tray and loaded it up. Then, as he'd done every day so far, he gave the woman his number.

"2528."

"Your account is out of money," the woman said.

"What?" Ozzy asked.

"No money. You need to put more in your account."

"How?"

"Really?" the woman said, disgusted. "Have your parent or guardian give you some money, or they can come here themselves and pay the office."

"Money?"

"Just leave your tray here and take this."

The woman handed Ozzy a brown paper sack. "It's free today, but not tomorrow."

Ozzy took the bag and left the line. He retreated to his normal spot by the back wall and windows. At first he was sad to lose what had been on the tray, but he was delighted to open up the bag and find a peanut butter and jelly sandwich, an apple, a bag of chips, and white milk.

Clark wriggled out of his pocket.

"I could use some air."

"You don't breathe."

"Still, that pocket's the worst. I know I can't smell, but I imagine it stinks in there."

Ozzy set an open book on the table and looked down. It was the best way to talk to Clark at lunch without anyone else noticing.

"My food number doesn't work anymore."

"I heard that."

"Yeah, well, I need some money."

"What about that box you found in the basement?"

The box Clark was talking about was a square metal

one Ozzy had discovered the other day. It had been hidden inside another box that was covered in piles of more boxes in the basement. There was a lock on the front and whoever had taken his parents must not have seen it, because it looked like it was worth stealing. Plus, it had the word *Funds* written on it.

Ozzy had tried to pry it open but with no success so far.

"There has to be money in there," Ozzy whispered.

"That's what I'm thinking. You could buy some lunch—or better clothes. Or a series of assorted metal objects."

"Let's find out if there's money in it before we start dreaming."

~

After school, Ozzy took the bus home, hiked to the cloaked house, and headed straight to the cellar. There were no lights in the cellar, and the four small windows it did have were high and covered with so much outside growth and vegetation that they barely let in any light at all anymore.

Ozzy grabbed a candle and struck a match. The room lit up, displaying his father's long metal worktable and hundreds of boxes. Most of the basement boxes had contained food at one time, but empty boxes were still stacked all over, stealing room and blocking the view.

The locked metal box was under two boxes in the corner. Ozzy pushed them off and lifted the large, heavy square box up. He carried it upstairs and put it down on the kitchen table with a thunk.

"Have you ever found any other metal boxes here?" Clark asked.

"Well, the box *you* were in was . . . well, that's not metal, right?"

"I don't find it attractive, so . . . no."

"Then I haven't found any other metal boxes."

Ozzy located a flathead screwdriver from one of the kitchen drawers and tried to pick the lock again.

"That's not going to work," Clark said. "Let me try."

Clark closed his beak and stuck the tip of it in the keyhole. His head twitched and his beak got stuck. Ozzy sighed, grabbed hold of Clark, and yanked him free.

Ozzy pulled a hammer out of a kitchen drawer and proceeded to bang the life out of the lock on the front of the box.

"You're not even denting it. Where'd you learn to swing a hammer?" Clark said. "What if I lifted it up and dropped it from a great height?"

"You can't lift this."

"What if *you* lifted it, or better yet, what if you took it to the top of the tree behind the house and let it fall?"

Ozzy picked up the box and walked out the front door. The forest was lime-green. The setting sun lit up the thin clouds and made everything hazy.

"This is a good idea," Clark said. "I can feel it. We need to know what's in there."

"What if it's like Pandora's box?"

"It's not—this is reality, not Greek mythology."

"I'm talking to a metal bird. Who's to say what's real or not?"

Ozzy walked back behind the stream and climbed over the black, mossy wall to get to the red alder tree that he liked so much. It was enormous; Ozzy had spent many days climbing and reading amongst its limbs. Clark flew straight up to the top as Ozzy pushed the square metal box up into the low branches.

Slowly he hefted and shoved the container higher and higher. The branches became thinner and the air lighter.

"Hurry!" Clark yelled down from the top of the tree.

"Why?" Ozzy yelled up.

"I don't know, it just seems wrong to yell 'slower!'"

"How about keeping quiet, then."

Clark didn't reply.

It took a few stops to rest, and some clever cramming to get the box through the branches, but eventually Ozzy reached the top. He looked out and observed the low clouds surrounding the house and forest like a field of pulled cotton.

Clark sat on a high branch, his beak clenched tight.

"You can talk now," Ozzy said.

"Thanks. Then let me just say—took you long enough. And: push it hard."

Ozzy positioned himself to best shove the square box out of the tree. Then, using his right leg and left arm, he kicked and pushed as hard as he could. The box dropped like a stone. He heard it falling through the branches and leaves, followed by a tremendous crack. From where he was sitting he couldn't see the ground.

"Do you think it opened?" he asked.

Clark looked at him and shrugged his wings. Then he darted down out of the tree and back to the ground. In less than thirty seconds he had flown back up to report his findings.

"The box hit a big rock and it's busted open completely. But there was just a bunch of paper inside."

"No clothes or money? Or maybe some food?"

"Don't you think I would have said that? It's just paper."

Ozzy made his way back down the tree. Thanks to the school cafeteria, he'd eaten more amazing food in the last week than he had ever in his life. Still, he would have loved to discover something delicious in the box. He had hoped his dad had locked up something good, like chocolate, or soda that didn't expire. So many of the boxes he had opened throughout his life had been filled with paper, so news of more was a terrible letdown.

Ozzy jumped from the low branches onto the ground. He could see the broken box. He also saw what looked like a meadow of small, green pieces of paper.

"That's money," Ozzy said happily.

"Really?" Clark said. "It looks like paper."

"Well, it's paper money."

Ozzy picked up a handful of hundred-dollar bills. "I wonder if it's still good?"

"You think it expires?" Clark asked.

"We could try some and see what happens."

"You mean eat it?"

"No, take some to school and see if they'll give me more food."

"Or," Clark said, "hear me out. Tomorrow's Saturday, so you can take some and see if they'll let you trade it for clothes at that store Sigi told you about."

Ozzy gathered every last bill while Clark tweeted and hopped around excitedly. There was a lot of money—well over fifty thousand dollars. Ozzy carefully stacked it all and then hid it in the starry stairs.

"Are we rich?" Clark asked as they looked at the money.

"Maybe," Ozzy replied.

"I feel snootier already."

"Maybe I can pay someone to help me find my parents."

"Still, you might want to change your clothes."

Ozzy closed the compartment and screwed the wooden ball back into the end of the newel post.

CHAPTER TWELVE

WELL, I HATE THAT IT'S COME TO THIS

The town of Otter Rock wasn't huge, but it had most of the things a town should have. There were restaurants and businesses as well as a few nice neighborhoods. Like the rest of the area there were trees everywhere. It wasn't more than a mile from the seashore, so the smell of the ocean also filled the air. Otter Rock had a picturesque Main Street, filled with nice stores where tourists could spend money on things that were suspiciously close to things they could probably just purchase at home.

One of those stores was Zell's.

As Ozzy stepped through the glass door, a small bell chimed.

Clark was hidden in Ozzy's pants pocket. They had argued over whether or not he should come in, but in the end Clark had won by pointing out that he had better style and could help with Ozzy's choices.

"Hello," a girl with pink hair and bare shoulders said. "How are you?"

"Hello," Ozzy replied.

"My name's Amy. Can I help you?"

"Your . . . hair's pink."

"Intentionally," Amy said, adding a smile to her words.

"I like it. I didn't realize people's hair could be that color."

"Mine can. Of course, if I had naturally black hair like yours, I might prefer that. Who cuts your hair?"

"Me."

"Well . . . we can talk about that later." She looked Ozzy up and down. "Right now you need some clothes."

"Um . . . these clothes cost money, right?"

The pink-haired girl frowned.

"Yes, they do, I'm sorry to say."

Ozzy took out a stack of hundred-dollar bills.

"Do these work?"

Amy smiled again.

An hour later, Ozzy left Zell's with a whole new wardrobe and instructions on what he should wear and when. Amy had even called the salon down the street and set up an appointment for Ozzy to get his hair cut.

"I don't think you need your hair cut," Clark said as Ozzy walked. "I've finally got it to be perfectly nest-like."

"Amy said it would make me look more polished."

"That does sound handsome. Just make sure they know you share your hair with a bird."

The salon was called Anthony's and inside, Ozzy met a girl with silver hair named Alyson. She gave Ozzy a haircut and washed his hair. It was the first time since his parents had been taken that someone had touched him. Lying back while warm water ran over his hair and Alyson gave him a scalp massage was extremely okay and very relaxing.

"Don't fall asleep on me," Alyson joked. "You need to be awake to see how amazing you'll look."

After the washing, Ozzy was taken back to the chair where she blow-dried his hair and then put sticky stuff into it. When she was done she sold him some shampoo and a few other things that he "absolutely needed" to maintain his new look.

As Ozzy stepped out of the salon he felt like a different person. His life had changed so dramatically in the last short while. He had been alone forever, hidden up at the cloaked house, and now he walked freely on the streets of Otter Rock.

When Ozzy turned down a side street, Clark flew up and landed on his head.

"Okay, this isn't bad," Clark said, kneading Ozzy's hair with his feet. "I can work with this. It's a little sticky for my taste, but that will wear off."

"Actually, I'm supposed to put sticky stuff in it every day."

"Then I'm going to have to wash my talons more often. Where now?"

"I thought since our money works, we could go to a restaurant and you could watch me eat something."

"No thanks, I'll stay in the trees."

Ozzy chose a Chinese restaurant, and although there weren't many customers, he thought the food was amazing. He expressed his opinion to his waitress, Tamera, at least ten times. And then, still not having a great understanding about money and what was expected, he left a hundred-dollar tip for a nine-dollar meal.

"Thank you," Tamera said.

"You're welcome."

On his way out, Ozzy nearly tripped over a wire rack holding a stack of magazines near the register. The cover said *ORVG: Otter Rock Visitor's Guide* in large letters. On the bottom of the cover, in white letters, it said FREE.

Ozzy picked up the top magazine in the stack. He flipped it over and saw a large ad for the local police department on the back. There was a picture of an officer on it, smiling, his arms folded, and a list of phone numbers a person could call if they were in need of help. Ozzy flipped through the *ORVG* and then slipped it into one of his Zell's bags before leaving the restaurant. He crossed the street and headed north.

"That's a huge smile," Clark said as he drifted in and settled onto Ozzy's shoulder.

"The food was just about perfect."

"You know, not to be 'that bird,' but you getting dressed up and eating a bunch of food wasn't really that fun for me. Maybe we could find a metal something I could take home and gaze at. I saw a lamppost a few blocks over that I felt like I had a connection with."

"We can't take home a lamppost, but I'll see what we can do. First, however, I have something I need to look into."

"I bet it's not metal."

"No, but they wear metal badges."

"Then what are we waiting for?"

Ozzy continued to head north toward the other side of town.

CHAPTER THIRTEEN

OFFICER FRIENDLY

The police station in Otter Rock was a square building made from cinderblocks with a pitched metal roof. It looked a little more imposing than welcoming, but Ozzy didn't let its appearance stop him from stepping through the front door.

For some time now Ozzy had thought about going to the police. Many of the novels his parents had left had been mysteries, and so he knew that there was a strong possibility that the police could help him find his parents. After all, his father and mother had been taken, and that was a crime that needed to be solved.

He hadn't gone sooner because for years he hadn't even known there was a town nearby, and once he had discovered that there was, he was old enough to have read stories that made him suspicious of what the cops could or couldn't do. His parents, after all, had been stolen from him by adults. And the smiling cop on the back of the *ORVG* in his green uniform made Ozzy a little uneasy. Still, he needed to take a chance.

With Clark tucked into his pocket, Ozzy tried to look confident as he strode up to the front counter. A woman with dark skin and short hair was busy doing something behind the counter. Her nametag said *Wilma*. Without looking up, Wilma said, "How can I help you?"

"Um, I was wondering, do you help people find people?"

"We do—are you missing someone?" Wilma looked up and took a long glance at Ozzy's birthmark.

Ozzy cleared his throat. "Does it cost money?"

"No," she said, looking at his eyes. "Now, who's missing?"

"My aunt and uncle used to live around here and I was wondering if the police had any information."

"Let's have you talk to Officer Greg. Greg!"

A pudgy man with no facial hair and round ears rolled the chair he was sitting in about halfway out of an office behind Wilma's counter. He had on a full uniform and a shiny gold badge. Based on his expression, he was considerably less friendly than Wilma.

"Yes?" Officer Greg said.

"This boy here needs some assistance."

Greg looked at Ozzy suspiciously. As he did so, the uncomfortable feeling began to grow in Ozzy's stomach.

"What can I help you with, son?"

"Yeah, I was just wondering if there was any

information about my aunt and uncle. They moved here about seven years ago."

"And they're missing?"

"Well, they haven't been seen for a long time."

Greg looked at Ozzy and sniffed. "Why don't you come into my office?"

"That's okay. I was just wondering." Ozzy began to back toward the door.

"Don't worry," Greg said. "Now come. Leave your bags on the bench there."

Despite wanting to turn and run, Ozzy set his bags down on a bench in the waiting area and pushed through a half-door at the side of the counter. He balled his hands into fists and followed Officer Greg.

Once in the office, Greg pointed to a chair for Ozzy to sit in and then pulled out a pen from a drawer.

"First off, how long have they been gone?"

"About seven years?"

Greg sniffed. "That's a long time. Are you sure you're telling the truth, or is this a joke?"

"No, it's not funny at all."

"Has anyone ever tried to look for them?"

"Maybe?"

"Listen, kid, I don't know what you think we can do. Frankly I'm not sure this isn't a gag. Maybe one of your friends put you up to it?"

"I don't really have any friends."

"Right, no friends. Just a kid looking for his aunt and

uncle who have been missing for years. You know, if you're going to make up stories, you should make them a little more believable. Seven years is a long time."

"Yeah, maybe I should just go. I wasn't trying to waste your time. I was just sort of curious if you guys might have some information that other people don't."

"Well, now, no need to jump up yet," Officer Greg insisted. "Just keep yourself parked right where you are. Let's get this figured out. So, tell me, what are your aunt and uncle's names?"

The oppressive feeling grew and then settled over Ozzy like a cold wet blanket. Officer Greg didn't want to help him—he didn't even believe him. Visions of being locked up and shipped away filled Ozzy's head.

"Maybe I should go and come back with my parents."

Greg set his pen down and stared at the boy.

"You seem a little skittish," the officer said. "Why don't you tell me what your name is?"

"Clark," Ozzy lied.

"Clark what?"

"Clark Bird."

"So, what's really going on here, Clark? You look nervous."

"I was just hoping to help my parents find my aunt and uncle."

"Right, and what are your parents' names?"

Ozzy had no desire to give out his parents' real names.

"I just call them Mom and Dad."

"Sure," Greg said, beginning to sound even more suspicious. "But that's not very helpful. There's a lot of parents named Mom and Dad. For example, mine are. But what are their given names?"

"Let just forget it," Ozzy pleaded. "I was only wondering if you had a computer I could use to look up missing people. But now I need to get going because I'm late for . . . well, I have to get home."

"We do have computers, but I need you to stay put for a moment. We take things like this seriously around here, so let me ask Sheriff Wills if he's heard of a couple that went missing seven years ago that are related to a couple named Mom and Dad."

Greg got up and left the office, closing the door behind him. Ozzy sat stiffly in his chair, not knowing what to do. Clark peeked out of his pocket.

"I don't trust that guy," the bird whispered.

"Me neither. This was a bad idea. We've got to get out of here."

"I told you we should have gone to scope out that lamppost."

Ozzy stood up and checked the office door. It was closed, but when he turned the knob, he could tell it wasn't locked. He peeked out the bottom corner of the small glass window in the door and saw Greg talking to another officer down the hall. Clark wriggled out of the pocket and sat on top of Ozzy's hair.

"Who's he talking to?"

"I don't know, but we need to leave. I think if I run, I can make it out before they're able to stop me."

"What about Wilma?" Clark asked.

"Her back's turned."

Clark looked out the window.

"I see something that might help," the bird chirped softly. "Open the office door a little bit so I can get out. When I turn the lights off, run."

Ozzy nodded. Then, as quietly as he could, he turned the knob on the door and pushed it open a couple of inches.

The hinges squeaked a little as they moved.

Officer Greg looked down the hall toward his office, but before he could see what was happening, Clark shot out of the two-inch crack and flew like a bullet to a long row of light switches behind the front counter. The bird hovered in front of the panel and kicked at the switches with his talons, quickly turning off all fourteen of them.

The police station went dark.

Ozzy ran out the office door, dodging Wilma as she spun around. He jumped over the front counter and grabbed his bags off the bench. Instantly Greg and Wilma were after him. He shoved the doors open, heading out into the light of the dying day. Clark flew next to his right ear, squawking at him, "Remember, they've got guns!"

The two cops were already out the doors and yelling for Ozzy to stop.

The boy froze.

At that moment, a small white car pulled into the

parking lot and rolled between Ozzy and the cops. A man wearing a felt hat and beard was driving. He glanced around, slowing down as he looked for a parking space. One of the cops banged on his roof to try to get him to move out of the way.

"Go!" Clark screeched.

Ozzy raced through the parking lot as the cops tried to scramble around the car. The boy bolted across the street. He ran across the backyard of a large house and jumped a short fence into the backyard of a smaller one. Clark flew up high and circled back to see if anyone was following them.

He saw Officer Greg and Wilma in the parking lot yelling at the man in the white car, who was yelling back about private property and suing for damages. Clark flew back down.

"You should keep running!"

Ozzy took the advice to heart. He ran for miles until he was lost in the forest and confident that he wouldn't be caught. When he finally made it home, he was exhausted and disappointed.

"At least your hair's still nice," Clark tried.

It was a small comfort.

CHAPTER FOURTEEN

EVERYBODY'S TALKIN' ABOUT YOU NOW

Ozzy related to Harry Potter a lot. Like him, his parents were gone. And he had a scar—of course, his was on his right arm and it was the result of a tree branch nicking him many years ago. Like Harry he was male. The comparisons pretty much dried up after that. Unlike Harry, Ozzy wasn't required to wear a uniform to school. So when the next morning rolled around, he got dressed in one of his new outfits, smeared some goop in his hair, and brushed his teeth with toothpaste that tasted like cherries. Then he stood in front of the mirror in his parents' room and marveled at the change.

"You look put together," Clark said. "I feel something inside of me. Something strange."

"Pride?" Ozzy guessed.

"No, I'm just not as embarrassed for you."

Ozzy reached the tracks and stood on the side of the Mule Pole Highway, waiting for the bus to arrive. It was

Friday and he was worried about his clothes and if they actually matched.

"Stop it already," Clark said. "They match."

Even with Clark's reassurance, something about the red shirt he was wearing with green pants seemed off.

"What about my hair?"

"Really? It looks hot."

"I don't trust you."

"Birds are inherently honest."

Ozzy tried to flatten his hair just a little.

The bus appeared down the road and Clark hid in one of Ozzy's pockets.

The long, noisy vehicle came to a squeaking stop just before the tracks. Mr. Goote opened the door to check for oncoming trains and Ozzy stepped on. Goote smiled at Ozzy as if he had said something funny when clearly he hadn't.

"You look like a cleaned up festive version of yourself."

"Thanks, I think," Ozzy replied.

He stepped down the aisle and took his seat.

"Merry Christmas," the boy with the half-shaved head said.

"Wait," Ozzy said. "What month is it?"

"It's butt month, but you're wearing red and green."

"Right—and those signify Christmas?"

"Geez, you take the fun out of teasing you."

All first period, people wished him Merry Christmas. Second hour was no different. But even with the festive colored clothes he was wearing people were much kinder to him. Students he had never noticed noticed him. A boy with a green backpack and long hair complimented his shoes.

Before lunch he went to the office and gave the secretary $100 to put in account 2528. She took the money without ever looking to check that Ozzy's name belonged to the number.

Then when lunch rolled around, he picked all the food he wanted and took it to his spot at the table by the far wall. Clark wriggled out of his pocket.

"It's weird how people keep talking to you," the bird whispered.

"I knew these colors were wrong. I should have . . ."

"Who are you talking to, Ozzy?"

It was Sigi—she was standing on the other side of the table, smiling.

"No one. Just myself."

"Again? That can be healthy or it can be a sign of mental illness."

"Probably some of both."

"I see you went shopping. And I like the haircut."

"Yeah." Ozzy self-consciously ran his fingers though his hair.

"It's a little holiday-ish, but you look amazing."

"Really?"

"Yeah, I've even had two friends ask me about you today."

"Is that good?"

"One of them's trouble, the other has issues, so . . . no."

"See if you can find a third with some sort of anger problem."

"I'm on it," she said. "Listen, I'd sit by you, but Christmas is over. Besides, I have to talk to someone about an assignment for math."

"Cool," Ozzy tried to say nonchalantly.

"I'll let you go so you can continue talking to yourself."

"I appreciate it."

Sigi walked off. Ozzy whispered into his lap.

"That was better, right? I mean, I think I even made sense when I talked to her."

"You didn't completely humiliate yourself. I'm very 'not as embarrassed of you.'"

Ozzy took a bite of his sandwich and smiled as he chewed.

CHAPTER FIFTEEN

WFH

After school on Monday, Ozzy walked over to Main Street. There was an electronics store called Volts near the Chinese restaurant.

The store was big and all of the signs and shelving inside were blue. Ozzy walked down the aisles trying to look like he knew what he was doing.

"Can I help you?" a man in a yellow shirt asked him.

"Yes, I want to buy a small computer for homework. Do they all run on electricity?"

The salesman looked confused.

"Yes, but many have a long battery life. A tablet might work well for you."

"Yeah," Ozzy said. "That's probably better. I've seen people at my school with those. Do they take electricity?"

"Yes," the man said slowly, looking puzzled. "But they can charge for a long time. You probably want one with wifi and cell data so you can watch movies and surf the net just about anywhere."

"Good, I'll take one. And a charger. And one of those little book lights you can clip onto your books at night. My science teacher uses one to read while he makes us watch movies."

The salesman tried to look interested.

After paying, Ozzy almost tripped over a small wire rack near the exit. Sitting in the rack were a pile of *ORVG*s. Ozzy looked around nervously. He had already taken one from the Chinese restaurant, but Clark had torn it up and made a nest out of it. Not knowing if it was against a rule to take a second one, he snagged another.

Ozzy left the store feeling dangerous and much more up with the times thanks to his new tablet.

Unfortunately for both Ozzy and Clark, when they finally got home, they discovered that the tablet wasn't charged. And since there was no electricity at the cloaked house, using his modern machine was impossible.

"This is the worst," Clark chirped as they both sat on the porch looking crestfallen.

Ozzy pulled out his old-fashioned notebook and scribbled something in it.

"Wait," Clark said. "Did you find something else you're not good at?"

"Yeah—I can't create electricity."

"I hate to be the bird of bad news, but it's entirely possible that you don't possess *any* special gifts."

"I'm aware of that," Ozzy said, already thinking of other things. "You know, I wonder if we could get something solar out here? Something to charge things with."

"Look in that magazine you swiped," Clark suggested. "Maybe there's an electricity store."

Ozzy went inside and came back out with the *ORVG.* He sat on the steps and flipped through it. He focused on the small classified ads at the back, looking for any mention of solar energy. On the last page he was happy to find someone who was selling a windmill.

"That could work," Ozzy said.

"Maybe, but I'm afraid I'll fly into it."

"What about . . ."

Ozzy was going to point out an ad for a car battery that could be used to power other things, but his attention was stolen by a tiny classified ad on the bottom of the page.

Wizard for Hire

Are you in a bind? Are your enemies at the gate? Is it time for some magic? Or perhaps you just need a good potion for sleeping. Call 555-SPEL

Ozzy shivered.

"Look at this!" He set the magazine down on the porch and Clark hopped onto the page and read the small words.

"'Babysitter needed. Must have strong nerves'? I don't know how good a babysitter you'd be."

"No, not that ad. The one below it."

Clark read the right one.

"Wait . . . so wizards are real?"

"I told you." Ozzy was excited.

"And you can just call up a wizard and they do things for you?"

"Well, we can't call because we don't have a phone. But I could call from town."

"Why do you want a wizard?"

"To find my parents."

Clark stared at Ozzy. "That is . . . the best idea I've heard in a long time."

"Right?" Ozzy said.

"Definitely right. This magazine has everything. Look, here's an ad for carpet cleaning."

"We don't have carpets."

"Sure, but if we ever did . . ."

"Let's just focus on the wizard. If anyone knows where my parents went, it's him."

"Or her," Clark corrected.

"A her would be a witch."

"Maybe he's married to one," Clark said. "Don't all wizards have to marry witches?"

"I don't think so."

"That's going to be my first question for him."

"I don't know if you should come when I meet him."

"Why, because a talking bird will confuse him? He's a wizard who may or may not have a witch wife. He's probably used to things like that."

"Okay. How about I just call him first?"

"Good, but it's getting dark and I haven't charged my

batteries like I should. So either light a candle or let me go settle into my nest."

"Just rest, we can't do anything until tomorrow."

"Goodnight, Oz."

"Goodnight, C."

Clark hopped inside and over to his shredded *ORVG* nest. Ozzy sat alone on the porch and listened to the soft wind twist through the trees. He looked up to the darkening sky, hoping to see into the present and view his parents, wherever they might be.

He saw nothing but a dark and cloudy sky.

Ozzy took out his notebook and wrote down yet another ability he didn't have.

CHAPTER SIXTEEN

IN A MINUTE THIS WILL ALL BE COMING DOWN

Ozzy left his tablet at home but took the charger so he could juice it up at school. After fourth hour he asked his literature teacher, Mrs. Jenkins, if he could plug it into an outlet behind her desk and pick it up at the end of the day.

"That's fine," Mrs. Jenkins said. "By the way, Ozzy, I wanted to find your parents' email address to let them know about the parent teacher conferences coming up, but the office doesn't seem to have any information for you."

"That's weird."

"I think so too. Your last name is Toffy?"

Ozzy nodded.

"And what's your home address?"

Mrs. Jenkins pulled out a pen from her desk.

"Actually, I don't like to give it out."

"I see . . . but does the office have it?"

"I'm sure they do. I mean, it would be weird for them not to."

"I agree, but we couldn't seem to find anything on you."

Mrs. Jenkins stared at Ozzy.

"Is there something you're not telling me?" she asked.

"I'm late for lunch."

Ozzy left the classroom as quickly as possible.

Mrs. Jenkin's behavior and questions left Ozzy uneasy, but the thought of food made him feel a bit better. He went straight to the cafeteria and picked out food while he worried. When he gave the cafeteria worker his number to pay, she looked up at him and asked,

"Name?"

Ozzy had never been asked that before by her.

"Ozzy."

"Last name?"

Ozzy cleared his throat. "Toffy."

The woman's brown eyes bore into his being.

"I have a note on my computer that you're supposed to report to the office."

"*I* am? *Now*?"

The woman nodded.

"Can I still take my food?"

The woman didn't nod.

"Okay," Ozzy said beginning to feel like he was stepping into a trap. "I'll just go to the office right now, then."

The woman had no further comment.

Ozzy left the cafeteria and headed down the hall toward his locker. Someone was on to him. Mrs. Jenkins had opened a can of worms. He was a fourteen-year-old with no parents pretending to be a sophomore. If anyone discovered he was living alone, they'd take his freedom away.

As he turned the corner he saw the principal and the school's police officer standing by his locker. Next to them was a boy named Jason who rode Ozzy's bus. Ozzy stopped in his tracks and hid around the corner to spy on what was happening.

"That's his," Jason said. "I've seen him put stuff in there."

"Open it up," the principal said.

The police officer stepped up and broke the lock with bolt cutters. There was nothing inside except the few textbooks Ozzy had borrowed for his classes.

"What else can you tell us about him?" the principal asked Jason.

"He really likes Christmas. Oh, and he gets off the bus near the train tracks. And he's got a weird finger."

Ozzy had heard enough. He turned around to run off and ran right into Sigi.

"Hey, Oz," she said loudly. "I was looking for you. One of my teachers asked me if I knew. . . ."

"I have to go."

"What? I . . ."

The principal came around the corner.

"Ozzy?" he called out.

"Sorry," Ozzy said to Sigi. "But I really have to go."

The principal reached out for Ozzy and Sigi strategically slipped between them.

"Principal Ward. I was wondering . . . are we still going to have tryouts next week?"

"Excuse me Sigi, but I . . ."

Ozzy moved backward. As the principal and officer lunged forward, Sigi accidentally put her foot in the way and both men went down.

"I am so sorry!" she said.

Ozzy took off down the hall.

"Stop!" the principal yelled, getting to his feet. "Stop!"

Ozzy weaved quickly around other students while being pursued by the principal and the cop. Fortunately for him, he had a head start and both men were badly out of shape. Ozzy burst through the doors leading outside and tore off across the lawn and toward the edge of the forest.

"Stop!" the cop yelled. "Stop!"

Ozzy did no such thing.

When he got to the cloaked house, Ozzy was winded and beside himself. To make things worse, Clark wasn't much help.

"So you just left the charger?"

"I couldn't help it," Ozzy said.

"But you promised me bird movies."

"Sorry, but it was bad. I can't go back."

"All right, all right—this it awful. Maybe we should go to the beach and try to relax."

"No, not until we talk to the wizard. Besides, the cops

are probably looking for me. I heard Jason tell them where I got off the bus."

"So? That's over two miles away from here and in a weird direction. There's no way they could find us."

"Still."

"Still, you have to get into town somehow and charge your computer."

"I'll wait till tomorrow and then go in to call the wizard."

"How are you going to call him?"

"I don't know. I can't use the phone in the school library now, but I did see one at the Chinese restaurant when I was there."

"And you can use it?"

"They might let me make a call."

"You better hope this wizard is real," Clark said. "Because your life is sticky."

"Thanks."

"And what do we do right now?"

"Hope they don't find us."

Ozzy had something to eat and then walked around the cloaked house just under a hundred times, looking for signs that anybody might have come looking for him. When he finally went to bed he was exhausted and fell asleep to the sound of his father speaking:

"There must always be a counterpart. Nothing in story or science operates alone. Good has evil, positive has negative, and nothing ceases to exist without something."

CHAPTER SEVENTEEN

DESTINY IS CALLING

Ozzy waited until noon the next day to begin his hike into town. He wore the most unremarkable outfit he could put together in hopes of not standing out. He wasn't sure if anyone would be looking for him or if someone like Officer Greg or the school cop had alerted others to be on the lookout. But he knew that Otter Rock was a small town, and it didn't take much talk or time to fill in everyone about everyone else's business.

When Ozzy got to the Chinese restaurant there were only two other people eating at a table near the back, and Tamera was working.

"Hello," she said, excited. "It's you. You left a very nice tip last time."

"I did?"

"And you're modest about it. What a nice young man. Would you like a table or a booth today?" she asked.

"Can I sit right there?"

Ozzy pointed to the booth closest to the front counter where the phone was.

"Sure."

He sat down and Tamera handed him a menu.

She walked off to talk with the other customers. Ozzy looked at the phone. It was just sitting there on the counter. He looked at the number he had written on his hand.

555-SPEL

Ozzy sat up as straight as he could. He leaned in closer to study the small letters on each button on the front of the phone. He quickly deciphered what numbers *SPEL* spelled and wrote the translation on his hand.

555-7735

Tamera was coming back.

"So, would you like something to drink?" she asked. "Water, soda?"

"I'll take that Sprite stuff, please, in a big glass."

"Large Sprite coming right up."

Tamera left and walked through a set of swinging doors that led into the kitchen. Ozzy was nervous, but it helped him to know that gaining the service of a wizard was probably never easy. Access to magic and wisdom always came with a price. He was on a quest—and most quests required sacrifices.

Ozzy leaned up to reach for the phone just as Tamera popped out of the kitchen with his drink. Ozzy moved his hand back and pretended like he was waving and not reaching.

Tamera smiled as she set the drink down.

"You're so friendly," she said.

"Thanks."

"Do you know what you want?"

"Some of that chicken that tastes like oranges."

"Orange chicken?"

Ozzy nodded. "And rice."

Tamera wrote down his order and returned to the kitchen.

It was now or never.

He leaned over and picked up the phone. Ozzy held it to his ear and heard the dial tone. Watching the kitchen doors, he dialed the number. It took a moment, but he finally heard ringing on the other end. It rang again and again and again.

Ozzy's hand was beginning to sweat.

Two more rings and then a voice spoke.

"Hello, you have reached the wizard. I am currently unavailable, but if you leave your name and number, I'll get back to you as soon as possible."

The call had gone to voicemail; Ozzy's heart sank. He didn't know what to do, so after the beep, he whispered into the phone.

"I'm looking for the wizard. It's an emergency and I have no way—"

"Hello, hello?" a live voice said on the other end.

"Hello?" Ozzy said back.

"Is this a real call?" the man asked.

"I hope so. I'm looking for the wizard?"

"If this is you boys who were harassing me at Walmart, I'll curse the lot of you."

"I don't know what you're talking about," Ozzy said honestly, trying to keep his voice down.

"Tony?" the man asked.

"Who's Tony?"

"My old neighbor. Thinks he can call me up and make fun of me."

"It's not Tony," Ozzy said, beginning to doubt his decision to call.

Tamera came out of the kitchen.

"I'll call you right back."

Ozzy hung up the phone as quietly as possible while Tamera tended to her other customers. She eventually made her way over to Ozzy and dropped off some soup and an eggroll.

"Are you okay?" she asked, staring at Ozzy's forehead.

He reached up and wiped the sweat away.

"I'm fine. It's just . . . the food's hot."

"I've never seen anyone sweat before the food's arrived."

"My whole family sweats. I mean . . . we're . . . big sweaters."

Tamara smiled and told him that the rest of his food would be out in a few minutes, then returned to the kitchen.

Ozzy reached across the counter and picked up the phone again. After dialing, he sank down in the booth, hoping to keep out of sight of the other customers.

"Hello," the wizard said. "Who is this?"

"My name is Ozzy, and I need help."

"Ozzy, huh? I used to know a man named Oswald. He had really poor nail hygiene. You know, when someone doesn't clean under their fingernails and dirt gets—"

"Sorry to interrupt," Ozzy interrupted, "but is there a place we could meet and discuss things?"

"Where are you?"

"In a Chinese restaurant."

"What town?"

"Otter Rock."

"Oh, you're at Tim and Sandra's place. They have the best egg drop soup."

Ozzy didn't know if they did or didn't, because he hadn't tasted the soup yet.

"So, could we—"

The front door to the restaurant opened, and two cops walked in. Neither one of them was Officer Greg, but they still made Ozzy's heart race.

The cops looked at the counter. Fortunately, they couldn't see the phone cord that was stretched back and into a booth. Ozzy sunk down even lower.

"So, could we . . . what?" the wizard asked. "I have to say, this phone call is highly unusual."

Tamera came out of the kitchen and saw the cops. She waved them over to a table five booths away from Ozzy.

"Could we meet somewhere?" Ozzy whispered into the phone, his voice barely audible.

"Hello?" the wizard asked. "Are you still there?"

"Yes," Ozzy hissed. "Could we meet somewhere?"

"Listen, there's a steakhouse in Otter Rock named Bites. I go there every Thursday at four. If you want to talk in person, I'll see you there tomorrow."

"Thanks, I'll—"

"Excuse me," Tamera said nicely. "That phone is for staff only."

She had walked over during Ozzy's hissing and caught him in the act.

"Oh. Sorry." Ozzy handed her the phone and she hung it up.

He looked at the cops. One of them made eye contact with him, causing his whole body to shiver. The cop whispered something to his partner.

"Are you okay?" Tamara asked Ozzy. "You're shaking."

"I'm fine. I guess I'm just not hungry anymore."

Ozzy took out a twenty-dollar bill and put it on the table as he stood up. At the same moment one of the officers stood and began walking their direction.

"Thanks," Ozzy said.

He slipped out of the booth and as calmly as he could,

walked to the door and left the restaurant before the cop got there.

"Hey, Tamera," the cop said. "Is your bathroom working yet?"

"It is," she replied.

The cop walked to the restroom, not caring a whit about Ozzy.

CHAPTER EIGHTEEN

THE END OF AN ERA

A dozen very important people sat around a long, dark, and very expensive table in the main boardroom of the Harken Corporation building. Charles Plankdorf sat at one end and Ray Dungee sat at the other. The people seated on the sides between the two men were also important, but they knew to hold their tongues at the announcement of a long-running and very expensive project being shut down.

"You need to understand," Charles said passionately. "This is a mistake."

"It has been too many years with no results to indicate that it's even possible." Ray's voice was unwavering.

"You *know* it's possible."

"I know it's over, but still you cling. We have other projects that need our resources, projects that are increasing our stock price nicely."

"Projects that pale in comparison to what could be," Charles said.

"This isn't up for discussion. The doctors have been taken care of, the records sealed where they can't do damage to our company. Any company scientists working on it have been reassigned. Our hope is that in a short time we will no longer have to think of it at all. Chalk it up to a learning experience. A long, expensive, and unsatisfying experiment."

Charles breathed out slowly.

"Are we clear?" Ray asked.

Charles nodded and the board moved on to other business.

CHAPTER NINETEEN

THE STRANGEST THINGS HAVE HAPPENED LATELY

Thursday the air was particularly wet. The clouds draped over the forest like soggy paper that could be torn with the slightest touch. Flowers had their faces closed and the birds were silent. Unless you count Clark.

"It's kind of eerie today, don't you think?"

"Yeah," Ozzy agreed. "It feels ominous. Like the perfect day for tracking down a wizard."

"Do you think he'll actually show?" Clark asked, sitting on Ozzy's shoulders as he walked through the trees at the edge of Otter Rock.

"I hope so," Ozzy said. "He told me he's there every Thursday at four."

"What do you know about this steakhouse?'

"Well, according to their ad in the *ORVG*, they serve the area's biggest onion rings and they're family friendly—whatever that means."

"Maybe some restaurants hate families."

"Maybe."

"Is he bringing his family?" Clark asked.

"I don't know—all I know is that he said I could meet him there today if I wanted to. I just don't want to walk in and have a bunch of cops take me away."

"Then maybe you need a disguise. You know, something to fool them."

"Like what?"

"You could wear one of your mom's dresses."

"No, thank you."

"Hear me out—we put you in a dress, some of those tall shoes, and a blanket for a shawl. Nobody will know it's you."

"That's not going to happen."

"Okay, what about that hat of your dad's in his closet?"

"That's a plate."

"Or you could make some sort of outfit from the cardboard boxes. They wouldn't be looking for a boy in cardboard."

"Come on, Clark, that's not going to work."

"Hey, at least I'm trying to be part of the solution."

"I could argue that."

"Okay," Clark said, "the outfit's fine. But if this guy turns out to be a real wizard, what are you going to do? You can't just tell him that you live in the woods and need your parents. Remember what happened with the cops?"

"I'm going to tell him that my mom's sister and brother are missing and that I need his help to find them. That way I won't have to admit that they're actually *my* parents."

"If this all goes well, do you think he could conjure up a . . . oh, I don't know, a bird? Maybe an orange metal one?"

"Orange, huh?"

"It's a very welcoming color."

"Well, if this wizard's the real deal he can do that and more."

"A blue one?"

"Now you want blue?"

"You said more. Maybe orange with blue wings?"

"I'm talking about in general. He should be able to help in all ways."

Walking through the trees above the school, both Ozzy and Clark could see the students getting out for the day. Ozzy had loved being around other people and now he was exiled.

"Are you ever going to go back?" Clark asked.

"I don't think I can."

"What about your charger?"

"Again, I can't do anything about that. I'll have to buy another one."

The bird and boy skirted around the school through the trees. They exited the forest well past Main Street and only a few blocks away from Bites Steakhouse.

"In you go, C," Ozzy said.

Clark flew into the front pocket of Ozzy's hoodie. He stuck his head out of the right side and looked up.

Ozzy waited for two cars to pass and then crossed the street and walked up to Bites. The restaurant was a large log cabin with a red metal roof and a wide parking lot. There were only a few cars parked there; the asphalt was black and wet.

A woman about ten years older than Ozzy saw him coming and held open the front door.

"Welcome to Bites," she said as he walked in.

"Thanks."

"Are you alone or waiting for someone?"

The question held a lot of weight for Ozzy. He felt alone and as if he had been waiting for someone his entire life. Now he was looking for a wizard.

"I think I'm looking for someone."

"Well, come in."

Ozzy stepped in and looked around like an explorer gazing out into the vast unknown. The walls were decorated with animal heads. Hundreds of single naked lightbulbs dangled from the ceiling to give the place light and ambiance. There were numerous tables and booths and a bar in the middle with a TV at either end. One television had basketball on, the other tennis. The place was relatively empty—a man wearing a suit sat at the bar, a couple at a table were talking loudly about music, and a man in a short off-white robe and pointy felt hat was sitting in a booth by a window.

"Do you know who you're looking for?" the girl asked.

"I do now."

Ozzy walked across the restaurant with his hands in

his hoodie pocket. He could feel Clark shifting to get a peek at things. He stepped up to the booth.

"Um, excuse me."

The man with the felt hat looked up and stared at Ozzy.

"I'm looking for a wizard," Ozzy said softly.

"Well, now you're looking *at* one," the wizard said with a smile. "I'm Labyrinth, but my friends call me Rin."

Rin wore his off-white robe over a black T-shirt and black jeans. His hat was made from grey felt and had a point at the top that drooped forward and down. His fingers were long and he seemed to be in better shape than most of the wizards Ozzy had read about. His face was appropriately weathered and covered with whiskers that were half black, half grey. He had blue eyes and long, curly hair that hung down in front of the left side of his face like withered weeds. A moment passed when Ozzy might have just turned around and left, but Rin's kind smile was friendly and unthreatening.

"Whew," the wizard said with a sigh. "I was worried you were one of those obnoxious kids who gave me grief at Walmart last week. Sit down, please."

Ozzy took a seat across from Rin. The booth had tall backs and was made from leather most likely stolen from some of the animals whose heads were hanging on the wall.

"You found the place all right?" Rin asked.

"Yes."

There was a basket of bread and cups of butter on the

table. Rin took a slice of bread and slathered on a nice portion of butter with a knife.

"I come here every Thursday." Rin took a big bite. "Have some," he said, spitting flecks of butter.

Ozzy wasn't about to say no.

"Your eyes," Rin said. "Very interesting. I'm guessing you're from the tribe of Mandor."

"I don't know what that means."

"Of course you don't—you're not a wizard."

Ozzy looked personally insulted.

"Sorry, that's a rough truth for anyone to hear. And who knows, in time, perhaps. I've been fortunate enough to have been a wizard for over ten years. If you don't believe me, then you can leave anytime and this meeting will have never happened."

"You mean you'll erase it from our memories?" Ozzy asked while buttering.

"No. I mean, yes. It will have happened, but it won't result in anything. But that's a wise question. I like people who think outside the cauldron."

Ozzy took a bite of bread and looked at Rin.

"That's wizard speak for 'think outside the box,'" Rin explained needlessly.

"I got it."

"You're advanced. I can sense that."

"I think I've seen you before," Ozzy told him. "I bumped into you on the street once. And you were at the police station."

"I get around," Rin admitted. "Or . . . it was the universe warming us both up to the possibility of me helping you in the future. Or it was a random coincidence. Who's to say?"

Rin took a big bite of bread.

"Your finger," he said through a mouthful of bread.

Ozzy looked at the birthmark on his pointer finger.

"That's not something you see every day. Which makes it a character trait of value. I know a woman who wears glasses even though she doesn't need to."

"Is that similar?"

"No, but all things are connected."

Clark stirred in his hoodie pocket, reminding Ozzy to get to the point.

"Right. I was wondering—"

Rin held up his hand to silence the boy.

"Before we continue, you need to know a few more things about me. This is actually my least favorite part of this interaction due to the fact that I hate to toot my own horn. Nonetheless, toot I shall. First, I have great powers, naturally. But I also have the wisdom of the ages."

Rin stopped talking.

"Is that it?" Ozzy asked.

"Let's see, great power, wisdom of the ages, yep, that covers it. In a very broad sense, of course."

The waitress came to the table and refilled Rin's water.

"What can I get you to drink?" she asked Ozzy.

"Do you have that Sprite stuff?"

"One Sprite, coming up."

"She's one of the better servers," Rin said as the waitress walked away. "There are a couple here who do a less than wizardly job. So—now that you know about me, let's hear how I can help."

Ozzy cleared his throat.

"I need to find someone."

"Excellent. That is well within the job description of a wizard. Who is this someone?"

Ozzy glanced around quickly. "If I tell you, will you tell other people? I mean . . . there could be repercussions."

Rin looked hurt. "Of course I won't tell anyone. There is a strict wizard-client privilege. Unless you've harmed someone, killed someone, or are looking to do something unlawful. Then it is well within my wizardly rights to blab."

"I haven't harmed anyone."

"Excellent. There will be no blabbery. Now, spill the beans before the pig lands."

"Is that wizard talk?"

"No, I ordered the pork omelet. I love breakfast at every meal. That's something unique to wizards. There's a property to eggs that helps our intuitiveness."

"Really?"

"Of course. Wizards don't make a habit of lying. Now tell me, who are you searching for?"

Ozzy looked around again to make sure the conversation was still private.

"I'm looking for my aunt and uncle. They disappeared about seven years ago."

"Interesting. And your parents don't know where they are?"

"No," Ozzy lied. "They've tried to find them but failed. That's why I'm hoping a wizard might be able to help. I haven't told them because I don't want to get their hopes up."

"High hopes are a wizard's creed. That and 'Undo unto others as you would have others undo to you.'"

The waitress was back to drop off Rin's pork omelet.

"Enchanting," Rin said as he gazed at it.

"Thanks," the waitress said. "I'll tell the cook. What about you, young man? Can I get you something to eat?"

The look and smell of the omelet was mesmerizing.

"I'll have one of those," Ozzy said pointing to Rin's meal.

"You got it."

The waitress walked off and Rin stared proudly at Ozzy.

"You passed the test."

"There was a test?"

"Yes, and you passed with broom-flying colors. The act of ordering breakfast for dinner is quite wizardly and not just some random happenstance. You would fit in well in Quarfelt."

"Quarfelt?"

"It's where . . . well, we should wait for that. Let's focus on you. Tell me more about this missing uncle and aunt."

"Their names are Emmitt and Mia Toffy."

Rin stopped eating and took out a pen and reading glasses from the front pocket of his robe. He put the glasses on and stole Ozzy's napkin to write on.

"Emmitt and Mia Toffy. Excellent."

Seeing Rin put on glasses made Ozzy feel even more at ease. Harry Potter had sported specs and he was a wizard.

"What can you tell me about them?"

"Well, they were probably in their early thirties when they . . . disappeared. They were both doctors and were living around here."

"Their address?"

"I don't know."

"Interesting. In Quarfelt there are no addresses. Just markers."

"I wouldn't know."

"Well-worded . . . Wait, I don't think you've given me your name."

"Sorry, it's Ozzy. O-Z-Z-Y."

"No need to explain things to me. I have the sight of a wizard. I saw the spelling before you told me."

"That's impressive."

"And your last name?" Rin asked.

"It's Toffy, like my uncle and aunt."

"Like the candy?"

"No, just a Y and no *E*s."

"Oh. T-O-F-F-Y."

"Right."

Rin corrected the misspelling on his napkin.

"Is there any reason why your aunt and uncle would have disappeared? I mean, maybe they want to be lost."

"No."

"Okay, then I'll find them."

"You will?"

"Sure. This is what I do. You might be surprised, but reality is no place for a wizard. I'm underappreciated and underutilized here. You would think that the world would put me to work, but they're all afraid of my power."

"So have you always lived here?"

Rin laughed as if Ozzy was a little kid with no knowledge as to how the world actually worked.

"No."

Ozzy's omelet came and the wizard and his client spent a few minutes devouring their soft omelets filled with bits of caramelized pork.

"This is amazing," Ozzy said.

"Yeah, it's called the Eggy Oinker. I'm not a big fan of the name."

"I agree."

Once they were finished, the waitress took their empty plates and refilled their glasses.

"So how does this work?" Ozzy said as soon as she was gone. "Does it take a long time? Do I pay you now? Do I help?"

"No, no, and yes, but not in that order."

"So it doesn't take a long time, I don't have to pay you now, and you don't need my help?" Ozzy guessed.

"No—it could take a long time, I need some money up front, and I might need your help."

"That's no, yes, no."

"It'd make sense if you were a wizard."

"So how much up front?"

"Let's just have you pay for this meal."

"Okay."

"Then I'll disappear for a while and when the quest is complete, you'll hear from me."

"How?"

"Do you have a phone?"

"No."

"An owl?"

"No."

"It would really help if you had an owl."

"I might have something even better," Ozzy said.

"I'm listening," the wizard said with a smile.

Ozzy looked around and then reached inside his hoodie pocket and carefully pulled out Clark.

CHAPTER TWENTY

TELL YOU EVERYTHING

"Whoa," Rin said, leaning in to examine Clark closely.

Clark was on the table, shielded by Ozzy's arms so that nobody else could see him. Clark spread his wings and fluttered his tin tail. He cocked his head to both sides and then tapped the table with his gold beak.

"Is that one of those drone things?"

"No, this is Clark."

"Is he remote-controlled?"

"No, I am not," Clark said. "You'd think a wizard would know that."

Rin looked excited.

"You'd think so, but you, my friend are a surprise and most definitely not an owl."

"Those mice eaters? I'm a raven."

"And he thinks for himself?" Rin asked.

"Yes, I do."

"You are much more wizard than I gave you credit for, Ozzy."

"That's what he wishes," Clark said. "But he's having a difficult time figuring out his ability."

"It'll surface eventually," Rin said, never taking his eyes off Clark.

"Do we have a deal?" Ozzy asked. "I'll pay for your meal and you'll find my aunt and uncle. We can communicate through Clark."

"How will he know where I am?"

"He's an excellent tracker. We can set up places for him to meet you."

"I like this. Let's have him meet with me behind the McDonald's tomorrow at two. I should know more then."

"Okay. Either my bird or both of us will be there."

The waitress was coming back over, so Ozzy scooted Clark off the table and onto the bench with his arm.

"Will there be anything else, Rin?" she asked.

"No, not today. But, as always, let me leave you with some advice."

"Of course," the waitress said, fully accustomed to Rin's ways.

"If tomorrow you find happiness, don't forget the sorrow that brought you there."

"I won't."

"More than fair. My work is done here. The boy will get the check."

Rin scooted over to get out of the booth. He stood

up and Ozzy was reminded of just how tall he was. The wizard was at least six foot three and the off-white robe he wore looked shorter than most any respectable wizard would be caught dead in. His shoes were well-worn red high-tops with writing all over them. Rin waved his arms over the table and then departed.

The waitress left the check on the table and Ozzy put some money down on top of it.

"Is fifty dollars a good tip?" he asked Clark.

"Seems a little cheap."

Ozzy left some more.

As soon as he was out of the restaurant and back in the safety of the trees, Clark came out of his pocket and flew alongside.

"So," Clark said. "Your thoughts?"

"I'm not sure. He sort of *seems* like a wizard. I think it just feels good to know that someone else might be looking for my parents."

"You know what else would feel good?"

Ozzy shook his head.

"If you got a charger and we could go back and watch some movies on that tablet."

"That *would* be good."

Ozzy made his way to Volts and bought a more expensive charger that used solar energy to store power.

Clark was beyond excited by the purchase. Not only would he get to watch bird movies but there would now be another piece of equipment like him at the cloaked house.

"Three against one."

"Three?"

"Me, the charger, and the cassette player all feed off the sun."

"And you guys are against me?"

"It's a figure of beak."

"Right."

They left the streets of Otter Rock and let the forest swallow them up completely.

CHAPTER TWENTY-ONE

THE FOREST FOR THE TREES

By the time Ozzy and Clark returned to the cloaked house, it was dusk, too dark outside to use the charger. Ozzy needed to light four candles just to make sure there was enough light to keep Clark charged. They sat on the porch staring up at the few visible stars.

"So do you think Mr. Wizard will find your parents?"

"I don't know. He seems a little off."

"He's a wizard. They're all nuts."

"Have you met one before?" Ozzy asked.

"No, but based on him that's a pretty good assumption. I'm actually just trying to say things that I think will help you feel better."

Their thoughts were interrupted by the sound of something thrashing around in the forest. Both Ozzy and Clark's heads jerked around to look towards the noise.

"Blow out the light," Clark whispered.

Ozzy did.

"I don't see anything," he whispered.

"Is it one of those deer things?"

"It could be a fox," Ozzy said. "Or some other animal. Come on."

Ozzy moved down the porch steps and toward the trees. Pressing his body up against a tall oak, he listened for any noise. They could hear some more thrashing and grunting.

"Animals," Clark said. "They have no sense of propriety or proper behavior. Do you know I once saw a fox defecating into the stream? Come on, that's disgusting."

"Shhh."

Ozzy knew it *could* be an animal. After all, the forest was filled with them. But tonight felt different. His guard was up due to his current circumstances.

"Listen," Clark said. "I—"

"What?"

Clark, out of juice, shut down. The day hadn't been sunny enough to keep him charged any longer. He dropped from Ozzy's shoulder and fell to the ground. The boy quickly picked him up and put him in his hoodie pocket.

There was something thrashing in the dark, followed by a strange voice swearing. It wasn't an unfamiliar voice—just strange.

"Labyrinth?"

Ozzy moved closer to the swearing. Ten steps later he could see Rin kicking at some moss and trying to find the shoe that had come off. Ozzy stayed back at a safe distance and spoke.

"Rin? What are you doing here?"

The wizard jumped. "Ozzy—you scared the spell out of me. I got tangled up in this brush and fell down. Now I can't find my shoe."

"Sorry, but what are you doing here? How did you know I'd be out here?"

"A wizard knows all. Also, I followed you from the restaurant. Sorry if that's weird, but a person doesn't meet a boy with a talking metal bird every day."

"You followed us?" Ozzy said.

"Yeah, before becoming a wizard I was an Eagle Scout."

"I have no idea what that is."

"It's something my mom earned for me. What it means is that not only can I sew and make toy cars, I can find my way in the woods. Which, by the way, is a helpful skill for wizards. You'd be surprised how many times it's up to me to guide my wizard pals through Quarfelt."

Ozzy looked around at the dark night.

"I'm not really sure how I feel about you being here. If my parents find out, you'll be in trouble."

"Right. I understand. The idea seemed good on paper, but in execution it has its flaws."

"I don't think it looks good on paper *or* in execution."

"Ah, there it is." Rin located his shoe and slipped it onto his foot. "You have to understand, as a wizard you can't be too careful. Those boys at Walmart would love to trick me into believing in metal birds and then making a fool out of myself."

"What actually happened at Walmart? It must have been horrible."

"I don't want to talk about it."

"That's fine. But you should go."

"Okay—to be honest, when I started following you, I thought you'd walk to some place on the outskirts of town. But then you just kept walking and walking. I considered turning around a few times but I wasn't sure I'd find my way back. Now, though, I know I'd better wait for daylight before I try to get back. Do you mind if I just sleep here on the ground until things light up?"

"How about I lead you back?"

"Even better."

Ozzy circled around Rin until he was a good ten feet in front of him.

"Come on, follow me."

"How can you see in this dark?"

"Easy. I grew up in it."

"That's a great ability."

"Really? I guess I've never thought of it that way."

They started walking, Ozzy always keeping ten steps ahead of the wizard.

"And you live out here?"

"That's not important."

"Really? Because I think it is. Are you sure you're not a wizard?"

"Pretty sure."

"Listen, if your family is out here doing something illegal, like making moonshine or fireworks, I want no part of it."

"We're not."

"Then why?"

"Again—it's not important."

"Fine, fine. Then answer me this: does the reason you live out here have anything to do with your aunt and uncle disappearing?"

Ozzy stopped. Rin did the same.

"They were last seen in this area."

"Interesting. In Quarfelt we always consider the last spot anyone is seen as sacred. So this is sacred ground."

"It's also the stuff of nightmares," Ozzy said, beginning to walk again. "And what is Quarfelt?"

"Most people aren't ready to hear about it, but since you live like a wizard, I feel I can trust you. Quarfelt is a place not far from here where all wizards live."

"Really? Like an apartment building?"

Rin laughed. "No, not at all. It an entire land that fits neatly in the cracks and shadows of reality. It's right around you and me now. We just can't see it because our minds are cloudy."

"Like Hogwarts?" Ozzy asked with some enthusiasm.

"I suppose," Rin said, "if that helps you understand.

It's a remarkable place, a breeding ground for wizards, and I was fortunate to spend almost ten years there."

"What brought you back?"

"It was time," Rin said with a sense of finality and pain.

"Time for what?"

"I don't think this is the place to discuss it," Rin said, trying to keep up.

"I think that the forest where you followed me is the perfect place to discuss it."

"Fine. Something bad happened in Quarfelt. Let's just say that I didn't finish a quest of great importance. And so now I'm here."

"Will you be able to finish *my* quest?"

"Of course. This is reality."

"How do you get to Quarfelt?"

"When the time is right you just see it. One day, I was working on computers in my garage and suddenly there it was—an unknown silhouette of mountains and forest right outside my home. I stepped into the foggy image and my life changed forever."

"Were you trapped in there?"

"No, once you step in, you have no desire to be anywhere else. It was as if I had struggled my whole life to know my purpose and in an instant, not only did I know, but I was engaged in achieving it."

"Brilliant," Ozzy whispered.

"Well put. Quarfelt *is* brilliant."

Rin stumbled and quickly regained his footing.

"You walk this far every time you come to town?"

"Yes," Ozzy said, turning his head to look back at Rin.

"Is there a road to your house somewhere?"

"That's not important."

"I think it is, because if there isn't, how do you get groceries or anything else to your place?"

"We manage."

"Wow. Would you like me to do a spell of stone and rubble? Maybe get you a nice path from your house to . . . anywhere?"

"No. Please don't."

"Fine—just know that I'm capable of it."

"Okay. So . . . will you ever go back to Quarfelt?"

"I hope so. As a wizard, it's my home. But I have things to finish here."

"Like what?"

"Who knows? Clear communication is not something wizards excel at."

The two kept walking. Rin stumbled again.

"This is one of the reasons why I wear a short robe," he said. "Have you ever tried walking through a forest—or the valley of death and light—in a long robe? Just awful. It's like a cape; it's no good in an epic battle. Sure, there are some traditional wizards who refuse to go short, but to me it makes much more sense."

Ozzy kept walking.

"Okay, yes. The long robe looks cooler, but is being a wizard just about the looks?"

Ozzy kept quiet.

"Anyhow," Rin said. "There are a few more things I would like to say about our quest."

"You mean our quest to lead you back to town?"

"No, the quest to find your relatives. You know, sometimes the answers we seek are more painful than the longing we feel."

Ozzy didn't reply.

"I read that on a billboard," Rin finally said. "Not that I wouldn't have known it without the billboard. Something that people don't think about is just how wise wizards are. Quarfelt is filled with sage advice and wise souls."

"I've always thought wizards were really smart."

"Thanks, Ozzy. My point is, your relatives disappeared for a reason. It might not be a good reason, or a happy reason, but some brushstroke of reality painted them into a mystery—and not all mysteries end up well."

"I understand," Ozzy said. "Can I ask you something?"

"Of course."

"I don't know anybody's life besides mine. To me, reality is a deep dark that I have to fight every day to make something beautiful and safe. But always, when the night comes and my brain whirrs, the black comes back. I know that the answer to this quest might be sordid and heavy, but I think knowing will make the rest of my life more hopeful and the darkness less intense."

"Wow, that could be on a billboard. Your family must really miss your aunt and uncle."

The sorrow Ozzy felt from the absence of his parents made it too difficult to keep talking. Rin said a few more things, but eventually they arrived at a point in the forest where Rin knew where he was and how to get home the rest of the way by himself.

"You got it from here?" Ozzy asked.

"Got it. Thanks again, and I'll see your bird tomorrow at two?"

"I'll probably be there as well."

"Good. Then I'm going home to work on the magic right now."

Rin walked off and Ozzy immediately turned and went back the direction he had just come.

FROM THE TAPES OF DR. EMMITT TOFFY: SUBJECT #3

Timsby

The weather in New York was mild, like a tepid soup with no seasoning. The zoo was filled with people who were interested in not being indoors at the moment—families with strollers, elderly couples with walkers, and everybody in between. The crowds were larger than usual due to the fact that today was the first day the new polar bear cub, named Winnie, would be on display. The community, it appeared, was itching to set their eyes on the young wonder.

Everyone crowded around the large outdoor display staring at the mother as she played with her cub. The oohs and aahs of the audience were audible and loud. Children pointed, parents smiled, and the zoo employees looked on as if they had personally had something to do with the birth of the bear.

A low wall surrounded the polar bear display. Behind the wall was a long line of shrubs, and on the other side of the shrubs was a shallow moat that kept everyone just the right distance from the mother polar bear and her newborn baby.

Timsby had come to the zoo with his wife. They were both taking the day off to see the cub, and had walked hand in hand through the zoo gates, hand in hand through the zoo, and hand and hand as they stared at Winnie.

But the handholding stopped when Timsby let go and pushed his way through the crowd to the wall.

"Honey?" his wife called out. "Where are you going?"

Timsby walked right up to the wall and in one smooth motion vaulted over it. The crowd's oohs and ahhhs changed to ohhs and noos. Timsby pushed his way through the scratchy shrubs.

"Get back from there, sir!" one of the zookeepers yelled.

But it was too late. Timsby leaped down into the shallow moat. His splashing caused the mother polar bear to take notice. The zookeepers panicked as Timsby's wife screamed.

Timsby stood up in the water and began to walk toward the bears.

Before he could get to them, four zookeepers entered the enclosure from the door. Two began to distract the mother bear while the other two successfully grabbed Timsby.

Miraculously he was hauled out without further injury or incident. He was taken to the police station two miles away and questioned for an hour.

Timsby had never done anything like that. He was a prominent member of the community with ties to multiple charities and associations. He was on no medication and had never been treated for any instability. He also had no recollection of—or excuse for—what he had done.

He was released into his wife's care and given a court date, then eventually fined and ordered to perform community service.

CHAPTER TWENTY-TWO

ALL-DAY BREAKFAST

"So what is this place?" Clark asked. "It smells funny."

"You can't smell, I thought."

"No, I can't, but it *looks* like it smells funny."

"It's McDonald's, and it looks that way because we're hiding behind the dumpster. I'm sure it's nice inside."

"Have you been in there?"

"No, but there's a coupon in the *ORVG* for a half-price Big Mac."

"What's that?"

"I'm not sure."

"Still, half off is hard to ignore. Why don't we go inside?"

"I told the wizard you'd meet him out here. Besides, I still need to make sure it's not a trap."

"Wow. Who do you think you are, Oz?"

"I'm not saying that I'm important enough to set a trap

for, but I can't be too careful. What if Rin's just an undercover cop?"

"Then why hasn't he already arrested you? Trust me . . . he seems like a wizard. That man couldn't be anything else. Can you picture him as a dentist?"

"Not really."

"What is a dentist, anyway?" Clark asked.

"They work on people's teeth."

"What a weird species you all are."

"I wonder if Rin will even show up."

"You thinking he just used you for that free Eggy Oinker?"

"I hope not," Ozzy said.

"You're still not convinced that wizards are real, are you?" Clark asked.

"I don't know. What I need is for him to find my parents so that I can ask *them* those kinds of stupid questions."

The white compact car they had seen before pulled into the parking lot. It had two doors and a blue stripe that ran all the way around it. Rin was driving. He spotted Ozzy and pulled into an empty parking space next to the dumpster.

"Hello," he hollered though the open car window. "You both showed up."

Rin turned off his car and stepped out.

"I wasn't sure if you would. I even brought some birdseed in case it was just me and the bird."

Clark was flattered.

"He can't eat," Ozzy informed him.

"I can chew."

"Good. Now, let's sit down so I can tell you what I've found."

The three of them moved to the McDonald's outdoor patio. Ozzy was so excited by the possibility of what Rin may have found he couldn't sit down. He stood next to the table and bounced on his toes.

"First off, did you know that your aunt and uncle lived in New York right before they moved here?"

"Yes," Ozzy said.

"And that he was an inventor and scientist and she was a psychologist?"

"Yes. I think I told you all of that," Ozzy said and begin to feel a little less excited.

"Well, look at this." Rin pulled out a piece of white paper from his bag. It was a picture of Ozzy's parents when they were young and still in New York.

"Wow," Ozzy said in awe.

He had seen a lot of pictures of his mom and dad. There had been a few different photo albums inside boxes at the cloaked house and there were other framed pictures sitting on the fireplace mantel. But Ozzy had never seen the picture Rin was holding.

"Where did you get this?"

"Conjured it up."

"From where?"

"It was taken by the university your *mother* and *father* worked at just before you were born."

Ozzy tried not to look shocked at what Rin had said. Clark didn't try at all.

"Uh-oh," the bird said.

Ozzy backed up, trying to decide if he should bolt.

"Listen," Rin said. "I'm not going to chase after you if you run, but before you do, I just want to ask you a couple of questions."

Rin's sincere expression helped Ozzy decide to at least hear him out.

"It appears that a while ago, Emmitt and Mia Toffy mysteriously left their home in New York—and nobody has heard from them since. There was some investigation done in the New York area, but no clues were found as to their whereabouts. It seems that the only person in the world who knows where they went is you."

The color from Ozzy's face disappeared and a new pale took its place.

"You also said that they've been missing for more than seven years," Rin continued. "If that's the case, have you been living by yourself all of these years?"

Ozzy could feel his emotions beginning to push up into the pale. This was not at all how he had envisioned this meeting going.

"Listen," Clark spoke up. "You don't know anything. I mean, you obviously know a lot, but that doesn't mean you can just go saying things."

"Is it true?" Rin asked. "Have you been living alone since you were six?"

"Seven," Ozzy said softly.

"I am so sorry."

"You should be, digging your beak into someone else's family business," Clark squawked.

"So how old are you now?" Rin asked.

"Fourteen, I think."

"Wow. This is a moment when even a wizard's wisdom is inadequate."

Ozzy was shocked, but he was equally surprised by the rush of relief he felt knowing that someone else knew the truth.

"How does a seven-year-old survive on his own?"

"I had no choice. I didn't know what else to do. It wasn't easy or fun, and I don't remember all of it now, but I do remember the terrifying feeling of being alone and scared and desperate. Actually, it wasn't until I discovered Clark that I began to have any semblance of comfort."

"Birds make excellent companions," Clark said.

Ozzy tapped Clark on his head affectionately. "What are you going to do? Are you going to turn me in?"

"For what?" the wizard asked. "I don't see anyone who needs to be turned in—I see a resourceful person who has survived something incredible. You are more than you imagine and no less than remarkable. Here's what we're going to do. We're going to find your parents. The only thing I ask is that from this point we are completely honest with one another."

"Deal."

"You must know, Ozzy, that to a wizard honesty is everything. And if we have to lie, we couch it in a riddle."

"Fine," Clark said. "If we're all confessing, I want you to know that I think that trash can over there is nice looking."

The trash can Clark was talking about was a big red metal one with a face painted on it. Ozzy shook his head with embarrassment.

"Sorry—Clark sort of gets funny crushes on anything bird-related—or made of metal."

"'Sort of'?" Clark said with disgust. "This could be a grown-up relationship."

"It's a trash can."

"Don't tell me who to love."

"You two really are lucky to have each other," Rin said. "You're like siblings."

"I'm older," Clark pointed out. "I was built before Ozzy was even born."

Ozzy tapped Clark on the head once more. Rin smiled at the exchange and then let his expression grow somber.

"Listen, Ozzy, I feel like now would be a good time to remind you of what I said yesterday. You know . . . the answer we might find could be something less than what you want. But with all you've survived, I think you understand that what lies ahead could end up with you being smothered in hurt."

"It's still an answer, and from there anything's possible."

"Well then, let me return to my cauldron and give these things a chance to simmer. By tomorrow I'll know where we must step next."

"And you promise you're not just setting me up to turn me in?"

Rin looked deathly serious.

"Quarfelt has taught me more than I can ever convey, but there is a loyalty that comes with fighting for the right thing. Our quest is as noble as almost any I have ever journeyed on. I might be a wizard that you look up to, but I am your companion now, and I won't rest until you have the answer you so desperately seek. Also, I kind of have this thing against helping the police too much."

"Thank you."

"There will still be a charge, of course, but I'll bill you by the quest and not by the hour."

"Fair enough."

"I prefer people say, 'More than fair,'" Rin said.

"Well then, that's more than fair."

"Hey," Clark said seriously, still staring at the painted trash can, "you know, I'm surprising myself, but I think I might be ready for a real relationship."

"Stop thinking about that trash can," Ozzy pleaded.

"Let's meet up tomorrow," Rin said. "Four o'clock at

Bites. I know it's not Thursday, but I think that's a safe place to meet."

"I'll be there," Ozzy said. "Wait—were we going to get something to eat?"

They went inside and Rin taught Ozzy how to order off the McDonald's secret menu. To Ozzy, it seemed like something only a wizard would know. They both got sausage McMuffins with three patties and hash browns sprinkled with cheese. To finish off the teaching moment, Rin let Ozzy pay for it all to show him how currency worked.

Then, to make Clark happy, they took their food back outside and ate it on the table next to the trash can.

CHAPTER TWENTY-THREE

WHO'S GOT THE BRAINS?

Ozzy wrestled with new feelings the entire hike home. It was exhilarating to know that Labyrinth was on his side. Not everyone had a wizard in their corner. It was scary to think that they might find answers, but the deepest dark came when Ozzy let hope creep into his soul. He knew all too well that some things, no matter how hard one hopes, never come to pass.

"You okay?" Clark asked as they entered the cloaked house.

"Fine. Actually, better than fine. The charger should work now."

Ozzy moved through the boxes and climbed the starry staircase up to his attic room. He popped open the round window on the dormer and climbed out onto the crooked overgrown roof to retrieve the charger. Ozzy had left it in a spot that would receive the most sun.

"Well?" Clark asked, having flown up from the outside.

"One hundred percent charged."

Ozzy climbed back in the window and sat on his bed. The afternoon sun spilled its wares in through the window and lit up the dark walls of the attic bedroom nicely.

Ozzy pulled the tablet out from under his bed and plugged it into the portable charger.

"How long do we wait?"

"How about now?"

He turned the computer tablet on and it came to life like a futuristic piece of machinery in the home of a woodland elf. The glow from the screen caused Clark to smile.

"I like this thing."

"No cheating on the trash can," Ozzy joked.

Ozzy opened the browser and typed in

Bird pictures

It took a moment, but then, like a rainbow bursting into the room, thousands of bird pictures filled the screen.

Clark's small eyes bulged.

"Wow. You've got to buy a printer so we can print some of those out and hang them in my room."

"You have a room?"

"Yeah—the downstairs. Which I've been meaning to talk to you about. Are we just going to leave things in boxes forever? Your parents probably didn't move all those in here just to leave them sitting around."

Talk of boxes reminded Ozzy of Clark asking once

about how all the things in the cloaked house had actually gotten there. He quickly typed in

Moving company Otter Rock Oregon

Two different names came up:

U-Haul Storage and Moving
Doyle and Sons Moving

"Somebody had to deliver all of these boxes," Ozzy said. "Maybe one of these places has a record of my parents moving here."

"Um, that was my idea, remember."

Ozzy clicked on the link for the U-Haul store and saw that it had only been open for three years.

"U-Haul's out."

He went to the Doyle and Sons website next. On the landing page in big letters it read:

Established in 1970

Ozzy wrote down the name and phone number for the business. Then he shifted his search to his parents. He typed in their names and pressed *Enter.* A few more entries popped up than at school.

"There must be a different filter out here."

"I have no idea what that means," Clark admitted.

"It means you can see more birds and do a more thorough search. Look at this."

Ozzy pointed to a mention of his mother in a book about psychology. It also had a quote from her.

"There is more to the human mind than synapses and contemplation. There are switches that exist, switches that can change emotions, thoughts, and even actions. Once we establish those connections, we can control ourselves in ways we never thought possible. Compulsive behavior will be a thing of the past."

"What's that mean?" Clark asked.

"That my mom was smart."

"We already knew that."

Ozzy found a few more mentions of his parents as well as the picture that Labyrinth had shown him.

"I don't want to be *that* bird again, but do you think that maybe instead of wizardry, Rin the Off-White just did an internet search?"

"It's possible."

Ozzy typed in.

Are wizards real?

There were hundreds of articles claiming that wizards were real. And hundreds that stated quite plainly that they weren't. Ozzy read through them looking for an argument that would convince him either way.

"It looks like most rational people don't think they are real," Clark said.

"Right," Ozzy agreed. "But sometimes rational people ruin everything."

"That sounds like something Rin would say."

Ozzy clicked on a link and brought up a Portland newspaper. There was a small banner ad across the bottom that was trying to drum up interest for an event at a shopping center.

**COME MEET THE CHEESE WIZARD
AT THE WASHINGTON SQUARE MALL!**

"There are *cheese* wizards?" Clark said in awe.

"I think that's one of the fake wizards."

Ozzy reached out to click off the page, but before he could, the banner ad changed into an ad for a Portland attorney named Timsby Lane.

"Timsby Lane," Ozzy whispered.

"Isn't that the street near the school?" Clark asked.

"No, that's *Thyme* Lane."

"Who or what is a Timsby?"

"My father mentioned a man by that name on one of his tapes. He was the guy who jumped into the polar bear cage, remember? I've never heard that name anywhere else."

"Sure, but you don't get out much."

"That's true, but still—Timsby?"

"I agree. It's a horrible name."

Ozzy set down the tablet and pulled out the box of cassette tapes he had near his bed. He dug through them until he found the one he was looking for. The tape player was sitting on the windowsill like it always was. Ozzy kept it there so that it could catch as much light as possible. He picked up the machine and put it on his bed. He ejected the tape that was in it and put in the tape he had found.

"I don't understand," Clark said. "How could it be the same person?"

"I'm not saying it is," Ozzy said as he fast-forwarded the cassette to find the spot he wanted. "I just want to see if I'm right about the name."

Ozzy pressed play.

"I will never give up on the dream of making this so. I find that terrible discoveries are often the most informative . . ."

Ozzy stopped the tape and pressed fast-forward again.

"I used to be impressed with this technology," Clark said. "But the tablet puts this to shame."

The machine clicked and whirred back and forth as Ozzy pressed play, then fast-forward, then play, then rewind, then play again.

"Or take, for example, the study of Timsby, subject number three."

Emmitt Toffy's voice filled the small attic bedroom like helium and made Ozzy feel light-headed.

"Timsby willingly displays the need for power and attention. As a young lawyer he cannot see the world outside the law and personal achievement. But as a subject he shows great possibility."

The tape stopped there.

"Do you think there's a connection?" Ozzy asked.

He looked at the tablet and saw that the page he had been on was no longer on the screen. Instead there were dozens of pictures of birds.

"What?" Clark said defensively. "I found the back button."

Ozzy typed Timsby Lane's name into the search bar. "There has to be a connection."

"No way," Clark said. "The Timsby your father was talking about was young."

"He was talking about that Timsby almost fifteen years ago."

"Right. I'm not great with ages anyway, since I'm ageless."

"There's always rust."

The screen revealed dozens of citations about Timsby Lane as a lawyer and about different clients he had helped. There was also some information on his family and the charity work he had done. According to one site, he had started his law career in New York.

That bit of information gave Ozzy chills. But what cracked the case was an article about him from almost fifteen years ago. It was a report on him jumping into a polar bear cage at the New York zoo.

"Just like the Timsby on the tapes did," Clark whistled. "That's something, right?"

"I'll say."

Ozzy and Clark did some more searching online, but they couldn't find anything else. Then they spent an hour looking at birds and various things made of metal. Clark enjoyed the search, but Ozzy's mind was a million miles away.

Timsby was his first solid lead, and with it came his first solid hope. It was a wonderful and dangerous feeling.

CHAPTER TWENTY-FOUR

A PLAN IS HATCHED

Ozzy walked into Bites with Clark in his pocket and new information to share with Rin. The wizard was already sitting at the same booth, drinking a soda. Ozzy took his seat and Rin smiled at him.

"You look like you learned something overnight," Rin said. "Maybe a full three-percent wiser than when I last left you."

Ozzy smiled and Clark climbed out of his pocket and hid behind the condiments on the table.

"I don't know if I'm smarter," Ozzy said. "But I might know something new."

"Let me tell you first—I spent a good amount of time consulting the cauldron and talking with the spirits that roam through my abode. I think there might be much more to the disappearance of your parents than meets the eye. There are pieces that you and I have yet to discover."

"Isn't that why it's a mystery?" Clark asked from

behind the steak sauce. "I mean, if there were no pieces to discover, we wouldn't be here."

"Such a knowing bird."

"Have you ever heard of a cheese wizard?" Clark asked, peeking out from behind the ketchup.

Rin thought about it for a moment, chewing on his lip as he thought.

"I'm not sure that I have. I do have a second cousin in Quarfelt who can do marvelous things with anything dairy related. I saw him transform a cow into a boulder once."

"Why would he do that?" Ozzy asked.

"In Quarfelt, good boulders are much more valuable than cows."

"Sounds like a lovely place," Clark interjected.

"We're getting off track," Rin said. "Please tell me what you discovered, Ozzy."

"I don't know if it means anything, but my father left behind dozens of cassette tapes. They were hidden in the stairs. They're recordings of him talking about his work and his experiments and inventions."

"There's actually a great tape where he talks about putting me together," Clark bragged. "Riveting stuff."

"I'm sure," Rin said kindly.

"Right. Anyhow, my father mentions a number of people that he knows or that he's working with in one respect or another. Usually he refers to them as subjects or test cases, but there are a few exceptions where he names names. One he mentions is a man named Timsby."

"Timsby?" Rin asked.

"Yes."

"Unusual."

"It gets weirder."

"Really?" Rin asked. "Because Timsby is pretty weird. Do you think his parents were trying to be clever?"

"That's not what I mean by weird."

"Maybe his father's name was Tim," Rin added. "And his mother's name was Amsby."

"Is Amsby a name?" Clark asked.

"The girl who used to cut my hair was named Ainsley."

"That's not the point," Ozzy said, trying to steer two drifting minds back to the conversation at hand. "The point is, I was doing research online and I saw his name pop up in an ad for his law firm in Portland."

"It seems like humans do a lot of making up names," Clark said.

"Please, Clark." Ozzy took a deep breath. "We need to keep focused. This isn't about the weird name. Also, since we're looking for leads, I think we should talk about the Doyle moving company. Somebody had to have helped my parents move everything out to my home."

"Okay," Rin said. "That's not a bad direction either, and it would be easy to check out both. I say we look into this Timsby thing after we pay a visit to the moving company. I know Beau Doyle and he owes me a favor."

"What for?" Clark asked.

"Let's just say I once worked a number on his competition."

"Who was that?" Ozzy asked.

"Well," Rin said proudly, "There was this other moving company here in town and I conjured up a couple well-placed spells so that they're no longer in business."

"That's not nice," Ozzy pointed out.

"They weren't very nice people."

"And the Doyles are?"

"Well, the Doyles are good in the sense that Beau Doyle was willing to pay me."

Ozzy rubbed his forehead with his thumb and two fingers. His grey eyes darkened to fit his level of concentration.

"You know what this means?" Ozzy said.

"I have less integrity than I thought?" Rin answered.

"Yes, that, but it also means there was another company that could have moved all of my parents stuff out to the cloaked house."

"Cloaked house?"

"That's what I call my home."

"No wonder I couldn't find it."

"You couldn't find it because you got tripped up in moss. But it's filled with boxes and somebody besides just my parents had to help move those. Especially since there are no roads for miles."

"Well, Beau Doyle's not exactly a friend, but he owes me," Rin said. "He'll answer some questions so we'll have some direction. That's a good thing, but no quest should begin on an empty stomach."

Labyrinth waved the waitress over and immediately ordered two Eggy Oinkers and two glasses of orange juice.

"Is one of those for me?" Ozzy asked.

"Of course. Also, you get to pay. I'm not sure how you have money, but it's really none of my business."

The waitress walked off, acting much less friendly than the one they'd had on Thursday.

"And I'd thank you for paying, but I consider the omelet as part of my fee. In a strange way *you* should be thanking *me*."

"Thanks," Ozzy said half-heartedly.

"You know, we have a saying in Quarfelt. 'Those who can, do. Those who can't, take from those who just did.'"

"That's a saying?" Clark questioned.

"In Quarfelt."

"Sounds like a wonderful place," Ozzy said.

"Indescribable."

Rin then took out a pack of regular playing cards and attempted to tell Ozzy his future. When nothing came to him, he bailed on the fortunetelling and they decided instead to play a game Rin called *fours*. After teaching the game to Ozzy, Rin lost two rounds. He pouted for a moment but then cheered up considerably when the omelet arrived.

The ways of a wizard are a strange and marvelous thing.

CHAPTER TWENTY-FIVE

DOYLE, DOYLE, DOYLE, AND TROUBLE

Ozzy had not been in a car since he was seven. The bus he rode to school was long and massive and not as fast or nimble as Rin's vehicle. They whizzed down the road, the experience feeling as magical as anything Ozzy had ever heard of a wizard doing.

"This was once an electric car," Rin said as he drove.

"Was?"

"Reality might not be my favorite realm, and I do care about the environment, but it was too slow. So I took out the engine and put in a better one. Now this thing has some real magic under the hood."

Rin pressed on the gas.

"Knowing that I'm helping my environment makes driving even more enjoyable."

"But it's no longer electric," Ozzy pointed out.

"Still, when it was purchased it was. You'll understand these things when you get older."

"Will I?"

"Listen, Ozzy," Rin said changing the subject, "when we get to Doyle's place, let's just tell Beau that you're my grandson."

"I can't say that."

"I know I seem way too young to have grandkids."

"No, you seem plenty old. It's just that I think I should stay in the car. The fewer people who see me the better."

"Right. I'll just have to make you invisible."

"You can do that?!"

"Of course. That's wizard 101 stuff. I once turned an entire building invisible. Then I forgot to turn it back. When I returned to take the spell off, I couldn't find it. Someone's probably really upset about that."

Rin drove down Main Street and turned just past Volts. He took another turn on a street called Ponce and then pulled up to a big metal garage with moving trucks parked outside. There was a massive *Doyle* painted on the side of the garage with "Let our family move your family" painted beneath that in smaller letters. Rin parked the car next to one of the trucks.

"Now, let's make you invisible."

"I don't know," Ozzy said.

"Don't worry, no one will see you. Keep Clark in your pocket and hold still."

Rin waved his hands and closed his eyes. His breathing became shallow and rapid. His eyes flashed open and he whispered a chain of words.

"Kiz-mon-al-mond-deen-lose-their-sight-wee-sea-unseen."

Rin opened his eyes.

"Well?" Ozzy asked.

"It worked."

Ozzy looked down at himself. He could still see his body.

"I can still see myself."

"Of course—you're not invisible to *you*."

"Are you sure about this?"

"One hundred percent. Come on."

Ozzy followed Rin into the front office of the moving business. Standing behind a worn and faded counter was a worn and faded man wearing dark glasses.

"Hello," the man said. "Can I help you?"

"You can, Beau," Rin said.

"Is that you, Brian?" the man asked.

"It's Rin, remember."

"That's right. Rin. I always forget about the change."

Beau didn't seem to notice Ozzy, but he didn't seem to be looking right at Rin either.

"I haven't seen you around. But then again I haven't seen anyone around."

Beau laughed at his own joke.

"That's still funny," Rin said. "I have a question for you. I'm working on a little project and I wondered if you might have a lead for me."

"Won't know if I do till you ask."

Rin took off his hat and scratched his head. It was the

first time that Ozzy had seen him hatless and he was surprised to see just how much hair he had. It was long and thick and all the color of charcoal. If Rin was thirty years younger and had a better outfit, he'd look a bit like a tall rock star. Rin put his hat back on and spoke.

"I'm wondering how far back your records go."

"Pretty far," Beau said. "We've got a lot of room to store things."

"I was wondering if you might have any information on a job you might have done about seven years ago?"

"Maybe. Back then it was only me and a couple of guys who did all the moving. Of course, I couldn't do much because of the blindness."

Ozzy gasped.

"What was that?" Beau asked.

"Just me," Rin insisted. "I've got a bit of indigestion."

"Happens to the best of us. Nice to know it happens to wizards too."

"Sure. Thanks for that, Beau. Anyway, I'm looking for a couple who may have hired you to manually move hundreds of boxes to a cabin deep in the woods. They would have been packed in over a number of miles."

"Doesn't ring a bell."

"Really? This would have been an unusual job."

"Do you have a name?"

"Yes—Toffy. Mr. and Mrs. Toffy."

"Let me go ask my son."

Beau got up and walked slowly out of the office through a back door, leaving Ozzy and Rin alone.

"I'm not invisible," Ozzy whispered. "He's blind."

"He might be blind, but that doesn't mean other people can see you."

"And why did he call you Brian?"

"That's a long story."

"How long?"

"I'll tell you later—I promise."

Beau came back into the office followed by another man who looked like a slightly younger copy, minus the dark glasses. Ozzy stood perfectly still, hoping the invisibility was a real thing.

"Hello, Brian," the second man said.

"It's Labyrinth—remember, Phil?"

"Right," Phil said. "Well, neither of us have any memory of any such job. And according to our records we've never done work for anyone named Toffy."

"Well, that's what I needed to know," Rin said quickly. "I'll be on my way."

Rin turned and began to push Ozzy towards the door.

"Wait," Phil said in a friendly voice. "Who's that you got with you?"

Rin sighed.

"You can see me?" Ozzy said.

"Of course," Phil said. "Are you related to Brian? I mean . . . Labyrinth?"

"Yes, he is," Rin said. "He's my nephew Crimsdale."

Phil stepped out from behind the counter. "Really? I don't remember you having any nephews."

"Well, I do, and here he is."

Phil extended his hand to Ozzy. "Nice to meet you . . . Crimsdale, was it?"

"Yes," Ozzy said, his face turning red over the dumb fake name Rin had given him.

"Well, Crimsdale and I need to go," Rin said again. "Family stuff."

"Hold on just a sec."

"We're pretty busy," the wizard insisted.

"Right . . . with your spells and family stuff."

Ozzy was trying very hard not to sweat. The way Phil was talking to them no longer seemed friendly.

"What's the story here? Why would you want to know about us moving things from so long ago? And I know your family, Bri—Labyrinth. You don't have a nephew."

"Genealogy is complicated," Rin tried. "He's the half-son of my third cousin completely removed."

Ozzy kept willing Rin to just stop talking and take out his wand.

Phil looked at Ozzy. "Is everything okay, here, Crimsdale?"

"Everything's great. Have a magical day," Rin said while pushing Ozzy through the door and outside. Phil called out after them but didn't make a move.

"Go faster," Rin ordered as they ran to the car.

"Crimsdale?" Ozzy asked, still baffled by the name.

"It was the name of my first goldfish."

"Crimsdale?"

"In Quarfelt it's a noble moniker."

"We're not in Quarfelt."

"Don't remind me," the wizard said. "Now get in the car."

Ozzy climbed in and Rin started the vehicle.

"Buckle up!"

Phil wasn't chasing them, but it still felt like a good idea to go fast. Rin pressed on the gas and the small car shot off like a rocket.

"Why didn't you just take out your wand and freeze them?" Clark asked as he hopped out of Ozzy's pocket and up onto the dashboard.

"It wasn't the right time."

"When is?"

"You need to understand something," Rin said loudly. "Being a wizard is a *responsibility*. You must choose your moments of power wisely."

"What about me being invisible?" Ozzy asked. "He was just blind."

"Was he?" Rin asked, trying to make it sound like a wise question.

"Yes."

"The invisibility must have worn off. The point is that we got the information that we needed and now we know the Doyles are no help at all."

"So what now?" Ozzy asked.

"We're going to see Ed."

"Who's Ed?"

"He used to own the moving company that I cursed out of business."

"You think he'll talk to us?"

"The adventure is in not knowing."

"Well, there's one thing I *do* know," Clark spoke up. "And that's that Ozzy and I both feel uncertain about all of this."

"Then let's see where uncertainty takes us."

Rin stepped on the gas and the little car careened down the highway.

CHAPTER TWENTY-SIX

A QUESTION OF GREAT IMPORTANCE

Rin headed away from town.

"Why are we leaving Otter Rock?"

"Ed lives in Bell's Ferry. It's about ten miles away."

"This is the direction I live."

"I know—I remember the hike well. My knees still hurt."

"Can your car make it that far?" Ozzy asked, having really no idea how cars worked.

"It's my ex-wife's car now . . . and yes."

"You were married?"

"For fifteen years. We got divorced about ten years ago."

"I'm sorry."

"Yeah, it wasn't a great time for me."

"But she still lets you use the car?"

"*Let* is a strong word. She's just not always around to

stop me. I souped it up, but she got it in the divorce. That doesn't seem fair."

"Don't you have a broomstick to fly on or . . . can't you travel by floo powder?"

"Wizards travel many ways. I left my broom in Quarfelt."

"Why?"

Rin was silent for a minute, letting the rumble of the car moving over the road be the only audible conversation.

"Is that a question you don't want to answer?" Ozzy finally asked.

"No, it's fine. You need to know that I had no desire to abandon Quarfelt. When I did, it was swift and I had to leave a number of things I loved behind—such as my broom."

"Sorry."

"Things happen for a lesson."

"Hey," Clark said, standing on the dashboard and pointing out the front window. "There's the train tracks."

The small car bumped over the tracks.

"That's where I used to get on the schoolbus," Ozzy explained. "Mr. Goote wouldn't stop for me so I just stood by the tracks. He has to open the door to check for trains because it's the law. That's when I would hop on."

"I'm not surprised you figured that out. Did you know that spirits board schoolbuses in just the same way? They float down the tracks and hop on buses when they need to change direction."

"Is that true?" Ozzy asked.

"Yes," Rin said. "Have you ever felt anyone else waiting with you at the tracks?"

"I don't think so."

"I have," Clark said. "Sometimes when I'm waiting for Ozzy at the tracks, I see things blowing around. Last week I saw a bag just drifting up and down."

"That was probably Harold."

"Of course," the bird said, having no idea who Harold was.

"It's quite remarkable that you two lived out here alone for so many years," Rin said sincerely.

"It didn't feel remarkable," Ozzy said. "It felt like reality."

"Still, it's hard to believe that you powered through such an ordeal. You can read, can't you?"

"Yes. My mother taught me to before she was taken. I read all the children's books we had in the house. After that, I read all my parents' papers, then all the books they'd left in boxes. It was a really great day when I discovered a few crates filled with fiction."

"That makes sense. Reading can sustain you in Quarfelt. A wizard can go weeks without water, but only days without books."

"Strangely, that makes sense to me," Ozzy said.

"Of course. It's reality that has everything backwards."

Each mile they drove, Ozzy could feel his life opening

up more and more. He had never traveled this far in this direction.

"There are kids out here that go to Otter Rock High," Ozzy said. "I know there are at least seven who rode my bus."

"I think the school district goes all the way to Bell's Ferry. When I was a teacher I had a few students who lived there."

"You were a teacher?"

"A long time ago."

"What did you teach?"

"History and math."

"Why'd you stop?"

"Well, let's just say that when you become a wizard, everything changes."

"I bet," Clark said. "You didn't dress like this before, did you?"

"No. I used to wear a dress shirt and tie just like every other wompin."

"Wompin?"

"The normals. You know—unwizardly humans."

"So kind of like muggles?"

"I suppose," Rin said. "But *wompins* is a better word."

"I disagree," Ozzy said.

"J. K. Rowling got a lot of things right about our world; she also made a number of improvements and mistakes. The residents of Quarfelt used to turn their noses up at her story, but not anymore. Now they have Dumbledore Days.

It's a week in May where all the wizards just go nuts. You know, put away your wands and robes and wear sandals and ballcaps."

"That's your definition of nuts?" Clark said, sounding bothered.

"Some of us braid beads into our beards."

"Sounds crazy," Clark chirped.

"How much farther?" Ozzy asked, more interested in the journey at hand.

"Just a couple more miles."

"So now that the Doyles are on to us, what do we do? I don't think it's wise for me to walk around town anymore. Plus, people are going to ask you questions about how you know me."

"Maybe," Rin said. "But you'd be surprised by how far out of the way people go to *not* talk to me. Let's just have a conversation with Ed and then go from there."

Ed lived in a modest trailer in a modest neighborhood tucked behind a short, flat, tree-covered hill. He welcomed Rin and Ozzy into his house even though his history with Rin wasn't great. Ed had bad posture and neglected teeth. He was older than Rin and not as kind-looking.

Ozzy and the wizard sat down on two padded dining room chairs that Ed pulled into the family room next to his La-Z-Boy. All three of the chairs were positioned around a large TV. Ed had graciously muted it so they could hear each other.

"Thanks for talking with us," Rin said.

"No problem," Ed replied. "It's a bad TV time. *Wheel* doesn't come on for twenty minutes and heaven knows I can't stand *Jeopardy!* Pretty sure some of those questions aren't even true. What can I do for you?"

"First off, I'm sorry about what I did in the past?"

"Listen, Brian . . ."

"Rin."

"Whatever," Ed said, seemingly bothered by the new name. "Like I've told you countless times, I don't blame you for my business going under."

"You have the charity of a wizard."

"It ain't that, it's just that I was no good with drumming up business. We were about to fold anyway."

"That's kind of you to say," Rin said humbly.

"Who's the kid?" Ed asked. "And what's the deal with his finger?"

"This is my nephew. And his birthmark is a sign of intelligence. He's working on a paper for school and is doing some research. That's why we're here."

"I'm not a man with great imagination, but I can't for the life of me imagine what I could know that would be considered research."

"It's about your old moving company," Rin explained. "Ozzy's doing a paper on a couple who moved here about seven years ago."

"I have a hard time remembering what happened last week," Ed confessed. "But if I can help . . ."

Rin looked at Ozzy and prompted him to speak with a nod.

"The people who moved here would have moved into a cabin in the undeveloped forest," Ozzy said.

"There's more than a few of those houses around here. People like to hide."

"Right," Ozzy continued. "This cabin is about five miles outside of Otter Rock and doesn't have a single road or drive going up to it."

Ed squeezed his bulbous chin like it was a tennis ball. His eyes twitched and he let out two soft snorts.

"They moved from New York and had hundreds and hundreds of boxes," Rin added.

Ed's eyes widened.

"You *do* know them," Rin said, having picked up on Ed's body language.

"Of course," Ed said. He sighed and took a big breath as if he was suddenly exhausted. "It was one of the hardest jobs we ever had to do. Me and my men hiked those boxes and furniture miles into the woods. There were so many boxes that it practically filled up the cabin. It took us forever to move all that stuff and my back hurt for weeks after. The man paid us in cash and told us he'd appreciate us not telling anyone they were there. I asked him how much he'd appreciate it and he gave me an extra five hundred dollars."

"Do you know anything about the man?"

"He had a wife and a child and he didn't want to give me much more information than that."

"No last name?" Ozzy asked.

"Not that I can remember. He must have been nuts, moving his family out there with no roads or electricity. Some people are crazy, but Oregon is like Mecca for the weird."

"Anything else you can tell us?"

"I know he owned a lot of land. We had to figure out how to get the stuff there and we were concerned about trespassing over other property, but this guy had bought hundreds and hundreds of acres around that cabin— from the highway to the cell towers.

"I remember the wife was real friendly and so smart. I was having difficulties figuring out what to charge them and she calculated the number of boxes and distance carried."

"Where did the boxes come from?" Ozzy asked.

"Not sure . . . I can't remember. They were all shipped by truck to our old warehouse in Otter Rock. Wait, I remember now. When they arrived, there was no return address on them and the driver of the truck wouldn't tell us where he'd come from. The boxes were unloaded in our warehouse and then the couple told us where to bring them. It was all a little odd, but that was kind of our specialty—off and odd. I suppose that's why things eventually went under for us."

"That and my spells."

"You're something else, Rin."

"Thank you."

"Why do you care about these people?" Ed asked Ozzy. "And why don't you just go talk to them?"

"They moved a long time ago," Ozzy said.

"Really? I wonder who had to move their boxes out. I pray it was dumb Doyle."

"Probably was," Rin lied.

"Anything more you can tell us?" Ozzy asked.

"No, and if you'd asked me about any other job, I wouldn't have remembered. There's something about carrying so many boxes for so many miles that stuck in my craw."

"One more question," Ozzy said. "Did you ever tell anyone else about them living out there?"

"No. That extra five hundred meant a lot to me. Of course, I can't speak for my employees. They might have said something even though they weren't supposed to. And seven years is a long time. Look at me—I'm talking now."

"Right," Ozzy said.

"Well, Ed, we should go," Rin said. "But before we do, are there any spells you might need or wizardly acts I can perform? How's your sleep?"

"I still don't believe you're a wizard," Ed reminded Rin.

"Oh, how ignorance clouds our intelligence."

"Whatever," Ed said, standing up.

"Wait," Ozzy said. "By any chance do you remember doing business with some men wearing green about the same time? Maybe they talked to your men?"

"No business, but—" Ed said excitedly, "I do remember seeing a group of men wearing all green at the gas station up the street years ago. It was weird because they looked out of place and they were arguing with the gas station attendant about filling up the van. All of them were in green. I would have thought they were hunters, but their clothes were solid green, not camo. Plus they were obviously not outdoorsy."

"What kind of van were they driving?" Rin asked.

"Red. I remember because it looked like Christmas when they stood next to it."

"I get that," Ozzy said.

"I remember now—I was with my employee Matt and he talked to one of them while he was buying some zebra cakes."

"Really?" Ozzy said, now working to keep his excitement under control. "What did they talk about?"

"I don't know . . . and you can't ask Matt because he died five years ago in a four-wheeler accident."

"Anything else?" Ozzy pleaded.

"It was a really nice four-wheeler?" Ed said, looking confused.

"No—anything else about the men in green?"

"Oh. No. That's it. Green men, red van, seemed out of place."

"Did any of them have beards?"

"Could have. I hate to be rude, but *Wheel* starts after these commercials."

"Right," Rin said. "Well, thanks for your time and for being so forgiving for things someone may or may not have done in the past."

"Again, I don't blame you—and I don't think magic is real."

"You're wrong about—"

"*Wheel*'s on," Ed interrupted. "See ya."

Ozzy and Rin left Ed's home and drove to the gas station up the street that was just off Mule Pole Highway. Ozzy went inside the convenience store, hoping that somehow the green men might still be there all these years later. They weren't, so he bought a few groceries, including some pepperoni, a loaf of bread, a couple Sprites, and a box of zebra cakes to console himself.

The purchase made the drive home a little better.

CHAPTER TWENTY-SEVEN

BREAKING CURFEW

Rin dropped Ozzy and Clark off on the highway near the train tracks. On the ride back they had made plans to meet at the Jack-in-the-Box the next day at one-thirty. It was on the edge of town, so Rin felt they would be safe meeting there.

"Plus, they have a breakfast sandwich that uses waffles for the bun."

Ozzy and Clark hiked back to the cloaked house wondering if they were making progress or spinning in circles. The afternoon was gone, and twilight was making a big showy push to be noticed.

When they arrived home, Ozzy made a pepperoni sandwich and ate it with some canned peaches for dinner. He washed it all down with two bottles of Yoo-hoo.

"You know, it might not be as easy for us to go grocery shopping now that the town's interested in who you are," Clark pointed out.

"That's true." Ozzy put a bit of a peach in his mouth and swallowed. "There are other grocery stores listed in the *ORVG*. We'll just find one that seems safe."

"So now that you've spent the day with Labyrinth, how do you feel about his wizard abilities?"

"I don't know. I just wonder why he doesn't do something with his magic wand or pull out a crystal ball and just tell me the answers himself."

"He did turn you invisible."

"In front of a blind guy," Ozzy reminded the bird.

"Still, that's something, and the words he used for the spell all rhymed. I think that's impressive. Plus, he hasn't told anyone about you."

"No, he's okay. I mean, I like the guy, I'm just not sure he's a high-level wizard. Actually, I'm not sure about wizards in general."

Ozzy took a big bite of his sandwich.

"He does like breakfast for dinner."

"Is that really even a wizard thing, though?" Ozzy said as he chewed.

"Sounds like it is."

"I'd like to know more about that Timsby guy. He's got the name and he walked into a polar bear cage—it's just like the tapes. And if Timsby exists, maybe we can find the other people my dad talks about."

"Their names were a bit more common."

"Still—what they *did* wasn't."

Ozzy left the kitchen table and headed to his attic

room. Clark hopped and fluttered behind him. Once they were up the stairs, Ozzy dug through the tapes and found the one he wanted. He placed it in the machine and . . . it didn't work. The cassette player hadn't been left in the window so it was dead.

"I think we should get some of that electricity stuff here," Clark tweeted. "I'd feel safer. What happens if somebody does come looking for this place?"

"Well, I'm hoping that if they do, they search on the other side of the highway. And this is private property."

"How much land do you think your parents own?"

"I don't know. If Ed's right, a lot."

"That makes me feel more important than other birds."

"You should already feel that way."

Clark smiled.

"You know, I don't know why you need to listen to any tapes," Clark said. "You must have all the names your dad talked about memorized."

Ozzy grabbed his tablet. It was still at full power. He opened the browser and typed in the name LISA followed by INTERRUPTING STAGE PLAY and pressed *enter.*

It took a few seconds, but the first link that popped up was from the *New York Daily News.*

Ozzy clicked on it and read it as if it were a race to the finish. Clark sat on his shoulder doing some reading of his own.

According to the article, Lisa was a prominent New

Yorker who, thirteen years ago, had walked up onto a stage and began performing. She had no history of mental illness and she had no memory of doing it.

"Holy nest," Clark said with a whistle. "Think of another name."

Another name, another coincidence.

"This guy was in Paris."

"I've never been," Clark said, as if disappointed that Ozzy had never taken him there.

"Neither have I," Ozzy said. "Remember? But this is much more than just coincidence. We need to tell Rin."

"He's probably busy eating pancakes somewhere. Besides, it's getting dark now and I spent so much time hidden in your hoodie that my batteries are going to run down pretty soon."

"Well, I could go alone."

"Go where? Do you know where Rin lives?"

"No. Maybe on a hill or in a cottage or in a round cottage *in* a hill?" Ozzy speculated.

"Really? I imagine him in, like, a little castle."

"I don't think Otter Rock has castles."

"It has a wizard," Clark reminded him.

"That's true."

"I guess we're just going to have to wait until tomorrow," the bird reasoned, his voice beginning to slow down and deepen. "You've waited all these years—now it's just a little longer because so often the more you wait the more you . . . um, I'm fading."

Clark closed his eyes and fell over onto the bed. The bird was out for the day. Ozzy carefully picked him up and carried him downstairs. He placed Clark in his shredded *ORVG* nest and then blew out the two candles that were burning in the kitchen.

The cloaked house was dark.

Ozzy considered sleeping. The last few days had been tiring, but sleep seemed like a foolish idea. He was uneasy now that there were people who knew the general area in which he lived. He wasn't worried about Rin, but knowing that there were police officers who wanted to know where he was made him jittery. After all, it wasn't like the cloaked house made him invisible. Seven years ago, five men had slipped through the trees and changed his life forever. Now, as Ozzy's life was finally beginning to get some traction, he needed to be smart and wary of everything that could cause him further pain.

Ozzy opened the front door and stepped down off the porch. Looking up, he saw a few stars but most of them were covered by small clouds that were lazily drifting across the dark sky.

If life was a puzzle, then the last couple of weeks had added more pieces than Ozzy's previous frame could fit. Each day was an expansion of the existence he once knew. Each day was bringing answers, but breeding new worries as well.

Ozzy walked through the trees.

It was dark, but his eyes adjusted like they always did,

and the outlines and shape of everything around him became very clear.

"Maybe I have super-sight," he said to himself.

Ozzy sat on a dead tree that was stretched out across the ground like a corpse in the throes of rigor mortis. He didn't want to, but his thoughts went back to the day his parents had been taken. So many life experiences had crowded the memory out and covered up the hurt, but in a couple moments, it instantly became an intense memory again. He tried to quell that pain by imagining that his parents were somewhere safe and simply unable to get to him.

The past was becoming more complicated—green-clad men who took people but wanted to pump their own gas, boxes sent from nowhere, someone named Timsby, Rin.

An owl hooted from the east and Ozzy moved his thoughts from himself to Harry Potter and his owl, Hedwig. Ozzy desperately wanted to be more than he was—he wanted to be like Harry.

"If I'm just me, then what's the value of any of this?"

Only the wind answered, and it didn't say a single intelligent thing.

Ozzy walked a wide circle around the house and listened for any intruders or disturbance, but eventually he grew tired and returned to the cabin.

He stepped in and locked the door behind him. Then, moving carefully, he tiptoed around boxes and through the kitchen.

His tiptoeing was pointless for two reasons. First, Clark couldn't hear anything when he was powered off, and second, Clark wasn't even there.

Ozzy looked around frantically. It was dark and the nest was empty.

"Clark! C!"

The metal bird had never woken up without sunlight. He usually faded and then had to be taken outside the next morning and put in the light. Candles could bring him to life as well, but there wasn't a single one burning.

"Clark!"

Ozzy ran through the house, looking around boxes and furniture. He climbed the starry stairs and checked his room.

"Clark!"

Just like the wind, the insides of the cloaked house didn't say a single intelligent thing.

CHAPTER TWENTY-EIGHT

I DON'T KNOW WHAT TO DO

The cloaked house felt empty. It was as if there were no boxes, no furniture, no rugs or cabinets—just a wooden shell with no feeling or warmth. A static hull void of any emotion or substance.

Apparently, the absence of one small metal bird made a big difference.

Ozzy couldn't figure out what had happened. His first thought had been that someone had come in and taken Clark. But there was nothing else disturbed and only the window in his attic bedroom had been open. His second thought was that Rin had come for Clark. The wizard liked the bird and he was a bit mad, so . . . it wasn't unreasonable to believe such a thing. It was possible that some animal had climbed through the open window and snatched Clark, but the bird was made of metal and had no scent of food or fowl. Any animal sneaking in would have been just as wise to have taken a dish towel or a book or the remains of Ozzy's pepperoni sandwich.

"Clark!" Still no answer.

Ozzy knew daylight would help. So he climbed the starry stairs and retired to his room, where he slept fitfully and with a large stick by his bed—just in case.

When the sun finally began to rise, Ozzy got up and searched the house more thoroughly. There was still no sign of Clark. He checked outside for strange footprints or animal tracks, but there weren't any.

Clark, it seemed, had just disappeared.

Ozzy cleaned himself up and changed into a blue T-shirt and black jeans.

He walked in circles around the cloaked house listening and searching for any sign of his bird. But by the time he left to go and meet Rin at Jack-in-the-Box, there was still not a single sign of Clark. Ozzy was beside himself.

"Dumb bird," he muttered anxiously as he walked. "You better be okay."

The walk to town seemed particularly long. The car ride yesterday had spoiled Ozzy. Walking was much less exciting than speeding along the road going eighty miles an hour.

"I need a car—or to learn how to fly!" he shouted to the universe.

Squirrels in the trees around him scattered, but the universe remained stingy and continued to pin Ozzy to the ground.

The Jack-in-the-Box was on the opposite side of town from the school and Main Street. It sat next to a pet store called Ma and Paws and a gas station that sold homemade beef jerky. Ozzy could see through the large front windows of the restaurant that Rin was already inside. He moved out of the trees and walked up the sidewalk to the front door.

Rin saw him through the window and motioned for him to hurry.

There was nobody else in the restaurant besides the workers behind the counter.

"Sit down, quick," Rin whispered fiercely while keeping his eyes on the window.

Ozzy sat across from Rin as the wizard worked over a plate of waffles.

"Have you seen Clark?" Ozzy asked.

"No," Rin answered with concern. "Is he missing?"

"Yes, he disappeared last night."

"Not good."

"What do you mean, 'not good'?"

"Well, things are getting a little stickier," Rin reported, syrup dripping off his fork. "Sheriff Wills had me come to the station for questioning last night. I guess Doyle went blabbing to him about us stopping there and acting strange. Then the sheriff said they were looking for a high school kid that fit your description. Now he's suspicious of me."

"Should I just turn myself in?" Ozzy said nervously.

"For what? And no—not yet. After talking to the police, I spent the night looking into this Timsby fellow. I even checked his genealogy. It turns out his father's name was Tim and his mother's name was Mairsby."

"Mairsby?"

"I know—it's awful. But there are a few connections to New York and possibly your father." Rin took a bite of his waffles.

"I think I found some of those connections as well," Ozzy informed him.

"I found mine with magic, how did you?"

"The internet."

"That's what I mean—that thing is magic. Anyhow, I don't know if we should, but we could make a trip to Portland, maybe talk to Timsby." Syrup dripped from his beard as Rin spoke. "It's not that far, and my sister lives there."

"You have a sister?" Ozzy asked. "Is she a witch?"

"No, her name's Ann and she's a fact-checker for a parenting magazine. But that's not saying she can't still be a real witch somedays." Rin looked pleased with himself about what he had just said. "That's right, I said it." He put his hand out so that Ozzy could give him knuckles.

Ozzy kept his hand to himself. "I don't know your sister."

"Right." Rin pulled his hand back. "Anyway, what do you think? If you want, I can go alone. But I just have no idea where that will lead to. Maybe your parents are in Portland?"

"Is there some sort of wizard thing you can do to see if they are? A spell, a trick? Can you look into your soda and glimpse their whereabouts?"

Rin shook his head sadly. "Oh, Oz, just when I think you're getting close to understanding wizard ways, you take a step back by asking something like that. Wizards are complicated and wise people. Quarfelt holds so many secrets and we are required to act in a way that benefits all mankind. I look in my soda now and who's to say the ripple effect doesn't destroy the life of another human somewhere? It's a precarious power and I choose only to use it when the time is right."

"Well, I can't go to Portland without first finding . . ."

Something smacked up against the window next to their table and scared the wizard out of them both.

"What the . . . ?!" Rin held his hand to his heart.

A bird slid down the glass and Ozzy could see that it was Clark.

"Hang on!"

Ozzy ran outside and picked up his friend. He quickly stepped around the corner of the restaurant so that he could examine him privately.

"Are you okay, Clark?"

The bird was dazed but otherwise fine.

"I hate glass," he said. "What a sadistic thing for people to use."

"Forget the glass—where were you?"

"I don't want to say."

"Why not? I was worried sick. I thought someone took you."

"No, I had more juice in me than you thought. In fact, I was fully charged when I faked sleeping."

"Why?"

"Can't we just be glad that I'm here?"

"Were you in the forest?"

Clark cleared his beak but didn't speak.

"Did you go into town? I mean why would you . . . Oh. You went to see the trash can."

"You don't know that."

"Well, did you?"

Clark put his head down. "Maybe."

Ozzy laughed. "I don't care if you go see a trash can . . . I just care that you're okay."

"I guess I'm okay, but it didn't go well."

"Rejected by a bin?"

"She just sat there staring at me until my batteries died. When I woke up this morning, people were throwing things away in her."

Rin had finished his waffles and grown curious. He made his way outside to see what was going on.

"Everything's fine," Ozzy reported. "Clark just wanted some alone time with a trash can."

"And it doesn't matter now, because it's over," Clark insisted.

"I'm sorry to hear that," the wizard said. "But since you're back we can all travel to Portland. Sure, we can hope to find out more here, but as long as the police are looking for you, it could be difficult."

"A trip would be nice," Clark chirped. "It might help clear my head."

"All right. Let's go to Portland," Ozzy said. "But I need to get a few things from home first."

"Of course," the wizard said. "And I need my yellow traveling robe. I'll drive you to the train tracks, then I'll stop over at my place and be back to pick you up around three. But before we do that, we should go back inside and get something else to eat." Rin patted his stomach. "Those waffles weren't that filling."

"Actually," Ozzy said, "if it's okay with you, I've always wanted to try going through a drive-thru."

"Say no more," Rin replied happily. "Hop in the car and we'll hit the thru. To the car!"

Clark flew up on top of Ozzy's head and began to knead his hair.

"I'm glad you're okay."

"Well, I'm not a hundred percent," Clark revealed. "But in time I'll love again."

Ozzy shook his head.

Clark held on with one foot and continued to work Ozzy's hair with the other.

CHAPTER TWENTY-NINE

WON'T YOU LOOK UP AT THE SKYLINE

The drive-thru was everything Ozzy dreamed it would be. He got a breakfast sandwich and French toast sticks. Rin got a waffle and egg sandwich and two orders of hash browns. Clark got a side order of onions because he had heard good things about the texture.

Rin dropped Ozzy and Clark off at the train tracks and Ozzy jogged home as fast as he could. He gathered a change of clothes and then went to the secret compartment in the stairs and stocked up on money.

He closed up the cabin with Clark on his head and started back to the tracks . . . where they waited for twenty minutes before Rin arrived.

"Sorry I'm late," Rin said as they drove off. "My ex-wife wasn't sure she wanted me to use the car. So I had to wait for her to leave and sneak the keys."

"Oh."

"It's kind of a game we play—I borrow the car, I use

her workshop, I take what I want from her garden, I . . . well, it's not much of a game. It's just me borrowing things."

The drive to Portland was a little over an hour long and the scenery and feeling of freedom was so exhilarating to Ozzy that it seemed to go much too fast.

Before he knew it, they were approaching the city, and buildings bigger than he had seen since he was a child in New York began to pop up all over like bulky beacons welcoming him to true civilization. There were more roads and cars than Ozzy thought existed in the whole world.

Rin wasn't the greatest driver on deserted roads and he was even worse in the city. Cars and trucks many sizes larger than the white wizard-mobile whizzed by them on all sides—honking and almost clipping them.

"Is this safe?" Ozzy yelled.

"Not really."

A large semi truck passed by on the left and the wake of wind it created caused the car to almost lift off the ground.

"This is insane!" Clark hollered, standing on the dashboard, his copper-tipped talons digging in.

The vehicle drove up over a tall bridge that spanned a wide river.

"That's the Willamette River," Rin yelled.

"I don't care," Clark squawked back. "Just don't let us die over—or in—it!"

They came down off the bridge and drove farther into the heart of Portland.

"I don't believe this place," Ozzy said with wide grey eyes. "It's like a scene from a book."

"It is beautiful," Rin added. "I can't think of anyplace I like better than here."

"So why do you live in Otter Rock?"

"I have commitments in Otter Rock. Besides, I don't want to live this close to my sister. She can be unstable."

"You mean the sister we're about to visit?"

"Yep."

Rin turned onto a side street covered by a canopy of trees. The buildings grew smaller and turned from square ones with sharp corners to homes with round-edged roofs and interesting architecture.

"Now, when we get there, we're going to have to tell my sister the truth."

"Right," Ozzy agreed.

"Even though she's not always the best sister, she'll be cool . . . probably."

"Just get us there so I can get out of this thing and throw up some bolts and wires," Clark pleaded.

"Poof," the wizard said. "We're here."

Rin pulled the car into a small driveway and parked it behind a green car with an orange bumper sticker that said *HONK IF YOU DARE*.

Rin tuned off the engine and looked at Ozzy and Clark.

"I have a favor to ask."

"Is it somthing you should have asked in Otter Rock?"

Ozzy asked. "Something you maybe should have asked before we were actually here?"

"I'm not sure, but it's not a big thing," Rin promised. "It's just that my sister, Ann, is a wompin, a non-believer. She thinks wizards aren't real."

"So she doesn't believe you exist?" Clark asked.

"Not at all. I've showed her all the things that I think she's ready to see, but as a wizard I know that some people just aren't built for the truth."

"Right," Ozzy said. "What's the favor?"

"Could we pretend that I brought Clark to life?"

"What?" Clark asked. "No way."

"Can't you just conjure up some creature or magical beast?"

Rin shook his head sadly. "Oh, Ozzy. Magic is not a piece of clay you can mold. Unless you're working with Spell-Doh. And we only need to pretend for tonight and tomorrow. My poor sister needs to see a sign to believe . . . and a talking metal crow is pretty hard to beat."

"I'm a raven."

"Right. So, what do you say?"

"What was all that talk about honesty?" Clark asked.

"It's well known in Quarfelt that complete honesty is one of the most dangerous of gifts. It's also one I haven't received yet. I'm honest in almost all of my dealings, but when it comes to my sister . . . I could use a little help."

"Fine," Clark said. "But if I do this, you owe *me* a favor.

Also, no telling me to do anything I don't want to do. I'm not your butler."

"I can agree to that, but what if she asks me to command you to do something?"

"Don't make it humiliating."

"Excellent. She's going to eat her words about me." Rin smiled wider than Ozzy had ever seen him smile before. "Ready?"

The three got out of the car.

"Maybe you should go under my hat, Clark," Rin suggested. "Then I'll let you out with a flurry for effect." He lifted his pointy grey hat.

Clark grumbled and flew to the top of Rin's head. Rin set his hat back down, completely covering Clark.

Ozzy followed Rin up a thin walkway to a yellow door. The wizard knocked three times and then took a step back.

They heard the sound of something moving around inside, followed by the door popping open. In front of them stood Rin's sister, Ann. She had deep black hair that was puffy on top and blue eyes that matched the color of her sandals. Her smile was welcoming like a warm meal. She was thin and wearing a pink skirt and a white blouse. Overall, she was much prettier, younger, and put together than Ozzy had thought she'd be.

"Brian!" Ann said happily.

"It's Rin now, remember?"

"Of course."

The brother-wizard and sister-fact-checker hugged in

a way most movies hope to capture. When the embrace ended, Ann stepped back and looked at Ozzy. Her shiny eyes welled up just a bit.

"You must be Ozzy," she said. "Come in, my brother's told me your whole story."

"He has?"

"Sorry," Rin whispered.

"He called last night and I just couldn't believe what you've been through. You poor boy."

Before Ozzy could stop her, Ann lunged forward and gave him a hug. As a fourteen-year-old boy, Ozzy was pretty certain that hugs were not for him. But being a fourteen-year-old boy who had lost his mother years before and had since then experienced very little human contact, the hug was like a clean, clear lake discovered after years of wandering through a dry, dusty desert.

"Now," Ann said after the hug ended. "Is anyone hungry?"

Ozzy wasn't, but he nodded yes.

"Good."

Ann waved them both all the way in and shut the yellow door behind them.

CHAPTER THIRTY

RELATIVELY SANE

The interior of Ann's house was interesting, to say the least—and charming, to say the most. It was filled with unusual knickknacks like unicorns and Star Wars figures that were set up in different poses around the room. There was a jukebox in the corner and her couch had mismatched cushions. Everything was clean, though, and it did have a kind of wizard's-sister feel. Ann led her brother and Ozzy into the open dining space next to the front room. She waved her hands and motioned for them to take a seat. Ozzy took a red chair on the side of the table and Rin sat in a blue chair at the head.

"Can I get you two anything to drink before we eat? Warm almond milk, maybe?"

"Is that something people like?" Ozzy asked her.

"Not everyone—I'm just not sure how to be a good host to someone who's been through such an ordeal."

Ann looked directly at Ozzy.

"Do you have Sprite?" he asked.

"I'm so sorry . . . this is a *no*-sugar house."

Ozzy looked around and wondered if she was talking about what the home was made from. If Rin was a wizard, maybe she was a witch with a tempting candy house, except her home was sugar-free to tempt all the little Portland kids who didn't eat sugar.

Ann noticed him looking around and felt a need to explain herself.

"What I mean is that there's no sugar allowed here."

Ozzy looked worried. "Is that the law?"

Rin's sister smiled. "It should be, but it's not. I just don't allow it."

Rin looked at Ozzy and rolled his eyes.

"I'll have water, if that's okay," Ozzy said.

"Water it is."

"I'll have warm almond milk," Rin said.

Ann walked off into the kitchen.

"What'd I tell you? My sister can be a real pill."

"She seems pretty nice, and aside from the toys in her house, not at all like you."

"Um, excuse me," Rin said, sounding offended. "I would *never* just open my toys and put them out like that. The value is in keeping them in mint condition. Did you see that first-run Han Solo just sitting on the coffee table? It's barbaric."

"I wouldn't know."

"Well, take it from a wizard—it is."

"Hey," Clark said from under Rin's hat. "When can

I get out of here? My batteries aren't as charged as they should be."

"Hold on," Rin whispered defensively. "I'm waiting for the right moment. It's going to be a whole big reveal."

"I like the sound of that," Clark said. "But could you hurry it up?"

"Shhh!"

Ann came back into the room carrying two plates of food.

"Are you shushing me?" she asked.

"No—I was starting to say *sure* and changed my mind."

Rin's sister set the food down in front of her two guests. "This is something I just came up with. Enjoy."

She then went back to the kitchen.

Ozzy looked down at his plate. He wasn't a food snob by any stretch of the imagination. He had grown up eating nothing but fish and freeze-dried food and the few vegetables he grew in his garden. He'd even consumed a lot of canned goods that were years past their expiration date. No, Ozzy was not picky. But what was in front of him now made his stomach turn.

"Is this food?" he asked Rin.

The plate was covered with a gel-like substance the color of faded green furniture. Sprigs of some type of root vegetable stuck out of the goo and a square, flesh-colored cube was plopped in the center of the plate.

"My sister's a health nut," Rin whispered. "Just push

the stuff around and pretend you're eating it. That's what I do."

Ozzy dipped his spoon in the goo and took a lick.

"Does she not use salt? It tastes like glue."

"She only uses seasonings she can grow herself."

Ann came back into the room with her plate and a pitcher of water. She filled everyone's glasses and took a seat.

"So . . . how is it?"

"Delicious, thank you," Ozzy lied.

"Reminds me of Grandma's farm," Rin said.

"Thank you, too."

Ann took a bite of her own creation and Ozzy could have sworn that he saw her wince just a bit. She finished chewing and spoke.

"So, at seven you were left alone?"

"I was."

"And you raised yourself without any help? How did you eat?"

"Our basement was filled to the ceiling with boxes of canned and dried food. I think my parents were planning to not go anywhere for a while. I also planted a small garden and the house has water."

"But no electricity?"

"No."

"You speak so well. How is that possible? I mean, I don't want to be insulting, but I imagined you sounding more like Tarzan or the Jungle Boy."

"I think I speak like I do because I have tapes of my father talking and I listen to them all the time."

"Oh, that's just so sad."

"It is," Ozzy said, feeling no need to hide the truth.

"You must have been so scared."

"Terrified. For so long, I thought it would always just be me. Sometimes I would see planes flying overhead, and the books I read suggested there was much more out there, but for the most part it felt like my world was the cloaked house and loneliness."

"The cloaked house?" she asked.

"It's what I call my home. It's a cabin, but over the years vegetation has almost consumed it to the point that it looks like it's part of the forest."

"Unbelievable. And now you're trying to find your parents?"

"I am."

"*Green* men took them?" she said compassionately.

"Well, men wearing green."

"So terribly sad. And look at me, making things worse by keeping you from your food. Eat up."

Ozzy took a small bite of the blobby square. Luckily it tasted like nothing.

"So good," Ozzy said.

"I love to cook. I think someday I'll open a food truck. Ann's Edibles."

"Will you serve this?" Rin asked, fidgeting with his hat.

"I might. Now, tell me why you two came to Portland?"

Ozzy wasn't usually prone to just talking and talking, but by doing so he could avoid the meal that Ann thought was edible. He told her more of his backstory and about school and Timsby. He would have gone on, but Clark was itching for the big reveal. The bird sank its claws into Rin's scalp, gently reminding the wizard to get on with it.

"Aagghh!" Rin yelped.

"Are you okay?" his sister asked. "Is the food too spicy?"

"I'm fine—I was just having another wizardly premonition."

"Really?" Ann said sounding doubtful.

"Yes, really. I feel the need to warn you that you should buy more sunscreen before the summer arrives."

"I have three tubes in the hall closet."

"You can heed my warning if you wish, or you can walk blindly into the future pretending you see more than you do."

Ann sighed. "So how is the wizard business these days, big brother?"

"It's just as it should be."

"And you still won't consider going back to teaching?"

"Ha," Rin said. "I teach every day and every moment."

"That's true," Ozzy said. "Earlier he showed me how a drive-thru works."

"That's why you two aren't eating more," Ann said. "I knew there was a reason."

"Sorry," Ozzy said. "I didn't know you would be serving food."

"No problem. I'm just so relieved that it's not my cooking."

Clark did some more scalp scratching.

"Yahhh!" Rin said. "I feel we should bring the conversation back to me. I have a strong feeling that you still don't accept me for who I am."

"I accept you, I just don't want to support something that won't benefit your future."

"What? Everything I do benefits the future of mankind. If Quarfelt taught me anything, it's that I have a duty to help every living creature. I think you still doubt my abilities."

"Maybe."

"Well, then maybe this will help."

Rin ripped off his hat to reveal Clark.

"Abracazum!"

It might have been a big reveal if the darkness of being under Rin's hat hadn't temporarily shut Clark down. So instead of a magical speaking bird gliding down onto the table, there was what looked like just a tangled mess of metal and wings stuck in Rin's hair.

"Are you kidding me?" Rin said, deflated. "Wake up, Clark!"

"Is that some sort of bird toy?" Ann asked.

"No. You'll see."

The sun coming through the windows brought Clark

back to life. He instantly began to thrash and struggle to get out of Rin's bushy mop.

"I'm stuck!" Clark chirped. "My talon's twisted around your hair!"

Ann screamed in surprise at the motion and voice of Clark.

"What *is* that?"

"It's Clark," Ozzy said. "He's a bird."

Ozzy stood up and helped untangle Clark from Rin's hair. As soon as the bird was free he flew around the room in a tight speedy circle.

Ann did some more screaming.

"Clark!" Rin shouted. "Behave!"

The bird swooped down and landed on the table next to Rin. He looked at Ann's startled face and took a gracious bow.

"Clark, at your service, miss."

"Is it a toy or a drone of some sort?"

"Excuse me?" Clark said.

"No, it's Clark. My wizard companion."

"It's made of metal," Ann pointed out.

"And some leather," Rin told her.

"I don't understand."

"I'm a bird," Clark said. "I can fly, talk, and think for myself. For example, I think your home looks like it was decorated by a child."

"Thank you," Ann said. "That's what I was going for. But how are you moving around and speaking?"

"Light. It touches my back here." Using his right wing, Clark pointed to the silver strip on his back. "The rest is magic."

Clark turned and winked at Rin.

Rin nodded in approval.

"I'm not sure what you *really* are," Ann admitted. "But you're remarkable."

"Now it's my turn to say thank you."

Clark flew around the room a couple of more times.

"I don't understand that," Ann said while pointing towards the flying bird.

"You heard the bird—magic," Rin insisted.

Clark glided in for a smooth landing next to Ann. She pulled back in her seat as if frightened.

"I won't bite."

"You can't tell anyone about the bird," Rin informed his sister. "I'm trusting you as family."

Ann nodded.

"Now, could we use your computer?"

Ann kept her eyes on Clark. "But you haven't finished your food."

"The drive-thru, remember?" Rin said.

"Right. I'll store it in the fridge for later."

Ozzy and Rin passed their food to Ann. Ozzy had always wanted to have a refrigerator. The ability to keep food fresh and eat it later was very appealing. Now, however, he wasn't so sure.

CHAPTER THIRTY-ONE

A SQUARE WINDOW

Ozzy was given the guest bedroom to sleep in for the night. It was a small room with a bed that looked and felt like a marshmallow. The sheets were made with a magic that rivaled anything Ann's brother had ever done. Like his attic room in the cloaked house, there was a single dormer with a single window. Unlike the cloaked house, this window was square and looked out over a neighborhood park. The window's view was best when Ozzy stretched out on the bed and looked up at the dark sky.

The stars looked so different than they did at home. There were fewer of them and they didn't seem as alert and twinkling. Ozzy had spent many nights looking at the stars, wondering how they could connect him to his missing parents. Now, as he rested in a beautiful bed in a different spot on the globe, he could see that despite the differences, everything was somehow hooked together.

Clark was standing on a wicker chair next to the bed.

He clawed at the straw seat, trying to make a comfortable place to rest.

There was a knock on the bedroom door.

"Yes?" Ozzy called out.

The door opened a few inches and Ann stuck her head in.

"I just wanted to make sure everything's okay."

"It is," Ozzy answered.

"It might seem out of place for me to say this, but wherever your parents are, I'm certain they would be very proud of what you've done."

"Thanks," Ozzy said, a feeling of warmth and safety overcoming him. At that moment, all he wanted was to never leave that bed again. He wanted to stay in a room with a window where he could watch the stars and a lady who checked on him to make sure he was okay.

"Goodnight, Ozzy."

"Goodnight."

Ann shut the door quietly.

"She seems *way* more normal than Rin," Clark whispered.

"Still," Ozzy said. "I can see how they're related."

"It's the noses. And what about tomorrow? Are you nervous?"

"Tomorrow could be big, or it could be a bust."

After dinner, everyone had gathered at the computer and Ann had found the address of Timsby's law offices and when it was open. She printed out a map with directions. It was only a ten-minute drive, and Ozzy couldn't wait to go there tomorrow.

"I just hope he's there."

"Yeah," Clark agreed.

"And that he'll talk to us."

"Why wouldn't he?" Clark asked. "You're a nice person with a question only he can answer."

"Thanks, but it might be weird to him to have a wizard and a boy he doesn't know just show up at his work."

"That seems perfectly normal to me. Besides, isn't Portland supposed to be weird?"

"That's true."

"You want to talk about anything else, or should I just shut down?"

"You can shut down if you want. I was just thinking how much things have changed for us. It used to be just you and me. The world seemed like a different place than what I see out the window now."

"It's the same place," Clark said. "There are just more things to fly into."

"Goodnight, Clark."

With a tick and a click, the bird shut down.

Ozzy continued to stare out at the starry sky, thinking about tomorrow and what it could mean. Eventually, sleep settled over him and the boy, like the bird, shut down for the night.

CHAPTER THIRTY-TWO

A RELATIVE IN THE OINTMENT

Timsby Lane sat behind a large wooden desk in his corner office on the thirty-third floor of the KOIN Center building in downtown Portland. He was forty-one, and greying more than someone his age should be. He'd been quite successful over the last fifteen years. His swanky surroundings testified to that. He was wearing a light blue dress shirt with heavy cufflinks at his wrists and an elaborately tied necktie that most style magazines would put in the "power" category. His face was clean shaven and, even sitting, he looked tall.

Timsby flipped through a pile of papers making tiny notations in the corners. It was only ten o'clock, but he was already thinking about taking off early and getting in some golf.

His desk phone buzzed. He pressed a button on the phone and leaned in.

"Yes?" he said.

"Sorry to bother you, Mr. Lane, but there's a . . . *wizard* here to see you."

"Excuse me?" Timsby said. "A wizard?"

"That's what he says."

Timsby checked the calendar on his desk to make sure it wasn't April Fool's Day. It wasn't.

"I don't understand what you're saying," Timsby said into the phone.

"Should I have him leave?"

Lots of people came to see Timsby Lane. He was not only an excellent lawyer, but he was involved in the community, with his fingers in many pies and other important pieces of the day-to-day in Portland. It wasn't unusual for clients to come see him, or for odd members of the community to stop by and ask for his professional help or a donation to their cause.

"Is he a client?" Mr. Lane asked.

"No, he's with a young man."

"Tell him to make an appointment and I'll meet with them later."

Mr. Lane went back to thinking about golf.

The phone buzzed again.

"So sorry, Mr. Lane, but he told me he wouldn't leave until you were aware that he was here to talk about two doctors named . . . Emmitt and Mia Toffy."

Timsby Lane sat up straight in his wingback leather desk chair. Emmitt and Mia Toffy were two names he hadn't heard in a very long time. His heart began to pound and it took a moment for him to gather his breath.

"Mr. Lane?" his assistant asked. "Are you there?"

"Send them in," he finally managed to say.

A few moments later, the heavy office doors opened and Labyrinth and Ozzy stepped in. Timsby stood up, still trying to compose himself. He was a lawyer and used to being cooly composed even when internally flustered, which is why he was so bothered by not being able to get his heart rate under control.

"Come in," Mr. Lane said. "Please, have a seat."

He motioned to the overstuffed leather chairs sitting in front of his desk. Before Ozzy and Rin could sit down, however, Mr. Lane came from around his desk and shook both of their hands.

"I'm Labyrinth and this is Frizzel," Rin said as his hand was being shaken, giving Ozzy yet another fake name. "We apologize for bothering you, but there might be something you know that we need to borrow."

Mr. Lane returned to his chair while his two guests settled into theirs.

"My assistant said your last name was Wizard?" Mr. Lane asked, thinking he had just heard her wrong.

"No," Rin corrected him, sounding as if Mr. Lane's assistant had made an embarrassing social blunder. "I *am* a wizard."

"I see," Mr. Lane said, willing to play along—to a point. "Well, if she was correct about the wizard part, I'm going to have to assume that she was correct about you mentioning the Toffys?"

"Well, as they say in Quarfelt, 'When you assume . . . you make a guess based on what you see and think.'"

"That's very straightforward," Mr. Lane said, having no idea what a Quarfelt was.

"I thought you'd appreciate it, being a lawyer and all."

"This is interesting, Mr. Wizard, but could we get to what brought you here?"

"Labyrinth. Or Rin," Rin said. "Did you know the Toffys?"

"Yes, and that's a name I've not heard in a long time."

"How long, exactly?" Rin asked. "We wizards work on a different time scale. I have a friend who took over five hundred years to create a spell that a first-level wizard could have created in three hundred."

Mr. Lane looked puzzled but still answered the question.

"I suppose it's been more than seven years since I've seen Dr. Toffy."

"And where did you last see him?" Rin asked.

"First, can I ask why you're interested? It's not every day that a wizard walks through my door and starts asking questions about my personal relationships."

Ozzy spoke up. "Actually, it started as a school project. I was researching inventors and I came across Dr. Toffy. There's not much about him and as I tried to find out more, I guess the mystery just got to me. I mean, I want to get an *A* on my project, but now more than anything, I want to find out what happened to him. I figured talking to you would show that I have gumption and get me an *A* for sure."

"Oh, I can respect that . . . Frizzel, is it?"

Ozzy reluctantly nodded.

"Sadly, however, I don't think the little bit I know will help your paper much."

"It's worth a shot," Ozzy said.

"It *is* worth a shot," Mr. Lane said, liking the gumption that Ozzy was showing in his pursuit of good grades. "I knew Dr. Emmitt and Dr. Mia when I lived in New York. I had just passed the bar exam and started working for a firm called Swilt, Leonard, and Wagon. Dr. Emmitt was one of our smaller clients and so he was given to me to take care of. He was only about five years older than me and, really, his legal needs were minor. But we became friends of a sort. I must have had dinner with him and his wife on three or four occasions. He used to invite people over to his house to socialize. He really liked to throw a party."

"Really?" Ozzy asked.

"Yes. They were good people and we had no reason to think anything was strange or amiss. Then one day, they were gone."

"Just like that?" Rin asked.

"Just like that," Timsby reiterated. "Because I was their lawyer, their landlord contacted me. He was concerned because their apartment was empty and they hadn't said anything about leaving. The only thing in the apartment was a short note."

"What did it say?" Ozzy asked.

"I can't remember exactly. Just that they were okay and that they wished everyone they knew well. It was a shock to those who knew them that they were gone. The police were called in, but no actual crime had been committed and the note explained . . . well, enough, I suppose. Once the curiosity died down, there was very little mention of them. My wife and I moved out here about a year after that."

"Can I ask you about the zoo?"

Timsby blinked and fiddled with the tip of his nose nervously.

"If you mean the polar bear incident . . . there's even less to say about that. I had an episode of some sort and wandered into a polar bear enclosure. I don't remember anything about it."

"Nothing?"

"I remember being questioned by the police and my wife wondering whom she'd married. What would that have to do with Emmitt and Mia?"

"Probably nothing—it just popped up when I searched for your name. You've got to admit it's pretty interesting."

"Well, no—it was horrible and I still don't understand it."

"Sorry," Ozzy said sincerely. "One last question. Do you still keep in touch with any of those dinner guests?"

"Heavens, no. There were about five of us and I only knew them through Emmitt and Mia. When the Toffys left New York, I never saw them again."

"Any names you can remember?"

"Wow, you *are* serious about getting that *A*," Mr. Lane said. "And no, I don't. There might have been a . . . Susan? And a Milo. Oh, right—one of them was Dr. Emmitt's half-brother."

"What?" Ozzy asked in shock.

"His half-brother," Timsby said. "Charles? Or John? He had a different last name than Emmitt and I can't recall it. He wasn't a pleasant person. He'd make bad jokes and then pout when people didn't react the way he wanted. He was at the gatherings, but he and I rarely spoke."

"So Charles . . . or John?"

"Maybe."

"And no clue about the last name?"

"Sorry, no."

Ozzy looked at Rin and tried desperately to telepathically communicate to him that he needed to put some sort of spell on Timsby that would help him remember. When the telepathy didn't work, he took another approach. He leaned over to Rin and whispered privately in his left ear.

"Is there anything you can do to help him remember?"

Rin looked puzzled for a moment before whispering back.

"You mean like bribe him? I don't have any cash."

"No, not bribe him—a spell."

"I did know a spell once that would have been perfect for this," Rin whispered. "But I can't remember it."

Mr. Lane cleared his throat. Rin and Ozzy stopped whispering and sat up straight.

"When people whisper in the courtroom, it makes me nervous," he said.

"Sorry," Ozzy apologized. "I'm just making sure I've asked everything."

"I'd say you've done a thorough job and then some. Now, I hate to break this up, but I've got a meeting to get to."

Mr. Lane stood up, which started a chain reaction of Ozzy and then Rin doing the same thing. Timsby came around his desk and shook their hands again.

"Listen, Frizzel, if you decide to go into the law, look me up. I could use someone with your tenacity for going the extra mile."

"No thanks. I'm going to be something else."

"Well, you're obviously too honest to be a lawyer, anyway."

Ozzy and Rin left the office. Neither said anything to the other until they were back on the street.

"That was interesting," Rin said, adjusting his hat.

"*Frizzel*?" Ozzy asked.

"It was the name of my house elf in Quarfelt."

"Still. And I wish you could have done some kind of memory spell. It's exciting that I have a half-uncle, but it might be hard to find him with the little amount of info we have."

"There are no problems too big to conquer if you keep the goal in mind."

"Really? What if your goal is to have a wizard use a memory spell on the one person who might possess a real clue?"

"Next time, you might want to not aim so high."

The wizard and apprentice returned to Rin's car, where Clark had been peacefully recharging himself and waiting.

"So?" he said after they were in. "How'd it go?"

"I have a half-uncle," Ozzy reported.

"Interesting," Clark said. "I have a full charge."

"And my doughnut meter's on empty," Rin said. "Who's paying?"

Ozzy raised his hand.

"How delightful. You wompins and your currency."

Rin started the car and they pulled out into traffic.

CHAPTER THIRTY-THREE

BOTHERED

After stopping for doughnuts, and then stopping for shakes, they stopped at Ann's. She tried to serve them a lunch that no one wanted to eat. So she packed up the food from the day before, the tofu eggs from breakfast that nobody finished (or began, really), and what looked like lasagna made of discarded salad and gave them to her brother to take back home to Otter Rock.

Ozzy was sad to say goodbye, but he was thrilled at the prospect of never eating her food again.

The drive back to Otter Rock seemed longer than the drive up had been. Ozzy had a thousand things on his mind and Clark kept interrupting by playing a game he made up called Beak Bug. The rules were simple. If you see a Volkswagen, you pinch someone with your beak. And since Ozzy and Rin were beakless, Clark pretty much ran away with the game.

About twenty miles out of Otter Rock, Ozzy said, "We

should strategize. You know . . . make a game plan about what to do next."

"Good idea," Rin said. "I'll drop you off at the train tracks, then I'm going to go to Bites. From there I'll go home to get a good night's sleep. That cot Ann had me sleep on was the worst."

"I don't mean strategize about your evening plans—I mean about finding my parents."

"Of course, of course. I'm with you. I need a little time to think and ponder and work at home. I might have some powerful ideas for what's next."

"Like what?"

Rin laughed. "Ozzy, you have such a tricky sense of humor."

"I'm not joking."

"There it is again."

"I *am* paying for all of this, remember?" Ozzy said. He was frustrated and the red creeping up his neck proved it. "I mean, so far everything we've done was accomplished by car and computer, not magic."

"Don't be so quick to dismiss ordinary things that might actually be magic. Do you think we walk around in Quarfelt just zapping things and casting spells? No, we pick up things that we've dropped, we walk to get the mail, and we shower standing up. There is magic in the force of gravity, magic in the mail system, and magic in the construction of pipes that provide water to stand under. When the time comes to use the kind of magic that books and movies fill people's heads with, you'll see it. And it will be that much more powerful because of the deft touch with which it was used."

"Sometimes you sound smart," Clark said to Rin.

"That's because I'm a wizard."

"My point is that sometimes you don't," Clark added.

Rin got a little pouty, Ozzy was already frustrated, and Clark was bored. So they traveled the remaining miles in silence.

When they arrived at the train tracks, Ozzy got out of the car quickly.

"Should we meet tomorrow?" Rin asked.

"How about you sleep on it and if you get any answers, get in touch with me magically and I'll respond."

"You got it," Rin said, completely missing the sarcasm.

Ozzy closed the car door and watched Rin drive away. He stood by the side of the train tracks as he had all those days for school. But now he knew there would be no bus to pick him up and give him a slight chance to think about something else or maybe see Sigi again.

Clark situated himself on Ozzy's head.

"You can't blame him too much," Clark said. "I mean, aren't wizards kind of known for being unstable?"

"Some of them."

"I know what will cheer us up. Why don't we go back to the cloaked house and look at pictures of birds?"

Ozzy crossed the road and walked into the trees.

"Are we making any progress?" he asked the bird.

"I think so. You're walking pretty fast."

"That's not what I mean. I mean, are we any closer to finding my parents?"

"Maybe."

"And you're sure you don't remember anything else about my dad? He built you."

"I remember some stuff, but not specifics."

A large fox dashed between the trees just in front of them. The shadows of leaves covered everything in cracks and fissures. Ozzy was down, but being in the forest he knew so well lifted his spirits.

"It's been so long since they were taken," Ozzy said.

"I can't speak to that. I was boxed up for a while, you know."

"Somewhere there has to be somebody or some clue to let me know what happened, doesn't there?"

"I hope you find it, because this rollercoaster of emotion is killing me."

"You're right. Let's not think about any of this for a couple of days. I mean . . . if Rin's as good a wizard as he claims to be, he can solve the case and then find us. I don't want to think about it anymore. In fact, let's go to the ocean tomorrow."

"Yes," Clark chirped. "You can build a real sandcastle, not like the one I tried to make."

"And maybe Sigi will be there."

"Now I'm pumped," Clark said. "The sand between my talons is just what I need."

The dimming of day made Ozzy sleepy and Clark a bit lethargic. Ozzy lowered his head and Clark hopped from his hair to his shoulder. As Ozzy was looking down, he noticed something he had never seen before.

"What's that?"

Ozzy stopped. He fell to his knees to better examine the ground. Clark jumped from his shoulder and did some investigating of his own.

"It's a dirt bike track." Ozzy said. "Someone was riding a motorcycle around here."

"Look," Clark said. "There's another."

To the right Ozzy saw a second tire track.

"And another," Clark announced. "I don't understand. Where would any motorcycles be going out here? There's nothing but our . . ."

The small bird squawked loudly as Ozzy jumped up off his knees and ran in the direction of his hidden home. Clark sprang forward and shot through the trees like a dart.

Jumping over moss and leaves, he quickly ran to the cloaked house. From twenty feet away he knew something bad had happened. From ten feet away he knew it was worse than he thought.

There were deep motorcycle tracks crisscrossing the dark soil in front of the house. The door had been kicked in and was hanging from the frame by a single hinge. Clark frantically flitted around the open door like an anxious hummingbird.

"Do you think anyone's still here?" he twerped.

"I'm not sure," Ozzy said. "The motorcycles aren't here. You fly in first."

Clark flew through the open door. Ten seconds later he was back out.

"I don't see anyone, but it's not pretty in there."

Ozzy stepped intrepidly through the front door.

The cloaked house had been discovered—and abused. All at once two things were clear: one, Ozzy's life was never going to be the simple existence it had been; and two, the beach tomorrow was out.

CHAPTER THIRTY-FOUR

TOOK EVERYTHING I HAVE

Whoever had broken into Ozzy's home had done so with little regard for what was inside. Boxes were tipped and torn. The couch and a couple of chairs had muddy footprints on them from someone using them as stepstools to reach higher and destroy more. All of the cassette tapes were on the floor, smashed and unspooled. Two of the kitchen cabinet doors had been ripped off and it looked like what few dishes Ozzy had were shattered on the floor. The map he had carefully drawn with Clark's help was destroyed.

The basement was just as bad—tools were missing and boxes had been smashed.

"Who would do this?" Clark asked, sounding as mournful as a metallic raven could. "I don't understand. What does this accomplish?"

They went upstairs to his attic room. His mattress had

been flipped over and the tape recorder and tablet were gone.

Clark squawked again, an unearthly and sad noise Ozzy had never heard him make before.

Ozzy sat down on his overturned mattress and put his head in his hands. He could do without the tablet—it was the tapes and recorder that hurt the most.

"I'm so sorry," Clark tweeted softly. "Maybe whoever did this is still out there. We could track them down."

Ozzy looked up. His grey eyes were filled with static.

"Whoever it was is gone now." Ozzy was angry. "We didn't hear any motors as we hiked in. It probably happened when we were in Portland last night."

"Me and my need to get away," Clark lamented. "Who could have done this?"

Ozzy was smart—according to the calendar he was fourteen, but if you factored in the experiences he'd had, he was advanced in age. He knew in his soul that whatever had happened to the cloaked house was somehow tied to him trying to find his parents.

"We need Rin," Ozzy admitted. "Do you think you can find him?"

Clark looked around. "As long as they didn't take my book light."

The bird flew down the stairs and was back up in a minute with the book light in his talons. He dropped it in Ozzy's hands.

"Where was this?"

"I may or may not have hidden it in the basement rafters. I guess I'm overly possessive. Flip it on."

Ozzy turned it on and a strong small light shone out.

"Perfect. Clip it to me and I'll go."

Ozzy clipped the light to Clark's rear and bent the small light to shine directly at the silver strip on his back.

"You know where he is?"

"He said he'd be at Bites, probably pigging out on that oinking egg thing."

Clark jumped to the window sill and looked out at the now-dark sky.

"Be careful," Ozzy said. "And if you have to stop for the night, make sure it's somewhere the rising sun will still hit you."

"I will."

"And don't mess with the trash can."

Clark looked at Ozzy and blinked his small eyes. "I'm a little insulted you even said that."

"Fine, I'm sorry. But still don't. Just find Rin, tell him what happened, and get back here. If he gives you any grief, tell him I'm paying for his time."

Clark saluted with his right wing and jumped out the round window. Ozzy watched the speck of light fly off and then come right back.

"What?" Ozzy asked urgently.

"Did that look cool?"

"What?"

"That salute, and then me just flying off?"

Ozzy was frustrated.

"It was okay. Go!"

Clark took to the sky and this time Ozzy watched the light fly off into the distance and not come back.

"Well, I'm not sleeping in *here*," he said to himself.

Ozzy collected some blankets and found his sleeping bag and pillow. He took them outside and went behind the house to the stream. He crossed a flat board that functioned as a bridge and made a place to sleep next to the black rock wall. His breathing was heavy and his heart was in shock. He wanted daylight to hurry so that he could better assess what had been damaged and taken.

His brain played through every possible scenario of who might have done this horrible deed. He had a few ideas, but he couldn't shake the thought that on the day he discovered he had a half-uncle, his house had been ransacked.

"There has to be a connection," he whispered to himself. "Timsby must have known more than he admitted."

Ozzy had read enough books to know that lawyers were often seedy.

"I shouldn't have trusted him."

The air was cool and every noise he heard caused Ozzy to get up and investigate. Once it was a fox looking for food in the dark. Once it was a squirrel running through the stream. And another time it was a fat owl who perched in a bent tree directly above the black wall. It hooted and fidgeted until Ozzy finally climbed up the tree and scared it off.

Ozzy got back into his sleeping bag. He scanned the sky, hoping that any moment a small pinpoint of light would return.

CHAPTER THIRTY-FIVE

SHATTERED MAGIC

Rin sat in a booth at Bites eating pancakes and sausage. The place was filled with locals and tourists eating, and drinking the kind of drinks that made people talk loud and get rowdy. As he took a huge bite of pancake, someone walked up to the table.

"Hello, Brian."

Rin looked up to see Sheriff Wills, a tall man with a thin mustache wearing a green uniform that was two sizes too small.

"It's Rin, and have a seat." The wizard motioned to the empty booth bench across the table. "Please. Conversation is so much better at eye level."

The sheriff sat down and the buttons on his shirt screamed.

"I thought you'd be here. Do you mind if I ask you a couple more questions?"

"Not at all," Rin said with a full mouth.

"Tell me again where you met that boy?"

"He called about my ad in the *ORVG*. We met here."

"What did he want?"

"He was having trouble with homework. His parents were giving him grief and he wanted to know if I could help with the research."

"Is that how wizards spend their time?"

"Wizards help wherever they can."

"Someone said you went to Portland last night."

"That's true."

"Why?"

"Ann lives there—you know that—and my mom. But I didn't stop in to see Mom, so I'd appreciate it if you didn't tell her I was there."

"Just went to see Ann?"

"A wizard doesn't 'just do' anything. Every journey we take has a purpose and . . . man, these pancakes are good. You want to try one?"

"No thanks, I'm not a breakfast person. Especially at night."

"I'm not surprised."

"Listen, Rin, I don't want to give you any grief. I'm just worried that you're getting yourself in trouble. Maybe you're a little unstable at the moment."

"That's a compliment in Quarfelt."

"See, that's what I mean. Are you still claiming that you don't know where this Ozzy Toffy boy lives?"

"I don't. I've never been to or seen his house. Where *does* he live?"

"We don't know."

"Has there been some kind of trouble?"

"Not necessarily. He was going to school for the last couple of weeks and now he's not."

"Certainly the school has more information about him than I do."

"Not a thing."

"Maybe you should be investigating that. How does a young man go to school without anyone knowing a thing about him? I just placed an ad in the *ORVG* like I always do and he answered. We met here and I drove him to Doyle's place. And since you and Doyle are friends, I'm sure you know what happened there."

"Yeah, you were asking about a couple who moved in years ago."

"Well, the boy was asking. He was researching a paper for school."

"A school he no longer goes to."

"That does seem weird. How's this—I'll give you a wizard's promise. If I see him again, I'll do everything within my legal power to get him to come talk to you."

"Fair enough."

"I'd prefer you say, 'More than fair.' That way the glass is at least half-full."

Sheriff Wills stood up and shook his head.

"You used to be so normal, Brian—I mean Labyrinth. Now the whole town laughs at you."

"I can't help it if people don't understand. It's not my worry to make life a place where there's no opportunity for others to grow and be challenged."

"You know, that Toffy boy also showed up at the police station a while back. He met with Officer Greg. Said he was looking for his aunt and uncle, but took off as soon as we started to question him."

"I don't know anything about that," Rin insisted.

"I believe you were at the station at that same time."

"Oh, that's right," Rin said. "I was reporting those kids at Walmart."

"So it was just a coincidence that you pulled into the police station as the boy ran off?"

"An interesting detail, and nothing else."

"You know, any normal person would want to help us."

"So would a normal wizard, but this is your journey, not mine."

"Weird, Brian, just weird. Maybe I should take you down to the station and keep you there for a while. I think that might . . ."

At that moment the front door to Bites opened and a woman screamed. Sheriff Wills spun around to see what was happening. A black bird had zipped in from outside and was shooting up into the rafters. More women screamed . . . and a few men. The bird dived down and through the bar area, avoiding a waiter who was trying to swat it with a rag and a woman who attempted to hit it with her purse.

The bird swooped back up and shot right through one of the hanging light bulbs. The bulb popped and shattered.

Now more men than women were screaming.

Sheriff Wills ran from Rin's booth and tried to act as if he knew what to do.

"Everybody stay calm! It's just a bird."

Clark aimed at another naked bulb and shot through it. The bulb made a louder popping noise than the last one. He swooped over Rin and winked.

The bird hit another bulb and then another. As the light bulbs exploded the restaurant began to grow darker.

"Shoot it!" someone yelled.

"No shooting!" Sheriff Wills yelled. "Everyone calm—"

Clark took out four more bulbs, one after the other.

Pop! Pop! Pop! Pop!

The vast majority of the restaurant's patrons were running for the door. Rin continued to eat his pancakes as fast as he could, shoveling the food into his mouth and covering the plate so no broken glass got in his food.

Pop! Pop! Pop!

Sheriff Wills ducked under a table directly to Rin's right.

"Some wizard you are! Why don't you *do* something?"

Pop! Pop! Pop! Pop! Pop!

Rin looked at Clark as he swooped overhead. He

pushed back his plate, slid out of the booth, and stood up. Then while looking upward he shouted,

"Fandel-cease-perdabra!"

The wizard clapped loudly as he recited the spell. Clark dropped from the sky and Rin caught him. Sheriff Wills saw the whole thing and couldn't keep his jaw from dropping.

Carrying the bird, Rin ran from the restaurant, everyone looking on in awe. Two customers opened the doors and Rin moved out of the restaurant to where the rest of the patrons were gathered. Once outside, and with a crowd of onlookers looking on, he opened his hands and held the bird up.

"Rindis-mindis-move!"

Clark lifted out of his hands and took off into the dark sky. Rin just stood there looking like an important statue.

To say that everyone was impressed was an understatement of epic proportions. It was only a wild bird that had broken a bunch of lights, but the gathering clapped as if Rin had stopped the apocalypse. Rin put his hands on his hips.

"Don't clap for me, clap for the fact that tonight has been more textured and unusual than expected. If there is one thing that I have learned it's that the expectations of men are often . . ."

The crowd of people had been impressed, but they weren't in the mood for a speech. They began to disperse. Rin stopped talking and tried to go back inside to pay his bill, but the owner told everyone to leave until they could get things cleaned up. He also informed them that their food was on the house.

"Well, then, my work here is done," Rin declared.

Rin walked off into the dark and disappeared into the trees at the edge of the parking lot for effect. As soon as the coast was clear, he circled back and snuck to his car. He crouched at the door and opened it. Clark peeked out from under the car, holding his book light in his left talon.

"Get in," Rin whispered.

The bird hopped into the car and up onto the dashboard. Rin pulled out of the parking lot without anyone noticing it was him. Once they were on the road, Rin looked over at Clark.

"That was remarkable!" he said, not trying to hide his exuberance in the least. "They were eating it up."

"You're welcome," Clark said.

"It couldn't have been better if we planned it."

"Probably not."

"Still, we should plan something else like that sometime."

"I'm up for it."

"Just incredible. That'll show Wills. Sometimes it takes the innocence of a bird to let the people see the wisdom of a wizard. I had a feeling tonight would go over well. The clouds were very expressive today." Rin laughed and then inhaled followed by a "Whooo."

"Why are you back in town, anyway?" Rin asked. "Visiting that trash can?"

"That's right, I have news," Clark said, slapping his small forehead with the tip of his left wing. "The cloaked house—it was ransacked."

"What?"

"When we got there this evening there were motorcycle tracks leading up to it and everything inside was torn apart. The worst part is that some things were taken."

"Where's Ozzy?!"

"He's fine, but he's back at the house. He wanted me to get you."

Rin did a sharp U-turn as Clark held onto the dash with his talons. The car shot down Main Street in the direction of Mule Pole Highway. Rin pressed on the gas and the car sped up.

"Do you know who did it?" Rin hollered.

"No."

"This is exactly the kind of thing we wizards hate."

The small car raced down the long road, away from town and toward the cloaked house.

CHAPTER THIRTY-SIX

THE DIFFERENCE IN DAIRY

Ozzy rolled over in his sleeping bag and felt something poking at his nose. Irritating. He brushed it away, but the poking intensified.

"Wake up," Clark chirped. "I'm back, and I brought the wizard."

Ozzy sat up and tried to get his bearings. He saw his bird standing near the stream, the book light clipped to his tail and shining in his eyes.

"You brought Rin?" Ozzy groggily. "Where is he?"

"He *was* a little behind me. I couldn't find you inside so I did a quick fly around. You've always liked this spot."

Ozzy climbed out of the sleeping bag and stood up. The bird and boy walked to the front of the small house. Even in the dark they could see Rin's faded off-white robe, hovering closer like a shabby ghost. Ozzy let out a sigh of relief at the sight of a wizard.

"Oz," Rin said, sounding like every kind wizard should. "What is this ordeal you've been subjected to?"

"Sorry to drag you into this, but I didn't know who else to get ahold of."

Rin put a hand on Ozzy's shoulder. "Don't be sorry—be amazed."

"About what?"

"Well, when we last parted, you said that if I was a true wizard I would find a way here. Well, here I am. Right where I'm needed."

"Thanks for making the hike."

"You are an interesting and important human. It is my honor."

It was dark, but Rin's voice was so sincere that there was no need to witness a corresponding expression to confirm it.

"It's dark out here," the wizard said, stepping back from Ozzy. "But even in the black, your home looks fantastical. I should have brought a flashlight with me."

"I have candles, but I don't want to light up our location right now in case someone comes back. I thought I'd sleep outside until I can go in tomorrow and really take inventory of what's been damaged."

"Smart. So the forest shall be our cover and our bed. Now, do you have an outdoor hammock or padded lounge chair?"

"No, but I have some blankets and soft dirt."

"Let me consult the stars."

Rin looked up and sniffed three times.

"Yes, the blankets will do."

Things felt considerably lighter with Rin there. The empty and uncertainty was less palpable.

The wizard, human, and bird all moved behind the house and crossed the tiny stream over the flat board.

Once they were each settled in their own spots, the clouds above broke up and drifted off. In their absence, there were stars as bright as any that had ever hung overhead. The billion points of light pulsated and blinked in a hypnotic fashion.

"Not that you don't have your own news here," Rin said. "But you would have liked the scene down at Bites. That bird is remarkable."

Ozzy looked over to where Clark had settled. The book light was off and he was out.

"What happened?"

"Well, in coming to fetch me, Clark gave the entire restaurant a show."

Rin told Ozzy everything. He filled him in on Sheriff Wills, acted out some of the customers screaming, and ended with the part where he didn't have to pay for his meal.

"So, it was good for your rep?"

"It was," Rin said.

"Any feelings or premonitions about who might have done this?"

"Someone with a dirt bike," Rin guessed. "Clark said there were tracks."

"Yeah, you'll see them when it's light. But what about any wizardly feelings?"

"I guess I am a little nostalgic for my family. Seeing my sister always makes me miss the good old days."

It wasn't what Ozzy was looking for, but he didn't push it any further. After a few solid moments of silence, Rin spoke.

"Oh . . . were you asking about my wizard feelings regarding who did this?"

"Yeah."

"Sure, I've got tons of those. Of course, you can't literally *weigh* feelings here in reality, so a ton is just an estimate. Interestingly enough, feelings actually weigh something in Quarfelt. It's necessary because of the need to exchange and use them for spells."

"Really?"

"Wizards don't lie, remember?" Rin paused. "That's not completely true. There are times when a lie is not the worst option. Have you ever reasoned with a dragon using only the truth? Not a good idea."

"There are dragons in Quarfelt?"

"Yes," Rin said. "How else would people travel across the sea? Flying cars? Remember, J. K. Rowling took a lot of liberties. You see, Quarfelt is very different than reality. To begin with, it's older than any place you can imagine. There are ruins and buildings there that are hundreds of thousands of years old. And the wizards who live in and amongst them are like me in many ways. They have spent time in reality, but fortune favors them with the ability to stay there as long as they please. I tell you there is no place like the mountains of Quarfelt in summer. Did you know that . . ."

Rin kept on talking. Ozzy would have stopped him, but the sound of his voice in the dark forest air and his tales of Quarfelt were intoxicating. Everything the wizard said sounded far-fetched and magical, but he was saying it with such sincerity and pride that it was hard not to believe every word.

About the time Rin started listing facts about the differences in reality's dairy products and the ones in Quarfelt, Ozzy drifted off.

CHAPTER THIRTY-SEVEN

TRY NOT TO THINK ABOUT IT

In the daylight, things looked even worse. The cloaked house had been thoroughly ransacked. The few things of value were gone and there was more mess than Ozzy wanted to clean. After going through the house with Rin, he sat down on the steps and tried his hardest not to let the weight of what had happened bring him down.

Clark rested on his head and Rin took a seat next to him.

"I know things look bad," Rin said. "But I just happen to have a trick for clearing up the grim feelings."

"Really?" Ozzy asked skeptically.

Rin pushed back the sleeves of his robe and shook his hands dramatically. Both Ozzy and Clark watched in anticipation as the great wizard prepared to say and do something magical.

"The trick is teamwork. Ozzy, you start collecting the torn boxes in the living room and I'll work on cleaning the footprints off the couch. Clark, you can pick up little broken pieces and take them outside. We'll work one room at a time and have this place put back together lickety-split."

"That's it?" Clark asked. "That's the trick?"

"Nifty, right?"

Rin stood up and went back into the house to find a bucket and brush to clean the couch.

"Come on," he shouted over his shoulder. "Working will make us all feel considerably better."

Ozzy stayed on the porch with Clark on his head.

"As far as wizard tricks go, I have to say the teamwork one is probably the lamest," the bird said.

"Yeah, disappointing for sure."

Ozzy stood up.

"Wait a second," Clark said. "Is he *singing*?"

The sound of Rin singing a song about cleaning drifted out the broken front door.

"That's going to get annoying," Clark squawked.

Rin got the couch clean in no time. Then he tackled the basement while Ozzy tried to find boxes that were still in good shape, and filled them with things broken beyond repair. In the daytime it was much easier to see how destructive the vandals had been. They'd turned over and searched through everything. Even some of the boxes that were filled with nothing but old papers and books had been tipped over and rifled though.

In the basement, Rin discovered that the little bit of

remaining dry food was still there, as well as one case of canned carrots.

"Do you want to keep these carrots?" Rin yelled up the stairs.

"Of course," Ozzy yelled back.

"They expired five years ago!"

"Keep 'em!"

Clark hopped around picking up pieces of broken plates and any other crumbs of trash and debris. He put everything he found in a half-crushed box that Ozzy dragged out onto the porch for him.

By noon, they'd gotten most of the first floor and the basement in order. There was a large pile of ruined boxes and unsalvageable paper in the front yard on top of the weedy lawn.

"We should eat something," Rin said as he came up from the basement. His robe, hands, and face had dirt all over them. He walked to the kitchen sink and began to wash up.

"There's not much to eat," Ozzy said. "The bread and groceries I had were destroyed. But we have some basement food."

"I'm hungry," Rin admitted. "But not five-year-old-expired-carrots hungry. Do you have any eggs?"

"No."

"You should get a chicken—endless eggs."

"A chicken *would* be a nice addition," Clark said. I'd love to have someone living here who really gets me."

"How about you run to my car and drive somewhere to pick up something?" Rin suggested.

"Really?" Ozzy said. The prospect of driving excited him. "I don't have a license."

"Ah." Rin executed a Frenchman's wave. "You're capable. Just don't damage it."

"I've never driven a car."

"It's much easier than a broom. Trust me."

"Um, you both know how I hate to be the voice of reason," Clark said. "Hate it. But did you forget that people are looking for Ozzy? Your car kind of stands out."

"That's true," Rin agreed. "So . . . instead, take Mule Pole back the other direction towards Bell's Ferry. There's that gas station and food mart where you can get us something to eat. I personally wouldn't mind a couple fruit pies. Oh, and some more zebra cakes!"

Ozzy thought about it. He had always wanted to drive a car. And he could run the two miles to the highway, drive to Bell's Ferry, and be back before too terribly long. Plus the lure of the zebra cake was strong.

Rin sensed his wavering and said, "Also, I'll keep cleaning while you're gone. That way, when you come back it will be like a fun surprise to see how much progress I've made."

"That *does* sound fun," Clark said.

"Okay, I'll do it," Ozzy said. "But I need to know how to drive."

Rin put his hand on the boy's shoulder.

"Sometimes the experience is the lesson. Just put your seat belt on first."

"That's wise and not at all helpful, so could you at least tell me what to do with my feet?"

"Yes," Rin said. "The right pedal makes you go. Wait, you do know right and left?"

"I learned that when I was four," Ozzy said, insulted.

"Sorry. You grew up in the woods so I wasn't sure. The right pedal makes you go and the left pedal makes you stop. Take these." Rin reached into his robe pocket and pulled out a keyring. He handed them to Ozzy. "Put your right foot on the left pedal and push it in. Put this key in the ignition slot and turn it to the right. That'll turn it on. Then move the stick thing into drive. Once that's done, you're good to go. Oh, if you need to go backwards for some reason, press the brake and put the stick thing into reverse. That's it."

Ozzy had watched Rin drive a number of times and he felt certain he could mimic what he'd seen.

"Now you two go."

"Ready, Clark?" Ozzy asked.

"I think so."

The bird and boy took off out of the cloaked house with Rin yelling after them. "Zebra cakes!"

CHAPTER THIRTY-EIGHT

SOME SHIRTS ARE HARD NOT TO NOTICE

Ozzy started the little white car with no problem. Clark looked impressed.

"Not bad."

"Thank you. Now for the stick thing."

Ozzy put the car into drive and the vehicle whirred lightly.

"This is happening." Clark jumped up onto the dash and dug in his copper-tipped talons.

The highway was clear as usual so Ozzy took his foot off the brake and pressed on the gas. The car lurched forward and onto the road. Keeping his foot down, they were soon moving at fifty-five miles an hour in the direction of Bell's Ferry.

Ozzy looked at Clark. "This really isn't that hard."

"Yeah, it looks easy," Clark said. "If I had arms and long legs and a body that was capable of sitting down, I'd be all over it."

To Ozzy, driving felt like another milestone in his life, another open door that he'd stepped through.

"Wait," he said. "What about the seat belt?"

Clark made a panicked squawk.

A sense of panic filled the car as Ozzy tried to steer and reach for his seat belt at the same time.

"I can't reach it!"

"Watch the road. Here, let me help."

Clark hopped down from the dash and bit down on the metal clip of the seat belt. He clawed and pulled his way onto Ozzy's lap.

"Ow! Watch it!"

Clark let go of the seat belt and it snapped back. Ozzy tried to grab it, but as he did, he turned the steering wheel with his other hand and the car swerved into the opposite lane.

"We're veering off course!" Clark yelled.

Ozzy overcorrected and the car jerked the other way onto the shoulder of the road.

"Hit the stop pedal!" Clark screamed.

Ozzy slammed down his foot and accidentally hit the gas instead of the brake. The car bounced off the side of the road and between the trees. The sound of branches scraping the side of the car were as bad as fingernails on a chalkboard. Ozzy turned into an overgrown meadow and then turned again to avoid a large boulder.

The third turn got them heading back towards the

highway. The car hit the upward-sloping shoulder of the road and bounced back onto the asphalt.

Ozzy located the brake with his foot and slammed it down. The small car came to a screeching stop in the middle of the highway—with nothing but the trees and sky to witness what had just happened.

"So that's what happens when you don't buckle up," Clark said. The mechanical bird was shaking like a nervous soda.

"That was the worst—"

"Car!" Clark interrupted.

Up ahead a semi truck barreled around the curve of the highway.

Ozzy put the car in reverse to back out of the lane.

"Wait!" Clark screamed. "Seat belt!"

Ozzy nervously grabbed for his seat belt. The semi blew its horn. It was getting closer by the second.

"Hurry!"

"What do you think I'm doing?!"

The seat belt wouldn't click in the first time or the second time or the third. But on the fourth try, it clicked. Ozzy pressed on the gas and the car almost went off the road in reverse. He slammed on the brakes and the vehicle stopped on the shoulder, the nose of the car sticking out into the lane. The truck blew past them, its horn blaring, creating a wind that caused the small car to shake almost as much as its occupants.

Once the truck was down the road, Ozzy exhaled.

"That was really close."

"I know—and I only have one battery life. I saw myself becoming part of this mangled car."

Ozzy put the car into drive and pulled out onto the road.

"You're still going to Bell's Ferry?"

"I'm still hungry."

The rest of the drive to Bell's Ferry was much less eventful. When they got to the gas station, Ozzy parked far away from the building so that he wouldn't hit anything.

Getting out of the car, they could see that the outside of the vehicle was scratched and dinged.

"Shoot," Ozzy said. "Do you think Rin will be angry?"

"Not if you tell him the scratches came during an epic wizard battle."

Clark flew into Ozzy's hoodie pocket and positioned himself so he could see out the right side. They went into the gas station food mart.

Inside, the shelves were filled with all types of cookies and chips in bright bags. There were two entire rows of candy and one that had only nuts and jerky. A woman and a small child were getting sodas at the soda fountain and a clerk was ringing up a bald man who was buying motor oil, circus peanuts, and a burrito.

Ozzy made a beeline for the zebra cakes. He grabbed four packs and a couple of granola bars. He got two large Sprites and a bag of cheese-flavored chips.

The clerk barely looked at him as he rang him up.

Transaction completed, he put the items into two bags and handed them over.

"Thanks," Ozzy said.

"No problem," the clerk replied.

Ozzy turned and walked to the front door. He stopped suddenly. Through the glass he could see the man he and Rin had talked to two days ago in his trailer.

"Ed," Ozzy whispered anxiously.

"What?" Clark whispered back.

It wasn't terribly surprising to see Ed there. After all, he lived just down the street from the gas station. The really surprising thing was that Ed had pulled up to the gas station on a dirt bike. And he was wearing one of Ozzy's dad's old shirts.

The question as to who had beat up the cloaked house was no longer a mystery.

CHAPTER THIRTY-NINE

CRACKING THE WINDOW

Ozzy backed up and moved behind the row of candy bars as quickly as he could. He hid behind a shelf of mints while keeping an eye on the front door.

Ed walked in like he owned the place.

"Mick," he said to the clerk. "How're things?"

"Fine. You?"

"Just thirsty. What's Powerball up to?"

"Over two hundred million," Mick replied.

Ozzy looked to his left and realized that if Ed was going for a drink there was a good chance he'd walk right past him. So he scooted down the row and crouched behind a beef jerky display.

Ed sauntered towards the refrigerators and didn't notice Ozzy. He opened one of the glass doors and pulled out a couple of large two-liters of Coke. The lady with the small child had finished getting their sodas and wanted something else near Ozzy.

"Excuse me," the woman said. "I need some of that."

Ozzy moved over so she could grab a fistful of Slim Jims.

"Are you okay?" the woman asked. "It looks like you're trying to hide from someone."

Ed turned around.

He and Ozzy made eye contact and for a moment neither knew what to do.

Ed moved first. He stepped away from the coolers and approached Ozzy.

"That you?" he asked, sounding almost friendly.

Ozzy stood up. Ed didn't *know* he lived at the cloaked house, and there was a chance he had no idea how connected Ozzy was to the place he had torn apart.

"You okay?" Ed asked.

"Yeah, sure," Ozzy said, trying as hard as he could to sound casual. "Just getting some snacks. How've you been?"

"Fine, fine. So, did Brian . . . I mean, 'the wizard' help you out?"

"He did."

"I don't think you mentioned that you lived out this way."

"Yep, just up the street."

"Huh. What street?"

"Forest Drive," Ozzy lied.

"Forest Drive? Don't know it. But the number of things I don't know's too long to talk about here. Well . . . have a nice day, kid."

Ozzy took his bags and exited the food mart as fast as he could.

"What's happening?" Clark asked from the pocket.

"Hold on a sec."

Ozzy quickly climbed into the car. He pulled out of the parking lot and back onto the highway. Clark shimmied out of Ozzy's pocket and hopped onto the dashboard.

"What was *that* about?"

Ozzy looked three times in the rearview mirror to make sure nobody was following them.

"That was that Ed guy."

"I saw that."

"He was wearing one of my father's old shirts."

"So—he *did* know your dad."

Ozzy was shaking.

"No—he was the one who messed up our home. He was even riding a dirt bike. Which means he's the one who smashed the tapes and stole my things."

"Why didn't you punch him?"

"Really? I can't even call the police."

Clark was hopping mad. "I can't believe this!"

"What do we do?" Ozzy said angrily. "I know—we'll tell Rin, he'll know what we should do."

"I think I need some air," the bird said. "Could you crack a window?"

Ozzy felt for the button on his door and then rolled down the passenger side window about four inches.

"Thanks," Clark said. "Oh—and I'll be right back."

“What?”

“I’m the twerp of reason and it’s payback time.”

Clark shot out the gap and into the great outdoors.

“Clark!”

There was nothing to do—the bird was gone.

Ozzy kept driving. He had no idea where Clark had gone or what he meant. Rin needed to know about Ed, so Ozzy pressed on the gas and flew down the highway.

CHAPTER FORTY

BEST SERVED COLD

Ed said goodbye to Mick and exited the Bell's Ferry food mart. He hooked the plastic bags holding his Cokes onto the back of the dirt bike and threw his right leg up and over the seat. Ed was a bit unsettled. He was at the food mart at least once a day and he'd never run into Ozzy before. He wasn't a smart man, but even he found it coincidental that two days after he had raided that hidden cabin in the forest, the very kid who had reminded him it was there showed up again.

"Whatever," he said.

He pressed a button and the dirt bike noisily came to life.

Something small and black passed between him and the sun creating a tiny, brief shadow. Ed looked up but nothing was there.

Rin and Ozzy coming to visit him had been a nice surprise. Ed was always in need of money, and the memory of the small cabin and the thought that it might be abandoned had been too strong for him to ignore. So he'd taken his dirt bike into the forest to find the house. It had been a long time, but he'd made so many trips carrying boxes years ago that it wasn't too hard to find again.

Once he was sure no one was there, he went through the house box by box looking for any kind of valuables. He didn't find a lot; some tools, picture frames, a couple of chairs, a cassette player, and a tablet. There was enough for him to have to make four trips back and forth to his house. He was hoping he could sell the haul to one of his less upstanding friends for a bit of cash.

As he drove home from the food mart on his dirt bike he smiled at his good fortune.

The smile didn't last long.

Something hit Ed in the back of the head, causing a good deal of pain and making his sunglasses fly off of his head.

Ed swore.

He slowed and stopped the bike on the side of the road and got off to see if he could find his glasses. He felt the back of his head. When he brought his fingers back to his face, there was blood on them.

"What the . . . ?"

Something slammed into the right side of his face. Ed spun around twice before regaining his footing. He crouched down a few inches, scanning the sky to see what it was. Walking slowly, his head on a swivel, he moved back up the road to where his sunglasses had flown off.

He saw the shades lying on the side of the road in the grass. As he bent down to pick them up something whizzed past his left ear. He heard it whisper, "Ed."

He stood up quickly and saw something fly into the nearby trees.

"Ed."

Twisting around, he kinked his neck—and still saw nothing.

"What is *happening*?" he cried, frustrated.

Cautiously, he walked back to the motorcycle and got on. He glanced around and started the bike back up.

Three seconds down the road, something hit him from behind again. He considered stopping, but now he just wanted to get home and get indoors. Something slammed into and stung his lower back. It took everything he could do to keep the bike under control. Ed pushed on the gas and went faster.

Clark dived in and smacked him on his back again.

"Go away!" Ed yelled. "Whatever you are, leave me alone!"

Clark didn't like being called a whatever. He shot down, and with the point of his gold beak, pierced one of the big bottles of Coke hanging from the dirt bike. Cold soda blasted from the hole and shot up Ed's back and into the air.

The bird looped around and poked another hole in the

second bottle. The spraying soda and numerous hits to the head were too much for Ed. He tried to slow down, but while braking, the front wheel wobbled. The whole machine went sideways and slid along the side of the road. Ed rolled off and slammed into a mound of old dirt.

He scrambled up screaming and swearing.

Then, looking like a man who had truly lost his mind, he waved his arms above his head and ran screaming away from his soda-squirting bike and into the trees.

With the satisfying feeling of accomplishment that comes from a job well done, Clark dusted his talons in flight and headed home. He'd never been a fan of theft or vandalism and felt pleased that he had righted a few wrongs with one bird.

CHAPTER FORTY-ONE

A SECRET ROOTED OUT

Ozzy parked the car in the trees near the tracks and hopped out. He started jogging and after a few steps switched to an all-out sprint. Part of him was relieved that it had been Ed who had invaded the cloaked house. Ed was less powerful than the police, or the men in green, or almost anyone.

Another part of Ozzy was livid.

It hurt his heart to know that someone like Ed had the ability to affect his life in such a painful way. Those tapes were irreplaceable and now they were gone forever.

Once he reached his home Ozzy ran through the front door.

"Rin! I know . . ."

The inside of the house looked amazing! The boxes were stacked in neat piles of different heights. It made the room look like a small mountain range. The couch had been moved to the middle of the room and two folding chairs from the basement were sitting next to it.

"I'm in here!" Rin yelled from the office.

The boxes in the office were stacked in a way that surrounded the desk and chair that Rin was sitting in.

"How'd you do all this?" Ozzy said, blown away by what he saw.

"Sometimes when others aren't around I cheat a bit."

"You used spells?"

"Who's to say?"

"Well, you could."

"Yes, I used a couple of spells."

"Wow," Ozzy said, looking at the boxes with new appreciation.

"Magic is very satisfying. Now, what were you screaming, 'I know' about?"

"I know who did this."

"Of course you do—I just told you it was me."

"No, not the stacking up, the tearing down."

"Who?"

"That Ed guy we met two days ago."

Rin sat, silently moving his lips and stroking his beard.

Ozzy told him everything that had happened during their stop at the food mart. The only part he left out was the near-accident he and Clark had almost had before they got there. Rin listened closely and at the end of the story closed his eyes and thought.

"Are you okay?" Ozzy asked after what felt like five minutes.

"Things are happening," Rin whispered. "Strings have been pulled that can no longer be woven back into the pattern they once were. Where's Clark?"

As if he had been lurking just outside the office waiting for a reason to come in, Clark flew through the door and landed on the desk.

"Where'd you go?" Ozzy asked.

"I wanted to right a small part of a big wrong."

"It makes me nervous to hear you say things like that."

"I'm perfectly aware of that. Let's just say . . . Ed might be hiding in a roadside ditch, crying."

"Is he?" Ozzy asked.

"No, but he's probably running and crying."

Rin closed his eyes again.

"What's he doing?" Clark asked.

"I think he's thinking."

Rin's nose twitched and his top lip went in and out a couple of times while his eyes remained shut.

"That makes me uncomfortable," Clark whispered. "Maybe we should go out."

"No," Rin said softly. "Stay just as you are."

The room was quiet. No running appliances, no fans, no TVs—just silence.

Rin's eyes flashed open. He stood up and reached into the front pocket of his off-white robe.

"I found this," he said, holding something orange.

"I moved a bunch of boxes and found it behind that wall. A tree root outside buckled the wood and I could see a small black box inside the wall. When I pulled it out, I found this inside."

Rin handed the object to Ozzy.

It was a solid-orange cassette tape with his father's handwriting on each side. Side A said *The Formula*. Side B said *The Problem*.

Ozzy stared at the tape. The thought of hearing his father say things that he hadn't heard him say before was exhilarating and almost worth the damage that had been done to his home.

"I don't believe it."

"I guess your dad was the kind of person who liked to hide things in the wall. It's lucky I was here to find it. Also, I found the deeds and maps to the land you own. Let's just say . . . most of this forest belongs to your parents."

Ozzy just kept staring at the tape.

"I don't believe it."

"Sometimes reality is blindingly incomprehensible," Rin said.

"Ed took the tape player," Ozzy said, looking at the tape closely. "I have no way to listen to this."

"Can't you buy a new one?" Clark asked.

"I guess."

"Not around here," Rin informed them.

Ozzy flipped the orange tape over in his hands, wondering how he was going to hear what his father had hidden.

"Someone must have an old one," Ozzy said.

The wizard closed his eyes again. They flashed open two seconds later.

"Someone does," he said, resignation in his voice.

"Who?" Ozzy asked.

"My ex-wife."

Rin looked weak and had to sit back down. His breathing was labored and uncomfortable. Ozzy didn't care—he wanted to hear the tape.

"Will she let us borrow it?"

"Probably," Rin said, sounding a bit like a big baby. "But she's already going to be mad at me for using her car."

Ozzy and Clark exchanged glances.

"Did you tell him?" Clark whispered.

"No," Ozzy mouthed.

"Tell me what?"

"Um. About the car . . ." Ozzy said. "There may or may not be a few scratches on it. And some dents."

"How many's a few?"

"Is twenty considered a few?"

"I think that's a bunch," Clark said.

Rin stood up again. He looked at Ozzy and tried to smile.

"The scratches and dents I can fix with magic," he said. "Let's just hope Patti's in a good mood. In the past she wouldn't even let me *touch* her old stereo. I guess a guy named Marco gave it to her when she was a freshman in high school and he was her boyfriend. Seems highly inappropriate to me."

"Him giving his girlfriend a gift is inappropriate?" Ozzy asked sincerely.

"It was if it made every gift I gave her for the next twenty years look bad. Neck pillows aren't cheap. Now . . . let's go before I change my mind."

Rin stomped out of the room and out of the cabin.

"This is going to be good," Clark said.

"I don't care; I just want to hear the recording."

Ozzy slipped the cassette tape into his pocket and followed the wizard.

CHAPTER FORTY-TWO

ASKING FOR FAVORS

Rin was *not* happy about the amount of scratches on his ex-wife's car.

"That's going to take *a lot* of magic."

He was too overwhelmed to cast any spells, though, so he climbed into the driver's seat while Ozzy took the passenger seat and Clark planted himself on the dashboard.

"Where does your ex-wife live?" Ozzy asked.

"Near the ocean in a house that overlooks the ocean near a pier that stretches out into the ocean."

"Do you not *like* the ocean?" Clark asked.

"It's fine."

Thinking about his ex-wife made Rin act more like a hurt child than a wizard.

"How long were you married?"

"Almost ten years, but if you ask her she'll say just over nine. Isn't that petty?"

"Very pretty," Clark said, having misheard Rin.

"Can I be honest with you two?" Rin asked while driving.

"I thought we promised each other days ago that we always would be."

"Right—but this is the kind of honest that evil would love to get its hands on."

"Go on," Clark encouraged him.

"Wizards have weaknesses. We're not human, but we *do* have things that can harm us. For example, I know a wizard who cannot master his allergies. On more than one occasion, epic battles were almost lost with his endless sneezing and sniffling."

"Oh," Clark said, disappointed. "This kind of truth."

"Yes. And a wizard's weakness is often what his enemies attack. Well, I have a weakness."

"What is it?" Clark asked.

"Patti, my ex-wife—I thought that was implied. Our marriage was happy, but it ended poorly. It was soon after that that I discovered Quarfelt. I spent years there becoming the wizard I am, only to discover that my one weakness was the very woman I once loved. She will stop at nothing to make sure I don't succeed."

"But she lets you borrow her car."

"Well, *borrow* is a strong word."

"She doesn't report you to the police," Ozzy pointed out.

"Not for this, at least. But she makes me human . . . and that is the one thing a true wizard must shake off."

A few miles later, they passed right through Otter

Rock. Rin turned onto a beautiful road that twisted between the trees and took them in the direction of the ocean. Ozzy could see the water on the horizon. A mile more and they were at their destination.

Patti's house was old and impressive. It had two stories and a four-car garage. There was a fountain in front of the house that sprayed water up in various patterns.

Rin parked the car on the circular driveway near the walkway to the front door. They all climbed out and began the impressively long walk to the front door.

"When we get in there, let me do the talking," he said.

"Of course," Ozzy replied. "I don't need to say anything."

"I'd like to say a few things," Clark chirped up.

"Hide the bird," Rin said. "There might be a time when I'll need him for effect, but until then, keep him hidden."

Clark reluctantly flew into Ozzy's pocket.

Patti's front door was massive and covered in ornately carved waves and fishes. Ozzy thought Rin would knock first, but instead he opened the door and walked right in. Ozzy followed and shut the door behind him. The home's entry was bigger than the cloaked house but considerably less interesting. It looked like a hotel lobby—or the entrance to a showy mall.

"Patti?" Rin yelled. "I'm here."

"This is a nice house," Ozzy whispered.

"It's fine. We lived here when we were married."

"Didn't you say you were a teacher? I read somewhere that teachers are underpaid."

"They are. Patti's rich. Her father owned all the beachfront around here at one time. Patti!"

Clark peeked his beak out to get a look at the surroundings.

A woman emerged from a hallway to the north. Her skin was the color of brown ink and her dark hair was short and neatly cut. She was thin and wearing jeans and a white tank top. She looked as if she couldn't decide whether to smile or frown about what she now found standing in her foyer.

"Hello, Rin."

"Hello, Patti."

"Who's this?"

"It's good to see you, too," the wizard said.

Patti looked at Ozzy.

"He's not holding you captive, is he?"

"No," Ozzy said with a smile.

"That would have surprised even me."

Patti was interesting and lovely, the kind of interesting and lovely that people wrote poems about. She was almost forty but looked nowhere near it. Her eyes drew Ozzy in as she looked at him.

"What's your name?" she aked nicely.

"His name's Rumton."

Ozzy looked horrified by the fake name.

"Nice to meet you, Rumton."

"He's my Little Brother," Rin explained. "I signed up for the Big Brother program and he's my first one."

"That's excellent. And how are you two getting along?"

"Perfect," Ozzy said.

The answer made Rin smile.

"Is there something you need, Rin?" Patti asked.

Rin looked nervous and less wizardly under the foyer lights. He also looked like he was out of answers. So Ozzy spoke up.

"I got a cassette tape from my real father but I don't have any way to listen to it. Mr. Rin said that you might have a tape player."

Ozzy pulled out the tape so that Patti could see it.

"Can't Rin just conjure up a new machine?" she said, smiling.

"Here we go," Rin said. "A wizard without worship."

"I'm just kidding, Rin. You're welcome to use that old machine. I think it's in the guest room closet. If you can find it, it's yours."

"Fine," Rin said. "Come with me, Rumton."

"You don't need his help," Patti insisted. "Let me make him something to eat."

Ozzy gave Rin a quick glance. There was no way that he was going to pass up food made by a pleasant woman just to go dig through a closet.

"We'll be in the kitchen," Patti said.

Rin stormed off.

"How hungry are you?" she asked.

"Pretty hungry. All I've had today was some zebra cakes."

"I bet I know who wanted those."

Patti's kitchen was so large it had three refrigerators. There were also three sinks and countless other appliances.

"This is one person's kitchen?" Ozzy asked. "Or do you share it?"

"I know, I know. It's too much. My father built this house years ago and I feel guilty living in it."

"Why don't you move?"

"I like how straightforward you are. Would you care for a sandwich?"

"I'd *really* care for one."

Patti went to one of the refrigerators and pulled out a bunch of food. Ozzy was in awe at how stocked and orderly the fridge was. She put the food on the large kitchen island and began to piece things together.

"Turkey?"

"Sure."

"Swiss cheese?"

"Yes." Ozzy had grown quite fond of cheese.

Patti placed a large amount of turkey on a piece of thick brown bread and then layered slices of cheese over it.

"How long have you been doing the Big Brother program?"

"Pretty long."

Ozzy had no idea what that was.

"You like it?"

"Sure?"

Ozzy knew that if he wanted her to stop questioning him he was going to have say something himself.

"I didn't think you'd look like you do."

"Again, so honest." Patti laughed. "Unfortunately, like a lot of places, there's not much diversity here."

"And you were married to Rin?"

"He went by Brian back then, but yes."

"Why'd you end it?"

"That's not a question with one answer."

"Was he a wizard then?"

"No, after we got divorced, he disappeared for a couple of years. No one knew where he went or what he was doing. Then he showed up in town one day wearing that . . . Well, you've seen how he dresses. He claimed to be a wizard and . . . that was that."

"He was in Quarfelt during the time he was gone?"

"He told you about that place?"

"A little."

"I think the Big Brother organization needs to do more thorough background checks. Mustard and mayo?"

"Sure. You don't think he's a wizard?"

Patti stopped spreading mayo to think a moment.

"I think he can be amazing when he wants to be, but I'm not sure I believe in wizards."

"It makes sense that if there are wizards there would be people who refuse to believe," Ozzy pointed out. "I mean, where's the mystique in something everyone accepts?"

"That's a big thought for a person your age."

"It's the same-sized thought for anyone, regardless of age."

Patti closed the sandwich up, cut it in triangles, and put it on a square plate. She set the plate down in front of Ozzy.

"Maybe the organization was wise to place Rin as your mentor. You sound as interesting as he is."

"Found it!" Rin said, walking into the kitchen. He had a big box in his arms and wore a triumphant expression. "You didn't think I would."

"I told you where it was."

"Still, there was sabotage in your doubt. Now we will take you up on your offer and graciously accept it as a gift."

"Excellent. I'm glad someone will use it."

"Right." Rin spotted Ozzy's sandwich. "Hey, did you make one for me?"

"No," she replied. "But you can."

"As a wizard, that's beneath me."

Using words Ozzy wasn't familiar with, Patty told him in a very straightforward manner what she thought of that.

"How about I split mine with him," Ozzy said, trying to make everyone happy.

Rin stared at the boy proudly.

"You passed the test," he said. "You have the generosity of a wizard. And your willingness to share gives me the humility to now craft my own." Rin turned to Patti. "Do you mind if I fry up a few eggs to put on mine?"

When they left the house they had multiple sandwiches, chips, and sodas packed into a wicker basket. Ozzy carried the food and Rin carried the stereo. As they strolled down the front walk back to the car that Patti let Rin borrow, Clark came out of Ozzy's pocket and took his place in his hair.

"Why did you ever leave her?" Ozzy asked Rin.

"If you must know, she left me."

"Sorry."

"I made a series of bad decisions, but I can't regret them now because . . . well, look where they brought me."

Ozzy glanced around and wondered what exactly he was referring too.

"The worst thing a person can do is to give space to regret. Why should the past have such crippling power? A wizard cherishes what lessons he's learned—regardless of how he came to learn them."

"Do you ever run out of things to say like that?" Clark asked.

"I wouldn't be a wizard if I did."

"Oh—and thanks for Rumton, by the way," Ozzy said.

"A respected surname in Quarfelt."

"Well, it's not my favorite here."

Rin put the stereo into the trunk of the car and climbed in. Ozzy opened his door and as he did he heard someone say, "Ozzy?"

The boy turned around and his jaw dropped. He'd thought so much about Sigi over the course of the last few weeks that he must have somehow conjured up a vision of her.

"What are you doing here?" she asked. Her expression was one part surprise, two parts happiness.

"I, I, well, I . . ."

Rin got back out of the car and stood up.

"Hello, Sigi," the wizard said.

"Hi, Dad."

Ozzy stood there in shock as his hoodie pocket rustled and made a very quiet squawk.

"Where are you two going?" Sigi asked.

"To the beach," Rin said. "Go inside. Your mother might need help."

"She doesn't and I'm bored. I'm coming with you guys."

"That's not a good idea," Rin insisted.

Sigi wasn't listening. She had already climbed into the small car and was looking back out and up at Ozzy.

"Come on, get in."

Ozzy was still frozen.

"Just get in," Rin said. "We'll figure this out at the beach."

Ozzy climbed into the back seat, not saying a word. He was thrilled to see Sigi, but he was paralyzed by the knowledge that she was Rin's daughter. The wizard had never *said* he had a kid, but in fairness, Ozzy had never asked. He wasn't sure if their being related made him more or less in awe of her.

Who was he kidding—he couldn't be more.

CHAPTER FORTY-THREE

VOICES FROM BEYOND

The sun was beginning to set when Rin pulled up to a small picnic area on the edge of the beach. There were only a few people walking at the edge of the water down the beach. The picnic area had two tables and a small restroom building.

Rin shut the car off and turned to look at Sigi and Ozzy.

"Listen, this isn't how I thought the night would go, but here we are. Sigi, it's nice to see you."

"It's been a while," she pointed out.

"I've been extraordinarily busy," Rin said defensively. "You don't understand what the life of a wizard requires."

"You're right—I don't understand."

Ozzy stared at both of them, still unable to speak.

"I'm helping Ozzy find his parents. It's a complicated situation that takes the deft understanding and wand of a wizard."

"Your parents are lost?" Sigi asked Ozzy.

He could only nod.

"Now, we've found a tape that he needs to listen to. So we borrowed your mother's stereo and we're about to borrow some electricity. But this is very private stuff and I think Ozzy would be bothered to have you listen in."

"I wouldn't be bothered," Ozzy managed to say.

"Fine, but as your father, Sigi, you need to know that this is a sensitive thing and I can't have you blabbing to your mother."

"Mom and I don't talk as much as you think."

"I'm sorry to hear that. Children need good communication with their parents."

Sigi's dark eyes went wide. "*What?* You haven't spoken to me in months."

"Well, I'm a completely different situation."

"You mean like how I'm supposed to be with you on weekends and this is the first I've seen of you in forever?"

"I thought you needed space."

"I hate to interrupt," Ozzy interrupted. "But is this a conversation you'd rather have without me around?"

Both Rin and Sigi looked at him as if he was crazy.

"Sorry," Rin said. "We'll put that conversation under a spell and move on to the business at hand. Now, Sigi, are you aware of Ozzy's bird?"

"I don't think so," she said, relieved to be moving on.

"It's remarkable and it might take you by surprise. Show her the bird, Ozzy."

Clark had heard them talking so he crawled out of the hoodie pocket and hopped up on the front seat headrest.

"Wow," Sigi said. "It looks like a raven."

"Thank you. Can you believe I've been mistaken for a crow?"

"You can talk?"

"I'm fluent in two languages—English and Chirp."

"Unbelievable. Where did you come from?"

"Ozzy's scientist-y inventor dad made me. I'm pretty sure I'm his finest creation."

"I can see that. Wait . . . are *you* who Ozzy was talking to when he was talking to himself?"

"Yep," Clark bragged.

"All right, this is very nice," Rin said. "But we've got things to solve. You can stay in the car or, if Ozzy approves, come with us."

"She can come," Ozzy said.

Rin retrieved the stereo from the trunk and Ozzy grabbed the food.

Clark realized where they were. "The beach!" He flew out of the car toward the water.

"He likes the beach," Ozzy informed Sigi. "We used to spend a lot of time here."

"I know," Sigi said. "That's where we first met. I don't know if you remember. Years ago my mother and I were hiking down near the rocky shores and ran into you."

"That sounds vaguely familiar."

Sigi smiled. "You're such a liar."

"I rarely go to the beach," Rin butted in. "The water gives my skin a rash. And traditionally, wizards aren't great swimmers."

"I didn't know that," Ozzy admitted.

"Well, you have a lot to learn."

The three of them carried their things to the closest picnic table. Ozzy set the basket down and Sigi took a seat on the bench. Rin kept the stereo in his arms.

"There's an electric outlet on the side of the restrooms," he informed them. "It's meant to supply power for the mowers and trimmers the caretakers use, but mostly the lifeguards just charge their phones with it. Sometimes I come down here to listen to talk radio. There's a cooking show out of Portland that has the best breakfast recipes."

Rin walked over and set the stereo down on the sandy concrete. He pulled open a metal door that protected the outlet and plugged in the stereo.

"Do you have the tape?"

Ozzy fished it out of his pocket and handed it to Rin, who put it into the stereo and prepared to press play.

"Hold on," Ozzy said. "Clark should be here."

Ozzy whistled loudly and in a few seconds the bird was back.

Sigi couldn't help staring at the bird, but Clark didn't mind the attention. He settled near her on top of the picnic table and made himself comfortable.

"Your hair would make a nice nest," Clark said.

"Um, thanks?"

"You're welcome."

The power cord was long enough that Rin could place the stereo on the edge of the table. Ozzy passed out the food and took a seat on the bench. In the distance seagulls squawked and the sun dropped down as it readied itself to take a soak in the ocean. With the sun sinking the sky could no longer hold onto its blue, replacing it with shades of silver and grey that matched Ozzy's eyes.

"This feels like a magical night," Rin said. "Can you see it?"

Ozzy looked around.

"It's as if everything in existence has been working up to this one moment," the wizard said.

"Could you just press play?" Clark asked.

"Right."

Rin pressed the play button, and *Side A: The Formula* began to play.

Immediately they heard Dr. Emmitt Toffy speaking. But even though the moment was magical, what they heard was not. Dr. Toffy just rattled off long strings of mathematical and brain chemistry formulas that would complete his greatest finding. He didn't say what the finding was, he just kept throwing out x and y and cosine and arc and serotonin and oxytocin . . .

After ten minutes, Clark finally spoke up.

"Is it just me, or is this really boring?"

"It *is* boring," Rin said. "Even as a wizard, I don't

know what he's talking about. Maybe we should fast forward to the good part."

Ozzy fast forwarded for a few seconds and when he stopped his dad was still being boring. He fast forwarded a little more—still boring. He kept skipping forward until finally they heard the doctor saying something other than numbers and letters.

"In conclusion, it is my finding that the formula works quite well to eliminate the dangerous willpower that so many never master, leaving the brain to make rational and life-changing decisions. It puts the brain in a position of complete control."

There were a few seconds of silence and then the tape clicked off.

The sun was almost completely beneath the water now. The street lamps near the picnic tables flicked on. The few people who had been out on the sand had packed up their things and driven away.

"Well," Rin said, "your father was obviously a genius."

"I don't understand," Sigi admitted. "Your dad was working on this formula? Was it a work in progress or had he figured it out?"

"Let's listen to the other side, shall we?" Rin suggested.

Rin flipped the tape and Clark insisted on being the one to press play this time. "It helps me feel included."

The tape began to play and all three were shocked when, instead of hearing Dr. Emmitt talking, they heard Ozzy's mother, Dr. Mia.

The sound of his mother's voice jolted Ozzy. He'd only heard her say the single line on the end of the one tape he had. Now here she was, saying more.

"Emmitt is greatly discouraged. The last test was a failure and nearly cost a man his life. There was a small alteration made to the formula and it appears that when changed, it reverses, giving power over the subject's brain to outside suggestions. In layman's terms, this means that when applied, you can make others do anything you wish. This is not an acceptable result. We fear drastic measures must be taken to make sure this never sees the light of day."

The tape continued to play but there was no sound.

"Is that it?" Clark asked. "I don't understand."

"There was a problem with their formula," Ozzy said. "When they discovered that, they decided not to pursue it. I don't see what the problem is. Do you think they moved out here to work on it in secret?"

"It seems to me like they moved out here to hide."

"Then I guess this tape sort of helps," Ozzy said, trying hard not to feel disappointed.

"I don't see how." Clark said. "And now I feel—"

"This could be our last recording." Mia's voice filled the air again.

The tape that had remained running was silent no more—all four of them leaned in closer.

"The most despicable thing has happened," Mia continued. "If this is found under suspicious circumstances, contact Charles Plankdorf immediately. He will . . ."

The tape was silent again.

"He will what?" Clark asked.

Ozzy fast forwarded through the rest of side B to see if there was an answer. When he reached the end, it clicked to a stop.

"He will what?" Clark asked again.

"I have no idea," Ozzy answered.

Both the bird and the boy looked at Rin. Sigi did the same.

"I'm stumped too," the wizard said.

"Don't you have a crystal ball or a puddle you can look into for answers?" Ozzy asked.

Sigi looked bothered by what Ozzy was asking.

"Be careful," Rin said. "She's my daughter, but she doesn't have much belief in my abilities."

"Actually," Sigi insisted, "I've just lived with my mother for too long and she has no belief."

"Well," Ozzy said. "I hired a wizard—I would love to see you pull out your wand or gaze into a crystal ball."

"Does that seem fair to the rest of mankind? How can a person cheating life ever bring balance to the universe?"

"So, no crystal ball?" Ozzy said sadly.

"No. I had one, but it cracked when I accidentally took it bowling."

"Really?"

"I thought it would improve my score."

"Never mind that," Clark chirped. "Who's Charles Plankdorf?"

"I'm not sure," Ozzy answered. "But didn't Timsby say that my half-uncle could have been named Charles?"

"I don't know. I was in the car charging my batteries when that happened."

"Not you, Clark."

"I think you're right," Rin said. "Charles or Jonathan."

"Since we don't have a crystal ball, we need a computer to search the name."

"We could go to the public library," Rin suggested. "No . . . that could be trouble, what with all the late fees I have. Wait," Rin said, sounding suddenly serious. "I sense something."

He closed his eyes and began to mumble.

"Yes, I do feel something. The veil between Quarfelt and reality must be really thin here. We're all connected and there are those in Quarfelt who wish to help us."

"Really?" Clark said excitedly.

"Close your eyes!" Rin commanded.

Ozzy, Clark, and Sigi obeyed.

"There's no need for vision now, we must hear the answer. Charles Plankdorf, Charles Plankdorf, Charles Plankdorf."

Rin repeated the name a few more times and then began to hum. Clark, because he was a mechanical bird with a warped sense of ethics, opened his eyes to peek.

"Hey, what's that?"

Ozzy and Sigi opened their eyes and saw Rin holding

a smartphone and typing the name Charles Plankdorf into a search engine.

"You have a *phone*?" Ozzy accused him.

"Of course," Rin replied, acting as if it was undignified for anyone to ask him that sort of thing. "What do you think you called me on, a troll verbalizing device?"

"That's cheating, Dad."

"No it's not, because the internet is the humans' closest form of magic. And I am currently using the internet to locate one Charles Plankdorf."

"But it's not *real* magic," Clark argued.

"Forget about that—did you find him?" Ozzy asked, more interested in finding Charles than talking about the phone.

"It doesn't seem to be a popular surname. In fact, there's only a single reference and there's not much on him." Rin held his phone closer to his face and began to read from it. "Charles Plankdorf appears to be a businessman who works for a company called Harken Corporation. He lives in Albuquerque, New Mexico . . . interesting. He's alive and grew up in New York . . . more interesting."

"You think he's the Charles my mother was talking about?"

"I suppose it could be. It says he's forty-eight years old."

"That age would fit with what Timsby said."

"There's not much on him, but there is a name and business phone number. And from the few pictures posted online, he appears to be wealthy. Look at his house."

The picture on the phone was of a man and a dog sitting on the hood of an expensive-looking car that was parked outside of an expensive-looking house. The home was beautiful, the car luxurious, and the dog handsome, but it was Charles Plankdorf's face that Ozzy found most interesting.

"He looks like my dad."

"He does?" Rin asked. "Actually, I think I can see a resemblance to you."

"That *has* to be him," Ozzy said. "So what do we do now?"

"How about we make a call?" Rin suggested.

He swiped the screen on his phone and pressed the number listed for Harken Corporation.

He looked excitedly at Ozzy and then at his daughter and finally at Clark.

"It's ringing."

Clark looked unimpressed.

The phone continued to ring. The small crowd of three people and a mechanical fowl waited impatiently to hear who would pick up. But no human answered, and after ten rings it went to voicemail, where a generic woman's voice told Rin to leave a message.

"Yes," Rin said into the phone, "there are many things in this world that fight for one's attention—let only the honest win."

Rin hung up.

"That's your message?" Ozzy asked.

"I'm trying to get people to really take a look outside of themselves."

"I think it means 'message' like who you are and how they can call you back."

"Really? Maybe that's why no one ever returns my calls."

Rin's phone made a chiming noise that startled him.

"Oh, I have a text from Patti."

As he read the screen, his eyebrows knitted deeper and deeper.

"What is it?" Ozzy asked.

"I guess Sheriff Wills just paid her a visit. He asked her a bunch of questions about me and you and she told them we were just there. Perhaps we should go in and explain things to them," Rin said. "You won't be in trouble and I can think of some spell to get me out of it."

"No," Ozzy said. "I tried talking to them once and it didn't end well. I have to at least make an attempt to find this Charles guy. After all, my mom just told me to."

"That's true," Clark agreed. "How far away is he?"

"Three states down and one over."

"Could I fly there in a few hours?"

"No," Rin said. "But we could drive there in about twenty hours."

Rin's phone beeped again and he read the new text.

"Patti said the sheriff wants me to come down to the station."

"Go," Ozzy said. "Tell them it's my fault. Tell them

everything, but I'm going to New Mexico. Can you drop me off at the bus station before you go to the police?"

Rin looked up at the stars in silence. He blinked a few times and then closed his eyes while keeping his head tilted back. He twisted on the picnic bench and turned to look directly at Ozzy.

"You're not going to the bus station. We've done nothing wrong and we're only attempting to right an injustice that was done to you. I'll take you there. To the car!"

They picked up the stereo and the food they still hadn't eaten.

"Sigi, I'll need to drop you off at the end of the street," her father said. "You'll have to walk a little bit, but I can't take you all the way home."

"Good, because I'm coming with you."

"I don't think so. Your mother will have my hide."

"Listen, Dad. I'm going. You're supposed to have me on the weekends. This is your chance to make up for all the times you weren't there. Show me that you really are what you say you are. You *have* to let me go."

"What do you think, Ozzy?"

"She was the only person who was nice to me at school."

"She also smells better than both of you," Clark said. "At least I'm guessing she does."

"What about the sheriff?" Ozzy asked. "We'll have to drive *through* town to get out of town."

"Hopefully he's doing something that isn't on our

route." The wizard adjusted his pointy felt hat. "Let's hope he's preoccupied somewhere else."

"If we're hoping," Ozzy said. "Let's hope my parents just come back and straighten things out."

They got into the car and buckled up.

CHAPTER FORTY-FOUR

GOING FAR AWAY

Rin drove away from the beach with Ozzy in the passenger seat and Sigi in the back. It was dark and there were no other cars around. They approached the road leading to Patti's and Sigi's house.

"You sure you don't want me to drop you off?"

"Positive," Sigi said.

"Well, you're going to need to call your mother at some point and tell her where you are. And I'm not making that call."

Clark turned on the car's dome light and sat on a headrest under it to soak up light.

"Oh, yeah, that feels nice."

"You might want to turn that off," Sigi suggested. "It'll give away who's in the car."

"I might want to *not* turn it off," Clark replied. "But I will."

The bird switched off the dome light and hopped up

into Ozzy's lap where he could use the light from Rin's phone.

"Hold on," Ozzy said. "I'm looking something up. According to this, Albuquerque, New Mexico, is nineteen hours and thirty-eight minutes away"

"That sounds about right," Rin said. "I've spent time there before."

"We'll have to stop somewhere for you to sleep."

"Oh, wizards don't need sleep in the way that humans do, but still . . . it might be prudent to pull over and catch a couple of naps along the way."

"This whole thing is a long shot," Ozzy said more to himself than anyone else.

"All rewarding things are."

"I'm sorry about my dad," Sigi said kindly. "He's always saying things like that."

"I don't mind it at all," Ozzy admitted.

"Well, then, you're different than any of my friends."

The route they needed to take out of town went directly down Main Street and up past the school. From there they could take a short road that hooked up to the Mule Pole Highway. The highway would then take them past the train tracks, past Bell's Ferry, and almost all the way out of Oregon. And then there were freeways that would get them the rest of the way.

"If we just get to the highway we should be okay," Rin said. "I can't imagine Sheriff Wills caring enough to chase us farther than that."

"I hope he doesn't chase us at all."

Rin drove through a neighborhood to avoid Main Street. Eventually, however, he had no option but to use it.

He turned out on to Main Street just past Volts. All four passengers began searching for any sign of police cars.

"This is nerve-wracking," Clark said, standing on the top of the dashboard. "Wait, is *that* a police car?" Clark pointed to a brown UPS truck parked behind a building.

"No."

"Well, then, I'm no help."

Clark hopped off the dashboard and back into Ozzy's lap so that he could shine the phone on himself again.

Otter Rock's Main Street was busy. The streetlights were on and cars were making their way to restaurants and movies while tourists were milling around on the sidewalks.

"Just act cool," Rin instructed.

"I have no idea how to do that."

"What I mean is just don't draw attention to our car." Rin was using his hands for emphasis and as he talked he accidentally honked the horn. "Whoops."

The people around them looked in their direction.

"I didn't know cars could *honk* like that," Clark said. "No wonder people like them so much. Reminds me of a goose I tried talking to once."

The traffic light ahead turned red and Rin had to stop. As they sat waiting for the light to switch to green, a police car drove through the intersection. As it crossed in front of them, the officer in the car looked at Rin and Ozzy.

"Shlip," Rin said, using Quarfelt slang. "I think he saw us."

The cop moved through the intersection and switched on his patrol lights.

"He's turning around," Sigi said.

Rin pressed on the gas and drove thought the light well before it had decided to go green. He turned onto Peach Street and instructed the car to go faster.

Clark jumped over Sigi to the back window.

"I don't see anyone following us," the bird hollered.

"They will be," Rin yelled back.

On cue, a set of bright flashing lights appeared behind them in the distance.

"Go faster!" Ozzy said.

Rin turned onto Mule Pole Highway without slowing down. The strong turn caused the small white car to lift up on one side. It came back down heavily on all of its wheels as Rin zipped around a truck that had the nerve to be traveling too slow.

"Everyone okay?" Rin yelled.

"I'm fine," Clark said.

"Don't tell your mom!"

"I won't," Sigi promised.

Rin pressed on the gas and flew down the highway. Behind them Clark could see the police car coming out around the truck. There was now a second one in tow.

"Two cop cars!" Clark reported.

"What do we do?" Ozzy asked. "We can't outrun the cops!"

Looking back though the windshield and the dark of night Ozzy could see that a third police car had joined the chase.

"Are they going to ram us off the road?" Ozzy asked nervously.

"No!" Rin yelled. "They don't just ram people."

"So, what do we do, drive until we run out of gas?"

"Use a spell," Clark squawked. "Use a spell!"

"Do you have actual spells?" Sigi asked.

Rin didn't reply—he kept his focus on the road in front of him. The traffic on the highway was as thin as usual, but Rin had to pass a couple of cars on the edge of town before the road opened up and there was no one in front of them any longer.

They sped down the highway without any impediments.

They were taking the same route Ozzy's school bus took on the way home, only much, much faster. Ozzy wished desperately that there were no cops behind them. He wanted Rin to just drop him off at the tracks so he could go home and sleep in his room. But there *were* cops behind them—and they were closing in.

"Can't you go faster?" Clark asked.

"It's a car, not a rocket," Ozzy answered for Rin. He had no desire for Rin to speed up any more than he already was. The small car felt like it was going to rip apart from the strain of moving so quickly.

“Maybe we should just stop near the train tracks and make a run to the cloaked house,” Ozzy suggested.

“There’s no way we’d make it,” Rin replied. “And if we did—what then?”

The little white car flew down the highway, the cops patiently keeping their distance but maintaining the chase.

“When are they going to start shooting?” Clark asked.

“They won’t shoot. But they’ll notify the cops in Bell’s Ferry. And they’ll set up a roadblock to stop us.”

“So we’re doomed?” Sigi said.

“Not by a long shot.”

“Are you nuts?” the bird warbled. “I need to make sure Ozzy stays safe, because if he’s locked up in jail or gets into an accident I don’t know what I’ll do.”

The cops were all running their lights and keeping back a good distance so as to not make the situation worse. They were aware that eventually the small car would have to stop.

Rin, Sigi, Ozzy, and Clark kept quiet as each tried to think of a solution. But with every mile they drove, the situation felt more and more hopeless. It wasn’t long before they were nearing the train tracks.

“The tracks are just around that corner.” Ozzy pointed up the road. “I think making a run for the cloaked house is our best chance of getting away. We can hide in the woods until they give up.”

“That’s not an answer—that’s a new problem.”

“At least he’s trying to come up with a solution!” Clark was freaking out. “Do you know what cops do to birds?

Seriously, do you? I can't get caught—I have a record. They'll punish me for breaking those lights at Bites."

Clark started flying around the inside of the car frantically.

"Knock it off!" Ozzy yelled as Sigi waved Clark away.

The bird bounced off of the windshield and hit Rin's hat.

"Careful, Clark!"

The road curved and they flew around the corner towards the tracks.

"Great mounds of magic!" Rin screamed.

Just up ahead, the railroad crossing lights were flashing, and for the first time that Ozzy had witnessed, there was a train on the tracks. The locomotive was flying across the highway just yards in front of them. Clark screamed and bounced back and forth against the windows.

"Ahhhhh!"

He smacked up against Rin, who was already more nervous than a wizard should be. The car swerved and Rin lost control. His foot missed the brake and the car jetted into the mounded shoulder on the side of the road. It hit the mound like a ramp and flew into the air, spinning upside down. The vehicle rolled all the way over in the air as it shot towards the train and landed, wheels down, on the back of an empty—and moving—flatbed train car.

Unaware of the fact that it had a new addition to its load, the speeding train sped on, continuing its uninterrupted course across Oregon toward California.

Sigi, Ozzy, and Clark looked at each other in disbelief.

One minute they'd been driving down the highway being chased by cops and now they were on the back of a train car being whisked away. Ozzy couldn't speak. His body was in shock and his brain was stunned.

"I saw my battery life flash before my eyes," Clark tweeted.

"What just happened?" Ozzy finally spoke.

"We caught a ride," Rin said. The wizard didn't seem the least bit surprised by what had just happened. "Is the food in the back okay?"

"That's *impossible*," Sigi said with a shaky voice. "What just happened is impossible."

"*Impossible?*" Rin asked. "That's such a weird word. Can't you see what happened? I mean, you were all there."

"I still don't believe it."

The train raced across the countryside with them parked on it.

"Humans," Rin said with a laugh. "That's why we wizards so seldom use magic. You refuse to believe."

"I— I— I—" Sigi tried to say.

"Don't tell your mom," he reminded her.

Rin casually reached back and grabbed a bag. He pulled it into the front and began to unwrap his second sandwich, acting as if it was just another night in the life of a wizard.

CHAPTER FORTY-FIVE

WHERE DID YOU GO?

All three cop cars slammed on their brakes and barely came to a stop before hitting the train or each other. The long freight train continued racing across the highway, clanking noisily and creating a moving wall that they couldn't get through.

Sheriff Wills and his officers got out of their cars.

"What happened?!" Sheriff Wills yelled.

The noise of the passing train was thunderous; the weight of the fast-moving machine shook the ground.

"I have no idea!" Officer Greg yelled back.

The three police cars had been tailing Rin's car for miles. Following protocol, they had stayed back a safe distance to make sure that they didn't cause any unneeded accidents or harm to other cars or themselves. They had contacted the officers in Bell's Ferry and a roadblock was in place. But as the cars had come around the corner, they had seen the crossing lights flashing and it looked as if the wizard's car popped and then just disappeared.

Sheriff Wills was stumped. "Did they get through?"

"They must have." Officer Greg wasn't confident about his answer. "I'm just not sure how someone drives right through a train!"

"Are you sure they didn't go off the road?" the third officer asked.

Sheriff Wills yelled back. "I'm not sure of anything!"

The three policemen walked along the sides of the highway looking for evidence that the car might have run into the trees while the unending train continued to block their passage. It was too dark to see much and, in their minds, the wizard had somehow made it across the track before the train.

"Unbelievable," Sheriff Wills said to his officers as they huddled together by the side of the road. "Earlier, Brian tamed a bird that busted up light bulbs and now he drove through a moving train. Maybe he *is* a wizard."

They all laughed uncomfortably.

More vehicles stopped behind the three police cars and joined the wait. There was still no sign of the end of the train.

"Bell's Ferry will stop them," the sheriff said. "They won't get far."

The locomotive rumbled as the railroad crossing signs flashed and dinged.

It was another five minutes before the train finished

crossing the highway. The flashing lights turned off and police held traffic a moment longer as they looked for signs of Rin's car on the other side of the track.

There were none.

Sheriff Wills got back into his car and raced to Bell's Ferry.

CHAPTER FORTY-SIX

I COULD TAKE A TRAIN

What happened with the police chase was something Ozzy and Clark and Sigi would never forget. Rin? Well, he acted like taking a dirt jump off the road and twisting upside down in a car before landing on a speeding railroad car was nothing out of the ordinary.

The train car in front of them had a large metal container on it, and the car behind them did, too. Somehow they'd landed unscathed on the empty one in between. Their small car shook and rattled as the locomotive rumbled along.

Rin put on the emergency brake for safety.

"You don't think that was unbelievable?" Ozzy asked for the tenth time.

"I guess once you've lived in Quarfelt you're not easily impressed. And besides, I told you previously that many spirits use the railroads for traveling through this dimension."

"Do they use it like that?"

"They use it however they see fit."

"I wish I had my phone so I could send out a snapchat of this," Sigi said. "No one's going to believe it."

"I personally think it's weird," Clark chirped. "Rin said we would get away and we did. That's weird, right? I mean there was a wall of train in front of us and a pack of cops behind us, and yet . . . here we are."

"It's almost impossible to believe," Sigi said.

"Sadly, you have more of your mother in you than you should."

"Do you think we're heading in the right direction?" Ozzy asked.

"We are," Rin replied. "This might actually save us time and gas money."

"And how do we get off whenever we stop?" Ozzy questioned. "What if when we stop, the sheriff's there?"

"What's the point of worrying about those things?" Rin said. "When the time comes, the answer will present itself."

Rin took a big bite of his fried egg sandwich.

"You don't think this is mind-blowing?" Ozzy asked.

"I do," Sigi said from the back seat.

"Look, you two, I know it appears as if we have unwittingly found ourselves on a great adventure, but it's important to know that this adventure started years ago. We are just now playing out the plot. Little things that were said, little things that were done—all those things, both granular and grand, shaped the choices and consequences that have led to right here. We are sitting in my ex-wife's car with my daughter traveling through the dark, hitching a ride on a train. That's not a surprise, because it was mapped out by actions that began long ago. The exhilarating part is that the little things we do . . . you treating Clark kindly, him causing me to lose control of the car, me finishing this sandwich . . . they are all starting points for new journeys that will propel us into the future."

Rin took another bite. After chewing a moment, he continued.

"You look at me and see a wizard. I look at everything and see magic."

"You have mayonnaise in your beard," Clark said.

Rin smiled and wiped off the mayonnaise with the end of his robe sleeve.

"Perfect example," Rin said. "We should all be excited to see how that very small thing, me wiping my face, might affect us in the future."

"I know it'll make it easier to look at you," Clark stated.

Sigi laughed.

Ozzy looked at Rin. He couldn't decide if he was wise or full of it.

The wizard finished his last bite of sandwich and then dusted off his hands.

"Now," he said. "You were wondering when I'd sleep, and it seems as if magically I now have some time to do so. This train is long and going fast, which means it must be traveling pretty far down the line. Sleep seems like a good way to spend my time."

Rin leaned the driver's seat back and closed his eyes. "I suggest you do the same," he said without opening them. "No one should be tired, because who knows what tomorrow may bring. Oh . . . wait, I do."

Rin shut his eyes and was out.

Ozzy leaned his seat back a little, but not so much that Sigi didn't have room in the back, and Clark got comfortable on Ozzy's stomach. Ozzy plugged the phone in to the car charger and held the glowing screen next to the bird's silver streak. Sigi leaned forward from the back.

"This is *not* how I saw my night going."

"Really?" Ozzy asked. "Riding the rails wasn't in your plans? I would think this was normal, since Rin's your dad."

"Actually, I hardly ever see him. He's not always been around during my life."

"Quarfelt?"

"Something like that. Your father must be amazing. I bet you're the only person in the world with a sentient raven. That's not normal."

"To be honest," Ozzy said. "I'm not really sure what is. The hidden house I live in, my parents' mysterious disappearance, me hanging out with a wizard and a talking metal bird. You being in the same car as me. Is all this normal?"

"Who's to say?" Clark whispered. "Remember that sign we saw next to Volts in Otter Rock? The one with the horse holding a TV, saying, 'All your nay-boors will be jealous'? Well, if a horse can talk, then anything is normal."

"I don't think horses can really talk," Ozzy said.

"Sure. Then how'd they get that picture?"

"I know the world has plenty of crazy things in it." Ozzy shifted onto his side to see Sigi better. "I've read books. I just wonder if what I'm going through now is extraordinary or commonplace."

"It seems to be commonplace for you."

Ozzy reached up and slid open the cover of the car's moon roof. He could see the stars and felt the click-clack of the track beneath him.

"Are you regretting the fact that you were nice to me at school?" Ozzy asked. "If you'd been mean, I probably would've just stayed hidden in the woods."

"I don't regret it at all. It's not always been easy feeling a little different than everybody else here. It was nice to find someone who was different in their own way."

"You mean different because your dad's a wizard? Because that's magical."

Sigi nudged Ozzy.

"No, different because of the color of my skin."

"Well, that's magical too."

Sigi smiled. She leaned back in her seat and closed her eyes. As if in chorus, the bird shut down, and the wizard was out as well.

Ozzy stared at the stars. The somewhat normal high school life he had enjoyed for a couple of weeks seemed like a past as distant as his parents. Still, somehow here he was with Sigi, and that reality helped him believe almost anything.

CHAPTER FORTY-SEVEN

HEAVY SLEEPER

The train traveled at full speed through most of the night. As daylight began to break, Ozzy woke up and put Clark on the dashboard so that he could catch some of the sun's first rays. He tried not to stare too much at Sigi as she slept in the backseat, but she was a firework he couldn't easily look away from.

Rin yawned like it was the most important thing a wizard could do. He adjusted his chair and sat up straight. His hat was still on, but his beard looked like it could use a wash and a good combing.

The terrain they were traveling through was hilly and treeless. The earthen banks on both sides of the tracks were high and wide.

It took a couple tries before Ozzy could get a phone signal to see just where they were.

"We're in California," he announced. "Does that seem right?"

"We may have gone farther than I wanted to," Rin admitted. "We should probably find a way off this train as soon as possible."

"Right," Ozzy said. "I figure when the train finally stops we'll have to get out and leave the car. I mean how can we . . ."

Rin started the vehicle and switched on the heat.

Ozzy looked relieved. "Oh, for a second, I thought . . ."

The wizard took the emergency brake off and turned the wheel to the right.

"Wait! What are you doing?"

Rin smiled and then pressed hard down on the gas. The car flew off the moving railroad car with Ozzy screaming. It landed hard against the raised ground at the side of the railroad tracks. The small white car then bounced and rolled down an incline towards a dusty road.

"You're insane!" Ozzy screamed.

The car fishtailed and rocked over the dirt, coming to a skidding stop on the hard soil of the small road.

The train just kept on going.

Rin put the car into park. Amazingly, Sigi was still sleeping in the backseat.

"I don't believe you!" Ozzy yelled.

"It's not necessary that you do."

"We could have died!"

"I see no proof of that. Besides, I couldn't just leave Patti's car on the train."

"He's crazy, right?" Ozzy asked Clark who had just now come to life.

"I don't know—what happened?"

"Well, do you see where we are?"

Clark bobbed his small head.

"And do you see that moving train over there?"

More bobbing.

"How do you think we got off it?"

"Does it matter?" the bird asked sincerely.

"What an intelligent answer, Clark," Rin said. "I'm very impressed by how wise you are."

The wizard put the car back into drive and began speeding down the dirt road.

"You realize that's something a maniac would do?" Ozzy argued, not willing to drop the conversation yet. "A maniac would drive his car off of a moving train with his own daughter sleeping in the back seat."

"Well, then," Rin said, "maybe I've misjudged maniacs all these years."

"It's just that I really want to live to see my parents again."

"Good for you. You should write that down. A goal written on the air is subject to the will of the wind."

"I think I'm going to be sick," Ozzy said.

Rin turned down a bigger dirt road and headed east.

"Where now?" Clark asked.

"We'll find a gas station and then find a road that takes us in the direction of Albuquerque."

Five miles later they turned onto an actual paved road and a few miles past that they saw the first signs of civilization. There were some old houses and a gas station at the crossroad where the road they were on met the highway they needed to take.

Rin stopped at the gas station. Before filling the tank, he announced that he needed to go into the store.

"I need to see a wizard about a griffin."

Ozzy sat in the car with Clark and a still-sleeping Sigi.

"I'm not sure we're doing the right thing," Ozzy said.

"It's the wizard, right?"

"Yeah. We almost died twice in the last twelve hours."

"If he was here he'd probably say something like, 'Most everyone dies every second of the day.'"

"Right. Or, 'If you almost died, that means you probably didn't.'"

"Good one. What about, 'Robes are cool and I wear a hat.'"

"Not great."

Clark hopped up onto the headrest of the driver's seat and fluttered his tin tail.

"I wouldn't worry about Rin. On that tape, your mother told you to talk to this Charles guy and Wizardy is helping you get there. How many people have a wizard on their side?"

Rin was back out of the gas station.

"We'll need some money to pay for gas," he said. "I'd

pay, but since this is a business trip I want to keep things on the up-and-up."

Ozzy handed Rin some money and he went back in.

"You're lucky your parents had money."

"I'd feel luckier if I had my parents instead."

"Soon you might have both."

Rin walked back out and began to fill up the car.

"I'd better use the bathroom myself."

"I'll never understand what you humans do in there."

"Well, that's a real upside to being a mechanical bird, I'd guess."

Ozzy woke up Sigi and explained to her where they were and how they had arrived at that point. She was madder about having slept through it than angry about what happened.

"You have a lot of your dad in you," Clark observed.

After using the restrooms, Ozzy and Sigi walked the aisles of the small gas station and purchased a few sodas, chips, and boxes of cookies.

When they returned to the car, Rin was done pumping gas and was putting the nozzle back on the pump.

"Wow," Ozzy said. "I didn't look at it when we got out, but the car has really been beat up."

"It does have an awful lot of character now," Rin said. "Patti never liked the color, so maybe she'll see this as a great opportunity to get it repainted."

"It needs more than just new paint, Dad."

The poor vehicle had been driven offroad by Ozzy and

had jumped onto and off a moving train thanks to Rin. It was scratched and dented, the front wheels were out of line, and the back of the car looked closer to the ground than it had before—but miraculously, it still ran.

Rin opened his door and got in. Ozzy and Sigi walked around the car and did the same thing but on the other side.

"I got some snacks," the boy reported as he put on his seat belt.

"Excellent, then the journey can continue," Rin said. "If we drive all day and make as few stops as possible, we can probably make it to Gallup, New Mexico, by late night. From there it's only another three or so hours."

They drove for a while and then entered the state of Nevada. Through most of Nevada, they listened to an audiobook that Rin had downloaded. The book was called *Margret's Weeping* and it was nearly as bad as its title. When it was finished, all four spent a long time discussing it.

"Why do you even have that on your phone?" Ozzy asked.

"It's on loan from the public library. I heard it was good."

"Now you've heard it was bad," Clark said.

"It had merit," Rin said, trying to defend the book. "What about the few parts where Margret wasn't crying?"

"She had nothing to cry about in the first place," Sigi pointed out.

"That's true," Clark tweeted. "All that money and two

parents and a house with another house in the back. That's what you need, Oz. One of those extra houses so that I can have my own place."

"Really? The cloaked house isn't big enough for you?" Ozzy asked.

"It's filled with all of that stuff. A bird needs room."

"It *is* quite cluttered," Rin joined in. "Have you ever seen that TV show *Hoarders*?"

"No, I've never watched TV."

"Never?" Sigi asked.

"Well, as you know, when the teachers didn't feel like teaching, they'd put a movie on. But that's it."

"Just like Margret," Clark said. "She never bought her own groceries."

"That's not a very good comparison."

"I agree," Rin said. "It's more like Margret's boyfriend, Keith. He never learned to care for anyone but himself, and Ozzy's never seen TV."

"Are you two aware of what makes things similar or not?" Sigi asked.

"You know, the books in Quarfelt are so different. You don't read them, you absorb the words. Sit on a pile of books, and in a matter of moments you're that much wiser."

"You *sit* on books there?" Clark asked.

"Well, holding them in your hands is more efficient and less likely to draw stares, but some wizards . . . well, you know wizards. Anything to be different."

"Are there schools in Quarfelt?" Ozzy asked.

"Of course. Great places of learning."

"Like . . . Hogwarts?"

"Not exactly—they're better run and they've outlawed floating candles. I guess dripping wax is very hard to clean up. You know, not everything that woman wrote is practical for wizards. I'd like to see Harry Potter clean wax off of the floor. But she told a good tale most of the time. I actually worked for the School of Mischief and Merriment in Quarfelt and believe me, there was no mirth to be had when book six came out and she had the nerve to do that to Dumbledore."

"I didn't like that part either," Ozzy admitted.

"So you've got regular books in that Quar place?" Clark questioned.

"Some made it in."

"What was your job like?" Ozzy asked.

"I taught the wand care class."

"Wait," Ozzy said. "You *do* actually have a wand?"

"Of course."

"*I've* never seen it," Sigi said stoically.

"I've never brandished it while you were around."

"Do you have it on you?" Ozzy asked.

"Of course. What kind of wizard travels around without his wand?"

"Can you show us?"

"I don't think I want to be brandished," Clark said.

"I'll show you later, perhaps. I'm driving and you

humans have designed these cars to require the driver's attention. Check my phone. I think I've got another book downloaded we can listen to."

Ozzy pressed the screen a few times and found the other title.

"*Darren's Mistake,*" he said with a groan.

"How about after we find out what this Darren chump did wrong, we spend some time listening to me chirp?" Clark asked. "Fair enough?"

"You know I prefer the term 'More than fair,'" Rin said.

Ozzy pressed play and they drove the rest of the way through Nevada and into Arizona learning about Darren's mistake and hoping they weren't making a few of their own.

CHAPTER FORTY-EIGHT

MAYBE IT'S TIME TO BELIEVE

The Mule Pole Highway near the tall yellow tree was lined with police cars on both sides of the road. It was morning and Sheriff Wills was there with most of his on-duty officers as well as three other officers from Bell's Ferry.

Rin and his white car had never made it to the roadblock.

When daylight arrived the police had gone back to the railroad crossing to look for clues. In the light of day, they were able to find tire tracks in the dirt on the shoulder of the road that went up the embankment and then just disappeared.

"I don't understand," Sheriff Wills said to Officer Greg. "Cars don't vanish."

"Maybe these aren't their tire tracks at all," Greg said. "They could have crossed the rails seconds before the train arrived. Which means they're hiding somewhere between here and the roadblock that Bell's Ferry set up. There aren't any other main roads but there are dozens of small dirt ones. We've had officers checking those roads all morning."

"The biggest problem with that theory," Sheriff Wills said, "is that even though it was dark last night, I saw the train already stretched out across the road when I turned the corner. How does a car beat a train that's already there?"

"I don't know, sir. They didn't go through it, and there's no debris or sign of an accident anywhere. Officer Wallow suggested that there might be a . . . portal of some sort."

Sheriff Wills looked bothered.

"He was joking, of course," Greg said.

"Of course."

"But," Greg added, "it's as good an explanation as any we have."

"What about the train?"

"It was on a long haul to Sacramento. We've contacted the railroad and they've spoken with the engineer. He had no additional information and no knowledge of any accident or damage to the train."

"Let's say these tracks are from the car. And say the car hit the mound going too fast and somehow flew *over* the train."

Officer Greg looked conflicted about what to say.

"Seems highly unlikely, sir."

"We saw it sort of weaving and then in a flash it was gone. Could it have hit that mound of dirt and then landed *on* the train?"

"Well, the angle's a little steep, and that seems almost as impossible as a portal, but they'll do a thorough search when the train arrives in Sacramento."

"Thank you, Greg."

"You're welcome, sir."

Officer Greg walked off and Sheriff Wills stood alone thinking. He had grown up with Brian . . . Rin. The two had been friends in grade school. Rin had always been resourceful and kind. Now, it seemed as if his onetime friend might actually *be* a wizard.

"Nah."

Sheriff Wills took out his phone and called Patti to fill her in about what they hadn't found.

CHAPTER FORTY-NINE

PROPELLED FORWARD THROUGH SPACE

By the time they got to Kingman, Arizona, it was beginning to get dark. Collectively they were all sick of driving and not in the best of spirits. *Darren's Mistake* was now their mistake as well. The book took *hours* just to reveal that when Darren had been a kid he had stolen his neighbor's pocket watch. And he felt terrible about it.

Patti had been texting Rin all day demanding to know where he was and wanting to talk to Sigi. Because wizards never text and drive, Rin had Ozzy type his answers and send them to her.

"Tell her that the wizardly winds have given me lift."

"Wizardly winds?" Ozzy asked. "That sounds like a medical condition."

"Right. Then tell her that we are safe and if the stars dictate, we will be back shortly with Sigi in tow."

Ozzy sent it off and she responded.

"She's furious. She also wants to know what happened

to her car by the train tracks. Sheriff Wills said it just disappeared."

"Tell her he isn't far off."

Ozzy sent it.

"Oh, but also tell her the vehicle's all right . . . -ish."

"Okay."

Patti's text back was a plea for Rin to stop whatever he was doing and call Sheriff Wills. Rin's text back was a plea for Patti to please check on his fish and tell Sheriff Wills to take a hike. They had done nothing wrong, and since it was now the weekend Sigi was supposed to be with him.

Ozzy didn't understand the reply Patti sent back.

"What does . . . here, look."

Rin took a quick glance at the phone.

"Oh. You probably shouldn't read that out loud."

Arizona was a beautiful state full of varied landscape and nice roads. They stopped at yet another drive-thru and Ozzy thought back to when he used to like them.

"This food is making me sick."

"Just keep eating it. Eventually you'll get over that feeling."

Ozzy choked it down and then spent a few minutes looking out the window at the passing landscape and wishing he had just eaten a meal from his garden and basement instead.

"You know what?" Rin said. "Let's call that Charles guy again."

"It's kinda late in the day," Ozzy pointed out. "He didn't answer before. I doubt he'll answer now."

"Let's just try," Sigi said.

"I'll dial if Rin talks."

"A true wizard knows when to be silent and when to speak. This feels like a time for the latter."

Ozzy found the number in Rin's outgoing calls list and pressed it. He handed the device to the wizard.

"It's ringing," Rin said.

There were a few moments of silence.

"It's still ringing."

"If it goes to voicemail, just hang up this time," Ozzy instructed Rin.

"It's going to voicemail."

"Hang up."

"It's telling me to leave a message again."

"Hang up!"

Rin couldn't pass up the chance to have his thoughts recorded.

"Yes," he said into the phone, "my message to you this evening is that when one door shuts it is usually for a reason. If it's not been locked, then it should be easy to open again."

Rin ended the call and everyone just stared at him.

"I see you all understand," he said, misinterpreting the mood completely.

"That wasn't your strongest message, actually," Clark told him.

"Should I call back and leave another?"

"No," everyone said in sync.

"Okay," the wizard said. "Now, we'll be driving for about another three or four hours before we stop for the night. Then tomorrow it'll take us three more hours to get to Albuquerque. In the meantime, who wants to play 'A Wizard Speaks'?"

"Is that a game?" Ozzy asked.

"Yes," Sigi said. "When I was younger he always made me play it."

Rin ignored his daughter's less-than-enthusiastic tone. "What you do is you look out the windows as we drive and if you see something magical you say, '*A wizard speaks and . . . he sees two blue cars in a row.*'"

Ozzy sighed. "You and I have such different definitions of magical."

"Try it," Rin encouraged. "It's very revealing. In no time it will become apparent that the whole world is sprinkled with magic."

"Okay, I'll go," Clark said. He looked out the front window. "A wizard speaks, and he sees an endless row of telephone poles."

"Brilliant," Rin cheered.

Ozzy looked at the long row of telephone poles in front of them that ran along the freeway. They were lit up by the cars' headlights. At the angle he was sitting they did look almost otherworldly and unending.

"This game is probably easier in the daytime," Ozzy

said. "That way you can see more than just what's lit up by the lights."

"Easier maybe, but not better," the wizard insisted. "It's a real marvel to discover that the things so nearby are much more than you once perceived. Your turn, Sigi."

"I've never liked this game."

"Come on," Clark chided. "Say something."

"A wizard speaks, and he sees a daughter who has spent her whole life having to explain her father to others."

"Very nice," Rin said. "How fortunate you are to possess knowledge to teach others. Some people go their whole lives never having the courage to explain anything. What about you, Oz? Give it a try."

The boy looked out the front window at the freeway before them. He saw the telephone poles and the lines painted on the road. He noticed the faded sky at the edge of the headlights' glow and felt the smooth turning of the tires beneath him. Sigi was breathing softly in the back seat. The ordinary moment began to feel ethereal and important. His brain buzzed softly.

"A wizard speaks, and he feels the weight of his body being propelled forward through space."

"Well done," Rin whispered.

"No fair," Clark said. "That's cheating. It's supposed to be what a wizard sees and not feels. Because if feels count, I'm feeling the same thing."

"Points for both of you."

Clark was okay with that.

The game continued and the miles ticked off. And each time a wizard spoke, the world became larger and less complicated and smaller and more intricate. By the time they reached the New Mexico border, Ozzy, Clark, and Sigi were surprised to already have driven so far.

"Time flies occasionally," Rin said. "But I have also seen it languish and whimper as it stomach-crawls across the floor. We'll stop in about an hour."

"Good, because this moving cage is killing me," Clark complained, as if he wasn't a mechanical bird who could just shut himself off at any point.

"Here," Sigi said, "rest on my lap."

Clark settled onto Sigi's lap and yawned.

"Are you doing okay?" Ozzy asked Rin. "You're not going to fall asleep driving, are you?"

"Of course not, that's not something that would ever happen to a wizard. Now, I've seen one or two drop from a broom while flying. There's something about the wind on your face that makes you tired. That's why you see very few wizards driving convertibles."

"Oh, that's why. I *did* wonder."

Ozzy smiled and closed his eyes.

CHAPTER FIFTY

FAKE PERSONALITIES

Gallup, New Mexico, is probably pretty, but it was so late when they arrived that they didn't see much of it. They checked into the Motel 6 and Ozzy and Rin were out the moment their heads hit the bed. Clark found a nice spot on top of a mini fridge in the room and shut down there. Sigi got her own room right next door and was out just as fast.

When they got up, they realized that Gallup itself wasn't much to look at after all. There were a number of fast food restaurants, some industrial looking buildings, and at least ten boarded-up gas stations. The land around Gallup, however, was beautiful—breathtaking deserts and flat mesas made from dirt the color of cinnamon and mahogany. Stretches of green topped the mesas like fuzzy toupees on a bunch of blocky heads.

They gassed up the car and then went through the McDonald's drive-thru to get breakfast. Rested and ready, they were on the freeway and heading towards Albuquerque by nine A.M.

"I feel a lot better," Ozzy said between bites of a sausage burrito.

"Breakfast will do that to you."

Clark chewed on bits of hash brown while standing on the dashboard.

"I like the texture of these. And they make my beak greasy."

After eating they brainstormed as a group. In a couple of hours they would be in Albuquerque and they still weren't sure exactly how things would go down.

"We can't just go in there all willy-nilly," Rin said. "It's smart to plan, wise to expect changes, and acceptable to be nervous about both scenarios."

"Okay—first we have to find where his office is," Ozzy said.

"That's easy. The map on the phone will take us right to the address," Sigi reminded him.

"Good. Second, we need to think about our approach."

"I would just drive on the streets that the phone tells you to," Clark suggested.

"Not our *actual* approach, but what we want to say," Ozzy clarified. "I don't know if it would be smart to go in there and tell him I'm his step-nephew and my missing mother told me to come see him."

"That's true," Rin agreed. "Honesty is pretty powerful stuff—we might want to spread it cautiously."

"We should tell him you're a rich inventor kid and pretend you invented me," Clark suggested.

Everyone stared at the bird.

"That's not a horrible idea, C."

"Of course it's not. That's why I said it."

"So why am I showing him my bird invention?"

"Because you're so proud of how beautifully it turned out."

"No, why am I showing it to *him*? It's not like kids all over the world go to Charles when they have neat-looking science projects."

"You think I'm neat looking?"

"Of course."

"Thank you."

"What's Charles's business, anyway?" Sigi asked.

"I'm not sure exactly what Harken Corporation is, but it says he works closely with the national labs who have a site in Albuquerque."

"So, he's a science guy like your dad," she observed.

"Maybe he's already invented his own bird," Clark tweeted excitedly. "This could be great."

"I don't think he did," Ozzy said trying to keep Clark's hopes realistic. "I don't know that we can get him to talk without saying who we are. But I would like to hold that information until we know more about him."

"Okay." Rin switched lanes and then switched back for no apparent reason. "Sorry. I didn't like that one after all. So . . . okay, here's what we do. We go into his office and tell him that we're a very wealthy and eccentric family, a father and his daughter and son. We let him know that we have more money than sense and that we're on a treasure hunt of sorts. We show him the orange cassette tape we have and say that we found it at an estate sale in Burlington, Vermont. Then . . ."

"Why Burlington?" Sigi interrupted.

"I don't know; I've just always wanted to live there. Plus, it's on the other side of the country, so we're not giving our position away. We tell him we searched for his name and that he was the only Charles Plankdorf to come up. Since we're so wealthy and don't possess the good sense to spend our time wisely, we decided to take a trip and see if he was the one mentioned on the tape."

"It might work," Ozzy said. "It's an interesting story and maybe he'll be intrigued enough to go along for a spell."

"I like your choice of words."

"Still," Clark chirped. "I think showing me off would be better."

"You can ride on my shoulder like a metal parrot statue," Rin suggested. "It will add to the oddity. Now, let's work on our backstory so we don't make any mistakes. For starters, I made my fortune in the diaper industry."

Ozzy shrugged. "Why not?"

The four of them worked out their history and who they would be. By the time they got to Albuquerque, they had assumed their new roles and were ready to perform the charade.

The city was spread out like a massive board game stitched together out of boards and pieces from every game in the closet. There were trees here and there and roads and freeways heading in every direction. In the distance the Sandia mountain range towered over the east horizon.

"That mountain has the world's longest tram on it," Rin said. "There's a restaurant up at the top. I remember that I didn't like what I ordered."

"Was it breakfast food?" Ozzy asked.

"Sadly no, but I once helped a woman in a castle here. She had trouble sleeping."

"Did you tell her some of your wizard-world stories?" Clark asked. "I know those make me sleepy."

Rin smiled. "Bird humor is so subtle. It wasn't a very authentic castle and the woman was unhappy with the results."

Harken Corporation was just off the freeway in a large, misshapen building with metal front doors and small windows. Rin parked the car in the parking lot and turned it off.

He looked at Ozzy and his daughter.

"Ready, Salvin and Honi?"

"Really?" Sigi said. "Am I Honi?"

"Yes, it means 'apple wedge' in Quarfelt. Now, come on, you two."

"Yes, Father," Ozzy said reluctantly.

Clark hopped onto Rin's right shoulder and they climbed out of the car.

CHAPTER FIFTY-ONE

I SEE THAT THERE IS EVIL

Lynette Tillman had worked for Charles Plankdorf and Harken Corporation for more than ten years. In all that time she had never seen a group of people quite like the three who had just walked in.

The older man was wearing a short open robe over a black T-shirt and jeans. He had on a pointy felt hat and a long dark beard that was sprinkled with grey. On his shoulder was a fake bird. The boy was tall and strikingly handsome. He had grey eyes that looked as if they belonged to a much older and wiser person. And the girl beside him was beautiful, with dark skin and sincere brown eyes.

"Goo day to you, madame?" Rin said using a fake accent that didn't fit any known accent in the world. "How ah ew this fine afternoon?"

"I am well," Lynette said with a professional smile. "Welcome to Harken Corporation. May I help you?"

"Yes, this is me son Salvin and a daughter, Honi. We three are hee to see a Meester Charles Plankdorf. Is he in?"

"And your business?"

"I've sold diapers the last wenty years."

"I see," she said. "What I meant to ask is—what is your business with Mr. Plankdorf?"

"Of course. Look at me bragging without needing to. We—my children und I, that is—have a question that we believes only Mr. Plankdorf can answer."

"Could you try the question out on me first?" Lynette asked, like the professional she was.

"I ood tell you," Rin said, trying desperately to keep up his weird fake accent. "But we . . . I . . . has traveled some deestance and we are very bit the eccentric beings we pears to be. What I try to say is we discovered a tape at an estate sale in Burlington, Vermont."

Rin paused for some unknown reason and Lynette just stared. "Have you ever been there?" he asked.

"No, I'm afraid I haven't."

"Nothing to be escared of, but if you get the chance you might put that on yis travel plans. Is a lovely town. The peoples is enchanting."

"I'm sure." Lynette looked as if she was having some fun with the conversation. It was a quiet afternoon and these strangers were providing a good story she could tell her friends later that evening. "Go on."

"Thank you I will. We found this tape and apond listening to, discovered it mentions the name of one Charles

Plankdorf. Not in a negative way, but in a way that made I want to drop what we are doing and search hims out."

"So, you traveled across the county to talk to a man who is mentioned on a tape you found in a box at a garage sale?"

"Estate sale, but yes, is gist of it. Not to toot my own horn, but I am exceedingly well-off and my fortune gives me the freedom to act on impulse and whim."

Lynette was tempted to just send them on their way, but she knew very well that her boss dealt in secrets. If there was any chance the tape contained something that could either harm or benefit him, it was worth the time to find out.

"Can you wait a moment?" she asked.

"Of course."

The assistant motioned to a waiting area with three handsome couches to the side of her desk.

"Please, take a seat, and I'll see what I can do."

"Thank you," Rin said.

Lynette walked off and the wizard and his fake family sat on the couches and tried not to look nervous.

"What accent are you trying to do?" Clark asked while standing perfectly still on Rin's shoulder.

"It's from the north hills of Quarfelt. Wizards are very adept at speech. In a way, we need to speak and understand every language there is. Magic does not have an official language."

"Whatever it is, it's really awful, Dad," Sigi said.

Lynette came back out.

"Mr. Plankdorf will see you," she announced as if they should be extremely grateful for the honor.

"Excellent," Rin said, standing up.

"May I take your . . . robe and hat?"

"Not on your life," Rin told her. "The robe is my blanket of security. I have brokered countless deals in this garment and I can see no reason to remove it now. And the hat hides a scar."

"Then please keep them on."

Lynette led them through the double doors behind her desk and down a long white hallway. At the last door on the left she stopped. Before opening it, she spoke.

"Mr. Plankdorf is a busy man. If you are wasting his time, he will sniff it out and ask you to leave immediately. And remember—there are cameras everywhere. We take security and order seriously at Harken Corporation."

"As one must," Rin said.

Lynette opened the door and walked into the room. Ozzy, Sigi, and Rin followed. The office was large and sterile looking. There was a glass desk, a few new books on a tall bookcase, and some modern furniture. Sitting behind the desk was Charles.

"Mr. Plankdorf, this is . . . I don't believe I got your name," she said to Rin.

"Sirius," he replied. "Sirius Knight."

"Sirius Knight and his son, Salvin, and daughter, Honi," Lynette announced.

Charles didn't stand up from his chair, but he did speak.

"Come in and have a seat. You have three minutes to tell me what you came to say."

"We will only need two," Rin said with a smile.

Lynette left the office and closed the door behind her. The trio walked towards the desk and sat in the chairs that were facing it.

Charles Plankdorf looked just like the picture they had seen online. He had a nice head of dark hair and puffy cheeks. His eyes were brown and his nostrils flared as he pinched his lips together.

"You say you have a tape?"

"We do," Ozzy said. "But before we tell you what's on it, can I ask you a question?"

"Fine."

"Do you know a Dr. Emmitt and Dr. Mia Toffy?"

The reaction in Charles's brown eyes and pale face was subtle but strong. There was no doubt that the names he'd heard meant something to him.

He pinched his lips tighter and then spoke.

"I may have known those individuals a lifetime ago."

"Well," Rin said. "Then what we have to say may be of interest to you."

Charles Plankdorf sat in his big fancy chair behind his desk and listened to every word that Ozzy and Rin and Sigi told him. He made no comments and kept his expression neutral.

His cellphone beeped a couple of times but he ignored it.

The story the trio gave was well rehearsed and sounded almost plausible. Ozzy wanted to drop the facade and just tell the truth, but he knew there was reason to be cautious. His parents had been taken, and somewhere in all the mystery there was an evil element that had enough dark in its heart to steal his parents and leave him for dead. They didn't show him the tape or attempt to play it, but they recited word for word what Mia had said at the end.

"So you see," Rin said, "we're just curious as to the fate of this woman on the tape. It seems as if her last words were in regard to you. When we searched for her online we found no information past the point when she and her husband quickly left New York."

Charles finally spoke.

"It is almost unbelievable to think that you and your children would travel across the country just to find out about what one woman said on the end of a recording that was probably made years ago."

"Well, as I mentioned . . . we are eccentrics."

"Yes, you mentioned that. Four times, I believe. I'm not sure a true eccentric would even realize that they are one."

"Fair point," Rin said, smiling. "I suppose I am more normal than I give myself credit."

"And shouldn't your children be in school somewhere?"

"We are privately tutored," Sigi said.

"The other children gave them grief about their importance," Rin continued to lie. "So I pulled them both out."

"And you say you made your fortune in diapers?"

"Ah, yes, but not wearing them—selling them. Now, do you know more about this woman or did we come all this way just to find out this is a dead end?"

Charles cleared his throat but didn't speak.

"May I ask you what your business here is?" Rin said. "This appears to be a very important and strange building. And there doesn't seem to be much about your company online."

"I deal in information," Charles said.

The wizard smiled. "That's good, because it's information we want."

Charles stood up.

There was no way for him to know that this moment had begun years ago. That the questions he was being asked had been formulating throughout Ozzy's entire life. He was unaware that what he was about to say would have any real impact on the three strangers that had interrupted his day in the most surprising of ways. He didn't know the weight his words carried, but he tossed them out anyway.

"I suppose it does no harm to inform you that Emmitt was my half-brother. His mother was my mother."

"Is he still alive?" Ozzy couldn't stop himself from asking.

Charles stared at the boy. His brown eyes connected with Ozzy's grey. For a moment it seemed as if he saw something new in Ozzy. He blinked and rubbed his chin while he continued to stare.

"Are you okay?" Rin asked.

"Fine. I'm fine," Charles said, shaking his pensive look away. "I don't know if Mia and Emmitt are alive or dead. They disappeared and no one ever heard from them again. It haunts me to hear of them now."

"What were they like?" Ozzy asked, trying his hardest to act uninterested.

"They were brilliant. Actually, too smart for their own good. Emmitt could build anything. No problem was too large and no obstacle stopped him. He was obsessed with the mind and people's free will."

Ozzy knew most of the information Charles was giving them thanks to the tapes he had listened to for years.

"Mia was beautiful," Charles continued. "Her understanding of the human condition was second to none. I only knew her the short year before they disappeared. They had a child when they left New York, a son. He would probably be about your age now, Salvin. How old are you?"

"Sixteen," Ozzy lied.

"Well, he would be a little younger."

"And they just decided to leave New York and move elsewhere?"

"What they decided was to leave everyone who loved them and not say a word."

"Sorry," Rin said.

"You played no part in that, so the apology isn't necessary. I moved away from New York shortly after that and I don't believe a single person has heard from them since."

"Other people's lives," Rin said reflectively. "It never ceases to amaze me how the world is filled with so many souls and each one of us has a catalog of stories to tell."

"Did these people have other family?" Ozzy wanted more information. "What about your and his mother?"

"My mother died about two years before they left New York, and I believe his father had passed away before that. We had no other siblings. I'm not one hundred percent sure about Mia. I never heard her talk about her parents or siblings. You'd think after so many years that would have come up."

Ozzy stared at Charles.

"You said you only knew her a year," the boy pointed out.

Charles momentarily looked at a loss for words.

"Well, a year's a slight figure of speech," he explained. "I saw them every other week and they held dinner parties once a month. We had a lot of interaction, even if it was a bit more than a year that I knew them."

Ozzy smiled and pretended that he was okay with the answer. But his chest tightened and he realized he no longer wanted to tell his half-uncle the whole truth.

There was a knock on the office door and a short man wearing a uniform of some sort entered.

"Come in, Eric," Charles said briskly. "I'm with visitors."

Eric walked up to Charles and handed him a folder. As Charles studied the folder, Eric looked at Rin and gave a friendly nod. He looked at Ozzy and froze. His eyes locked with the boy's and his hands began to tremble slightly. He glanced down to get a better look at Ozzy's hand.

"Thanks, Eric," Charles said. "You can go."

Eric continued to stare at Ozzy's eyes.

"You can go," Charles snapped. "Leave us."

"Yes . . . yes, of course."

Eric shook off whatever he was feeling and left.

"Now," Charles said to Rin once the door was closed, "how about you let me see that tape and I'll get someone to track down a way to listen to it?"

"No," Ozzy said suddenly, "I mean . . . we can't. We don't have it with us. We left it at the hotel."

"Oh," Charles said sounding suspicious. "What hotel?"

"The Marriott," Rin said, catching on to the fact that Ozzy now felt a need to keep the secret a bit longer. "What's up with this town not having a more upscale place for us to stay?"

"Well, I *would* like to hear it," Charles said. "After all, it's my half-brother's wife talking about me."

"No problem," Rin said. "We were going to go back and get it once we realized we'd left it at the hotel, but we figured we'd make sure you were truly connected to the Toffys first."

"I see."

"We'll run get it now," Ozzy said. "Will you be here the rest of the day?"

"How about I follow you to your hotel? You can grab

the tape and then we'll have a late lunch or an early dinner together."

"That's very generous," Rin said. "But I'm eccentric and I don't like people following me. So we'll retrieve the tape and return later this afternoon."

"Are you sure?"

"Yes," Ozzy said.

"Well, I would have loved to get something to eat with you three, but it might be best for me to keep working."

"Excellent," Rin said. "Just one last question: Why do you think Mia wanted anyone listening to that tape to talk to you?"

"I can't imagine. Maybe she knew I had a connection with her husband."

"Sure, that's probably it," Rin said, slapping his wizard forehead with his right palm.

"Now . . . can I ask you a last question?" Charles said.

Rin nodded.

"Why do you have a bird on your shoulder?"

"First of all, I appreciate your noticing. Second of all, it's to let others know I'm eccentric before I even open my mouth."

"Mission accomplished," Charles said. "I'm not a huge fan of birds, but it works for you. Now, have my secretary give you my personal number and be sure to leave yours. That way if there's a change of plans on either side we can notify one another."

"We will," Ozzy said, standing up.

Charles stared at the boy's eyes again.

"What color would you say your eyes are, Salvin?"

"I'm afraid you already asked your last question for the moment," Rin said in a friendly tone. "Your words, not mine. Save it for later."

Rin stood and followed Ozzy and Sigi out of the office.

CHAPTER FIFTY-TWO

WORRY AND HOPE

As soon as Rin and Ozzy had left the office and the door was closed, Charles picked up his phone and dialed a number.

"Come to my office at once," he ordered. "There's a situation."

Charles hung up the phone and stared at the air in front of him with an expression of anger and worry. For years he had worked tirelessly and spent millions of dollars trying to recreate the formula his half-brother had once discovered. It was his obsession to figure it out. There had been countless setbacks and he had done things that he would have rather not done in the quest to find the answer. But even after all the trials, a team of scientists at his command, the code had not been broken and the project had been canceled.

Now, three strangers had walked through his door claiming to have a tape that could contain answers, or at the very least a reason for Harken Corporation to start working on the project again. The excitement he felt was intoxicating.

He picked up his phone once more and pressed a button.

"Are they gone?" he asked Lynette.

"Yes, Mr. Plankdorf. They just left."

"Did you get their information and give them mine?"

"I did."

"Good, now find out as much as you can about this Sirius Knight. He claims to be some sort of diaper mogul. I need to know exactly who he is."

"Of course."

Lynette went to work on her end and Charles leaned back in his chair and let his brain process this new information. It could be nothing, but as Charles knew, few things ever were.

Most smoke, he had discovered, was accompanied by fire. And if this was a real breakthrough, then the course of mankind could be close to taking a big step forward.

His office door opened and three men came in.

"I have things I need you to do."

Charles gave them their orders and sent them out to get what he wanted.

CHAPTER FIFTY-THREE

BURRITOS AND BREAK-INS

Ozzy, Rin, Sigi, and Clark climbed into the beat-up white car. All four of them exhaled.

"Why didn't you tell him who you really are?" Rin asked. "I thought that was the plan."

"I was going to, but then something he said made me rethink it."

"Was it the crack about not liking birds?" Clark asked.

"No. He said that he knew my mom for years and he also said he'd only met her the year before she disappeared."

"He said it was a figure of speech," Sigi reminded him.

"No, it's more than that. Also, did you see the way he reacted when I first said my parents' names? It wasn't a look of caring or sadness; it was a look of fear."

"I did notice that," Sigi said. "So now what?"

"We drive away and pretend we're going to get the tape."

Rin started the car and pulled out of the parking lot. He got on the road leading back to the freeway.

"I don't know what it was," Ozzy said. "I wanted to tell him the truth, but something about him seemed way off."

"Then you did the right thing." Rin looked proud. "I can think of nobody better to trust than one's own self. Or maybe Snilf—he's the current high wizard in Quarfelt."

Rin merged onto the freeway.

"Maybe we should eat something," he suggested. "It'll clear our heads and give us a moment to regroup. We'll kill two birds with one stone."

"I hate that expression," Clark said.

"So sorry," Rin apologized. "Now, I wonder who serves a decent breakfast around here."

Sigi looked on the phone and found a place with good reviews called Frontier Restaurant.

"It says they have the best breakfast burritos in the world," she reported.

"That's a statement no wizard can take lightly."

Using the GPS on the phone, they found the restaurant. It was located across the street from the University of New Mexico, a large school consisting of adobe buildings and tall cottonwoods. Rin parked on a small neighborhood street two blocks behind the establishment.

"You coming in, Clark?" the boy asked his bird.

"Yes, and you're ordering me something with texture. Maybe some hash browns."

Ozzy put Clark in his hoodie pocket along with the orange cassette tape.

The restaurant was filled with all sorts of interesting and diverse looking people so Rin and his wizard garb fit right in. They ordered breakfast burritos and pancakes. Then they found a table by the far wall and waited for their names to be called.

"So, are you going to show Charles the tape or not?" Sigi asked. "I mean, is there any harm in him hearing it? Maybe he just doesn't trust us now, but when he finally hears it he'll really open up."

"Perhaps," Rin said.

Clark shifted and stuck his beak out of the hoodie pocket so as to feel less confined.

"I just don't see where we go from here if this doesn't give us any answers," Ozzy said. "I'll have to go home and hide out in the cloaked house for the rest of my life."

"That is, if the sheriff hasn't found your home by now. He's looking for us and his efforts will be more aggressive than in the past. Ed found it. He could have easily blabbed. But then again, Sheriff Wills is pretty inept. I doubt he'd hike more than two miles for anything."

"What about you, Rin? What are you going to do?"

"Technically, I haven't done anything wrong. But Patti's not going to be happy about me taking Sigi on this trip. So, if Quarfelt doesn't take me back, maybe I'll finally move to Portland. Heaven knows they could use a wizard."

Ozzy heard Clark sigh and then spoke. "If this is a

dead end then I don't know where to look for my parents next."

"You know, it's possible they can't be found," Rin said seriously. "I hate to bring that up, but there are things hope and magic cannot do. We may wish for things to be one way, but there are billions of conflicting wishes that may want it another."

"I know! I know my parents are probably dead," Ozzy said defiantly. "I'm not stupid. They loved me, and I can't believe they would ever stop trying to find their child that was left behind . . . unless they just couldn't."

"Wizard!" a man called out from the front counter.

"That's us," Rin said needlessly.

They got their food and returned to the table. The conversation they had been having was heavy and reason for quiet introspection, but the food was too good to keep any of them quiet.

"There must be a sorcerer in that kitchen," Rin said. "I can taste the alchemy."

"What's that green stuff in the eggs?"

"Green chile," Sigi said.

"I think it's my new favorite thing."

After stuffing the burritos down their throats and every last bit of pancakes into their mouths, Ozzy left a good tip and they walked slowly back to the car.

Clark took his place on Ozzy's head.

"I think that might have been the tastiest thing I've ever eaten," Ozzy confessed.

"It's in the running," Rin said. "Quarfelt has some pretty spectacular food."

"Really? Like what?"

"They have this berry called the Loom. It can be both sweet and savory. Prepared by the right hands, it's incredible."

"So . . . do you believe in Quarfelt?" Clark asked Sigi.

"No, but if it helps my dad to travel there occasionally, I'm okay with that."

"Believing is different for everyone," Rin said.

"Um," Clark tweeted from the top of Ozzy's head. "I think we have a problem. Did any of you guys leave the car doors open? Because they are."

Ozzy ran to where the white car was parked. Both doors were wide open and all of their belongings were spread out on the road.

"What happened?" Sigi asked, looking around.

The inside of the vehicle had been thoroughly picked through. The glove compartment was empty, the floor mats had been flipped over and the back hatch had been popped open.

"I don't see anything missing," Clark said as he hopped to the ground and took inventory of all their stuff lying there.

"They were looking for something specific," Rin said. "Where's the tape?"

Ozzy reached into his pocket. It was still there.

"I have it," he said quietly without taking it out.

"Why would someone somewhere you've never been want an old tape?" the bird questioned.

Ozzy looked down at Clark.

"Oh. You think Charles did this?"

"Or he had someone do it for him," Rin suggested.

"But how did they know where we were?" Sigi asked.

"There was a car following us," Clark said. "I was going to say something, but the sunlight in the back window was intoxicating. I got a little drunk on glow."

"It doesn't matter now," the wizard spoke. "What has happened has happened. Now we must gather the mess and get away from here. If they followed us this far I'm sure they still have an eye on us."

All four looked around nervously.

"Use your wand," Clark suggested. "Levitate all of our stuff back into the car."

Having no faith in Rin's wand, Ozzy and Sigi bent over and scooped up the things that had been pulled from the car. Rin got into the driver's seat and started the vehicle.

"Let's go."

Ozzy and Sigi got in.

"Where are we going?" Ozzy asked.

"We need to find out if someone's following us," Rin said. He pulled away from the curb and drove off. "And if they *are*, we need to lose them."

"Fine," Ozzy said. "But if somebody *is* following us, don't lose them by doing a barrel roll onto a moving train."

"I can't promise anything."

CHAPTER FIFTY-FOUR

CEMETERY GATES

Clark jumped to the back window to keep an eye on the rear while Ozzy and Sigi scanned the area for any sign of someone nefarious.

"I don't even know what I'm looking for," Ozzy confessed.

"I do," Clark said. "And you have at least one vehicle following you."

Ozzy looked out the window and saw a large black SUV move into the lane directly behind them.

Rin pressed down the gas pedal and turned right quickly.

"I don't get what's happening!" Sigi yelled. "Why are they chasing us?"

"I can't say for sure," Rin yelled back, "but I think Ozzy's half-uncle wants that tape at all costs. Hold on!"

The wizard took another turn and increased his speed.

"They're getting closer!" Clark reported.

The black SUV flashed its headlights and sped up.

"This isn't going to end well!" Ozzy yelled. "Let's stop and reason with them. If they know that Charles is my uncle maybe they won't hurt us."

"We're not stopping," Rin said with authority. "We're going to play this hand out. Of course, it helps that I've seen what's coming and know we'll be fine."

"Really?" Ozzy said. "That's good, right?"

"Hold on again!"

Rin turned the car once more and the tires on the right side almost lifted off the ground. Ozzy wasn't buckled in, and he slammed up against the passenger's side door. Rin straightened up the steering wheel and zoomed down a wide four-lane street.

"What have I told you about seat belts?" the wizard chastened.

The SUV tried to pass them on the right but Rin moved in front of them. They backed off and tried passing on the left. They sped up and brought their vehicle even with Rin's. A man with short hair and out-of-style glasses was in the passenger seat of the SUV. He motioned with authority for them to pull over.

Rin obeyed faster than they wanted. He turned so sharply that the little car went up on two wheels. The SUV couldn't make the turn and it raced on to the next possible one.

The car came down on all four wheels and raced along a small street that led to an old cemetery. Rin turned into the cemetery and quickly drove down one of the thin lanes between the graves. He pulled the car up to a large shade tree and turned it off.

The three humans breathed loudly.

"For a wizard, you're a pretty good driver," Clark said.

"Thanks. Now we'll wait here for a while and then make our move when it feels safe."

"What's our move?" Sigi whispered.

"I don't know yet."

The cemetery was large with big overgrown cottonwood trees along the lanes and thousands of headstones. There were small paths for single cars to drive around, and a big mausoleum in the center of the graveyard for people to bury those souls who didn't want to actually be buried.

"This is a beautiful park," Rin said.

"I don't think it's a park, Dad."

Rin begged to differ. "It has grass, trees, gravestones, and it's open to the public. It's like a park with interesting things to read sticking out of the lawn."

"Whatever it is, it's a bad spot for us," Ozzy said. "I can't believe how wrong this day is turning out."

"You must be joking," Rin said. "This day is just getting better and better. Do you realize that while we were eating that wonderful breakfast burrito we had no clue what to do next? It felt like we had come all of this way for nothing. Then those gentlemen were kind enough to go through our car and chase us."

"Really?" Ozzy asked. "That was *kindness*?"

"They handed us hope," Rin said. "Now we know there's more to Charles than he let on. That tape must be important, and it must hold clues that we didn't pick up."

"Or it's the formula on side A that Charles is after," Sigi said.

"I bet that's it," Clark agreed. "Bad people like formulas. Ozzy once read me a book about a crooked general who had a secret formula."

"That was the biography of Colonel Sanders, and you're talking about his chicken recipe. I don't think he was evil."

"He looked evil—pointy beard, crazy glasses, weird tie."

Ozzy ignored his bird and carried on talking with Rin.

"That formula on the tape is why my parents moved to Oregon to hide out. It's the answer, but I just don't understand it."

"Right. And it's a formula for what?" Rin asked. "Also, why did you read a biography of Colonel Sanders?"

"It was mixed in with a bunch of cookbooks I found in the cloaked house. As for the formula, I bet it has something to do with the brain. All of my dad's tapes are about the brain and how powerful it is. The brain was my mom's specialty as well." Ozzy was getting excited. "It probably controls the mind. All of those people who did things they normally wouldn't must have been influenced by what my parents discovered."

"Uh, oh," Clark said. "They found us."

The black SUV drove into the cemetery through the

same gate. It drove slowly down the small paved lane two rows over. Rin and Ozzy slid down in their seats.

"That seems pointless," Sigi whispered. "They know what this car looks like better than they know your heads."

She was right. The men in the SUV spotted their car and drove over onto the same path. Rin quickly put the car into drive and drove down the lane towards the back exit of the cemetery.

"This might not be a good idea," Ozzy said, pointing out the front window.

In the distance a long line of cars with their headlights on and a hearse at the front was slowly driving in through the far gate. From where they were, Ozzy could see that the gate was too narrow for two vehicles to go through at once. And since everyone was coming their direction, they were trapped.

"We can't turn around!" Clark yelled. "The SUV is right behind us."

"I guess there's only one option."

Rin pressed on the gas and sped forward at an alarming rate. It actually would have been an alarming rate on the freeway, but it was beyond alarming to be going so fast in a cemetery down a one-way lane filled with oncoming cars toward a stone wall with an opening that wasn't much wider than a single vehicle.

"Don't do this!" Ozzy yelled.

"It's already done."

The cars in the procession saw them coming and tried

to move over as far to the left as they could. Rin squeezed between the vehicles and the gravestones on his right. It was a tight fit, but he was doing it. The SUV followed suit. They were considerably bigger than the white car and kept hitting gravestones on their right side.

"That is so disrespectful," Rin said as he looked at them through his rearview mirror.

The procession of cars trying to come into the cemetery were honking and Ozzy could see people in their vehicles shaking their fists and yelling at them as they passed. He looked up the lane and witnessed a long pickup truck just beginning to enter the small entrance in the stone wall.

"We won't make it!" Sigi yelled.

"I believe you're wrong," the wizard testified.

Rin pushed the pedal all the way down and the small car jammed through the opening, barely missing the side of the truck and scraping the stone wall.

They burst out of the cemetery and onto the road. Ozzy and Clark looked behind them as the large SUV tried to do the same thing. It shot forward and attempted to squeeze between the truck and the wall. Unfortunately for them, it was too big. The massive SUV squealed and hissed as it quickly came to a stop, wedged impossibly tight in between the truck and the stone wall.

Clark tweeted joyously.

"They're never getting out of that," Ozzy said.

Rin pressed on the gas while handing Ozzy his cell phone.

"Take my phone and look up 'Randall' in the contacts."

Ozzy took the phone and searched through the contacts for a Randall. He was surprised how many people Rin knew.

"You know a lot of people."

"Wizards are in high demand."

There were three Randalls listed.

"Which one?"

"Randall Mortley," Rin said.

"I got it. Do you want to call him or something?"

"No, map his address. We're going to pay him a visit."

Ozzy pressed 'start navigation' and held the phone so Rin could see it.

"You didn't tell me that you still knew someone in Albuquerque."

"It didn't come up," Rin answered, driving quickly.

"You think he can help?"

"I don't know—the last time I saw him he was upset with me."

"For what?"

"For being his son."

"You have a *father* and he lives here?" Ozzy said in disbelief.

"Brian had a father. Rin? I'm not so sure."

Sigi was shocked. "I have a grandpa?"

"You met him years ago. I think you were two."

Clark hopped up onto Ozzy's right shoulder and whispered in his ear.

"Wizards have dads?" the bird whispered.

Ozzy shrugged.

"I thought they were hatched," Clark added.

The car continued to move quickly through the streets of Albuquerque, making its way to the coordinates on the phone. The map on the screen showed where they were on the route; on the bottom it read:

"Time till arrival: twelve minutes."

CHAPTER FIFTY-FIVE

TROLLS AND DARKNESS

Rin's father lived in a neighborhood on the west side of Albuquerque. His house was small and the front lawn was just rocks with a few weeds growing up through them. It was an average-looking neighborhood, but the windows of all the homes had bars over them.

"Why?" Ozzy asked.

"I think there's a lot of crime here," Rin replied.

"I believe that," Clark said. "We've not been here even a full day and already our car's been broken into and some guys in a black SUV chased us."

Rin parked the car in the driveway and turned it off. He took a deep breath and then very slowly exhaled.

"When was the last time you spoke to your dad?" Sigi asked.

"It's been a few years," Rin said. "He's one of those humans who refuses to believe in magic."

"Is that why I've never heard about him? I thought Mom said your dad was dead."

"Patti never liked him, so he drifted out of my life. When I went to Quarfelt, I learned to accept that my father is dead to me. I'd love to see him accept who I am."

"I'd love to just *see* my dad," Ozzy said.

"I don't have a father," Clark added.

"My father barely knows me."

"Thanks, you guys," Rin said sincerely. "Let's do this," he said, steeling himself. "We'll go inside and I'll call Charles to see what he has to say for himself. If we need to, we can use my dad's computer as well."

"What about me?" Clark asked. "Should I show off a bit? Maybe give your dad a look at how magical I am?"

"It might be best if you stay hidden until we get a reading on his mood."

"Fine."

The four of them got out of the car and Clark worked his way into Ozzy's hoodie pocket.

"Who am I?" Ozzy asked Rin as they walked to the door.

"That's a question that takes a lifetime of living to answer. You're asking me to describe the sun on the first day I see it. The definition would be simple and lacking in any real perception. One must live first before being penciled into a dictionary."

"No . . . who am I for your dad? Are you going to give me a weird name again, or do we just tell him the truth?"

"Let's go with a short of version of the truth."

Rin rang the doorbell and then waited on the stoop with Ozzy and Sigi.

The door eventually opened to reveal Rin's father, Randall. He was a short, old man wearing overalls and a white T-shirt. He had big hands and ears and what hair he had on his head was white and sticking up. If Rin looked like a wizard, then his father looked like a troll. He wasn't a million years old, but if one was rounding up, he was close.

Randall blinked a couple of times and then glanced at the people on his porch like they were a foreign movie he didn't understand.

"Brian?" he finally said.

"Dad," Rin replied coolly.

"My word, what on earth are you doing here?" Randall asked. He stuck his head out the door and looked around for any other surprises.

"It's just us," Rin assured him. "I was in town and thought I'd stop by. Can we come in?"

"That's okay, I guess," Randall said, sounding bothered. "But don't turn on any lights."

"We won't, but can we pull our car into the garage? I don't want anyone stealing it."

Randall looked at the beat-up car and sighed. "Fine."

While he was inside opening the garage, Sigi asked, "Why does he like it dark?"

"I'm not sure. He's hidden his whole life from any sort

of relationship or honesty. Some people have a difficult time existing."

Once they were inside the house there was only a tiny, single lamp with a low-watt bulb turned on at the far end of the family room. All the windows had blankets over them and no natural light was making its way in anywhere. Ozzy took a moment to wonder if this was where his life would end. A wizard had taken him to see a troll and the troll was hiding him away in a dark cave.

"I'd apologize for the dark, but it's my house and so I don't have to," Randall said. "The light bothers me. Come into the family room and have a seat."

There were no couches or love seats, just a puffy recliner and a TV with a coffee table in front of it. The family room butted up against an equally dark kitchen where there was a counter with two barstools. Ozzy and Sigi grabbed the barstools and sat on them. Rin took a seat on the edge of the coffee table.

Randall the troll groaned as he settled into his recliner.

"So," he said, "I can see from your getup that you still think you're a sorcerer."

"Technically a wizard, but sorcery is in my wheelhouse."

"What do you call yourself again?"

"Labyrinth is my name, but most of the people I'm close to call me Rin."

"Your mother and I gave you a proper name and you traded it in for *that*?"

"I didn't trade it in—things change."

"Who are these two kids?" Randall asked, switching topics.

"I'm Sigi, your granddaughter."

"Interesting. I saw you as a baby. I'd apologize for being such a lousy grandfather, but I've never been good with family. Now I'm too old to feel bad about it. How's it been having a wizard for a father?"

"Okay, I guess."

"Are you a witch?"

"Not that I know of."

"And the boy . . . is he related?"

"No, this is Ozzy. I'm out here helping him locate his family."

"Nice to meet you," Ozzy said.

"So is that what wizards do these days? Startle their parents with surprise visits and help kids find their families?"

"Sometimes."

"And the boy's not a wizard in training?"

"No," Rin anwered.

Ozzy was actually a little disappointed to hear Rin say that.

"You know, I never really went in for all that make-believe and fantasy stuff," Randall sniveled. "When you first told me about being a wizard, I thought at least what you're doing might be interesting. But the last time I saw you, you were here and you made that smoothie for that woman in that big stone house who couldn't sleep."

"It was a nightshade shake."

"Well, it's boring. Now you're helping families find one another? Boring again."

"You sit all day in a dark house," Rin pointed out. "I don't think you're one to talk."

"I sit here and claim only to be an old man who is easing into the last days of his life. I never claimed to be a wizard."

Clark slipped out of Ozzy's pocket to get a better look at the arguing and to see the troll for himself.

"Listen, I know this is a surprise," Rin said. "And I'm aware that you don't approve of my career choice, Dad. But do you think it would it be okay if we stayed the night?"

"I've got four bedrooms and it's just me, so fine. No skin off my back. Just don't go turning on needless lights. House guests," Randall mused. "I didn't see this coming. How's Patti?"

"Good, but as you know, we're not together anymore."

"She was a catch. Such a smart girl. And your sister?" Randall asked.

"Doing well. She's still a fact-checker at the same magazine. We just saw her a couple of days ago."

"At least I have one child with a normal job," Randall jabbed. "Tell her that it wouldn't hurt her to come visit me every once in a while."

"I'll pass that along."

"What about . . . well, you know—"

"Mom? She's doing great."

"Are you going to mention that you saw me?"

"It'll probably come up."

"Good. Just leave out the part about me not liking lights. That comes off as weird for some reason."

"Right," Rin agreed. "Well, this is great reconnecting, but we need to make an important call."

Randall made a passive-aggressive sniffing noise. "Go ahead."

"We'll just move to another room so we don't bother you."

"Really? I'm eighty-two years old and nobody has come by the house in weeks. The last person to drop by was a kid selling pest control. I must have talked to him for an hour before he finally just turned around and ran off. Don't you think I might enjoy listening in on any phone calls you're making?"

"It's the kind of call you might not want to overhear."

"What—are they out of wands at the wand shop?"

"No, it's a serious situation."

"Make your call right here. I want to hear what a wizard thinks is serious."

Rin looked at Ozzy and shrugged.

"I guess it's all right," Ozzy said. "Just call Charles and you talk."

Rin straightened his hat and then got the card from his robe pocket. He dialed the number Lynette had given him and held the phone to his ear.

"Hello?" Charles said gruffly.

"Yes, Charles," Rin said into the phone. "This is Sirius Knight. I must say that our afternoon didn't go over quite as we planned. Do you mind telling me why there were men chasing us on the streets of Albuquerque? Or why they rifled through our vehicle?"

"I have no idea what you're talking about," Charles replied.

"I think you do. We had planned to give you the tape, but now we're not so sure we can trust you."

"Let's cut to the chase," Charles said. "I'll stop pretending I didn't have someone search your car and you stop pretending whatever it is you're pretending."

"I don't know what you're talking about," Rin said. "And I'm thinking about being offended by all of this."

"Feel any way you please," Charles said. "I just want to check out that tape. I'm sure it's nothing, but I don't like having my name out there on things I can't control."

"Well, we want to bring you the tape, but your men jumped the gun."

"Listen . . . I made a mistake. Just tell me where you are and I'll send someone to get it."

"I don't like that scenario. I believe we'll take the evening to think about it. If we feel like it, we'll drop by your office tomorrow and let you listen. If we don't, then you will never see us again."

"I know about the diapers," Charles said.

"What?" Rin asked, embarrassed. "That was just for a couple of weeks after a minor surgery. Who told you?"

"You did—you're a diaper mogul, remember?"

"Oh. Those diapers."

"I know you're not who you say you are. And as a man who deals in secrets with the government at the highest levels, I can make your life very complicated. Why don't you tell me where you are and I'll send someone over to pick up the tape."

"Why don't you cross your fingers and toes and hope we decide to stop by tomorrow. I need to go."

"Wait," Charles said angrily. "Just so you know, I have far more information about Emmitt and Mia. If you don't drop by, you'll never know what it is."

"I'll keep that in mind," Rin said cheerfully.

The wizard hung up the phone and looked over at his father. It was dark, but for the first time in a long time, it looked as if Randall was impressed.

"Now, that was all right," Randall grumbled happily. "I never knew you had any of that in you."

"Well, if you had ever stuck around long enough anywhere you might have found that out long ago."

"Fair enough," Randall said.

"He prefers 'More than fair,'" Clark said, having forgotten that he was supposed to be hiding.

"Who said that?"

Rin looked at Ozzy and then down at Clark, who was sitting on the bar.

"Have I introduced you to Clark?" Rin asked his father.

The bird flew through the air and landed near the lamp on the other end of the room. He put his back facing the bulb and chirped.

"Ahh, that feels much better."

"You have a talking bird?" Randall asked in amazement.

"Not just any bird," Ozzy said. "Clark."

Clark charged up a bit and then flew over and landed in the old man's lap.

"Clark, at your service."

Randall stared at the mechanical bird and then looked up at Rin.

"I may have misjudged your career," he said.

"Luckily there is no time limit on change."

Rin and Ozzy and Sigi told Randall everything, not leaving out a single car flip or breakfast burrito. By the time the sun began to go down, Rin's father had a new appreciation for his son's line of work.

"Well, you should be safe here tonight," Randall said. "But I'm not sure I'd trust that man. Maybe it would be best to not see him tomorrow. You could hang around here and I could get to know Sigi a bit."

"We can't," Rin said. "We have to find out if this is a dead end. If it is, I have to get Sigi back and make a few things right in Oregon."

"But first we've got to meet up with Charles again," Ozzy argued. "He knows more about my parents. What if there's a chance that they're still alive?"

Rin, Sigi, Clark, and Randall were suddenly quiet. Everyone knew how impossible that sounded, but nobody wanted to point it out again.

They all sat there in the dark wondering what to say. Their dilemma was temporarily put aside when someone knocked three times on the front door.

CHAPTER FIFTY-SIX

GOOD FROM BAD

The dark family room made the knocking seem ominous and unsettling. Five pairs of eyes looked to the door in stunned silence.

"Were you expecting anyone?" Rin whispered.

"No, but I wasn't expecting you. Maybe it's your sister."

Ozzy stood up from the barstool he was sitting on and walked across the room to the door. He looked out the peephole. It was dark outside and there was no porch light.

"Should I open it?"

"Wait," Rin said. He stood up and pulled something from the inside pocket of his robe. "Go ahead."

"Is that your wand?" Ozzy said excitedly. "You actually have one?"

"Of course I do. It's an authentic Gruntvole and very expensive."

Ozzy stared at it as best as he could in the dark.

"It has a steel core and is surrounded by alder wood," Rin bragged. "I got it in Quarfelt. Now, open the door."

Ozzy took the doorknob and pulled.

"*Risindus milindus*!" Rin yelled, waving his wand towards the open entry.

The spell wasn't necessary because there was no one there.

Ozzy and Sigi looked out the door while Rin put his wand away. On the ground there was a large manila envelope. The boy bent down and picked it up.

"There's a letter for you here."

"Bring it in," Randall insisted.

Ozzy brought it in and closed the door. Rin took out his phone and, using the light of the screen, looked at what the front of the envelope said.

"Nothing," Ozzy told him.

He handed the envelope to Randall. Rin's dad took the envelope, opened the clasp, and pulled out a stack of papers about ten sheets deep. They were bound with a silver clip at the top and the front page had one word on it.

Toffy

There was a yellow note clipped to the front of the papers written in faint pencil. The poor lighting made it almost impossible to read.

"Hit the switches, boys," Randall ordered. "It's time to shake this darkness."

Clark shot to a row of light switches and clawed them all on. The family room and kitchen lit up like magic.

Looking around, it was clear to see why Randall liked the lights off—his home was in serious need of dusting.

"Here," Randall said, handing the papers to Ozzy. "That's not my name on the front. *You* read it."

Ozzy took the papers and sat down on the coffee table. He looked at the yellow note and read it aloud as Sigi and Rin looked over his shoulder.

> I know who you are. Your eyes gave it all away. I have lived with the shame and horror of what I was a part of for too many years. I won't pretend that this makes up for any of the pain you've suffered, but I believe there are answers here you deserve to know. Charles had me track your phone to find this location. I have not told him where you are. With this delivery, I now plan to never return to what I have been doing at Harken Corporation. I wish you safety and peace. Your parents were the kind of people this world needed. They would have been amazed with you. So sorry.
>
> ERIC

"Who's Eric?" Rin asked.

"He was the man who interrupted that meeting with Charles," Sigi answered.

Ozzy stared at the note. Then he slowly set it down and looked at Rin.

"I told you this could become painful," the wizard said with compassion. "It's not too late. You can try to return to the cloaked house and spend your days hidden and safe while living off the memories and hope of whatever you wish. Or you can read what's there and most likely see things that will provide answers . . . but also conjure up dark things that you have waded through your whole life."

Ozzy took a moment to breathe. Clark flitted up and parked himself on the top of Ozzy's head.

"Wow," Randall said. "This is some heavy stuff you wizards do."

Ozzy picked up the papers, folded back the first page, and began to read.

CHAPTER FIFTY-SEVEN

YOU ARE WHAT YOU READ

By the time Ozzy had finished reading the pages aloud, a few prominent points stood out. Emmitt and Mia were brilliant and perhaps a bit . . . mad? They had discovered a formula that could help people have better control over their own free will. The formula had the potential to cure apathy and misunderstanding. They wanted to build a perfect world where everyone was able to think their way into prosperity and happiness.

They had tested the solution on the unsuspecting patrons of their dinner parties. After a few initial snags, all signs indicated that the formula worked perfectly. Then on one of the final tests, Timsby had not done what he was supposed to do and instead jumped into a polar bear cage and almost died.

They stopped all testing completely, but Emmitt's half-brother, Charles, had caught on. He had seen the endless potential for the formula to control others for his benefit. Like his own father, he longed to be in control and make decisions that weaker people couldn't make themselves. He wanted his half-brother to team up with him and, in a sense, rule the world. But Emmitt wanted no part of that.

The two half-brothers fought and Charles tried to kill Emmitt.

Finding no other option, Emmitt and Mia moved out in the dead of night. They took their child, their belongings, and hid themselves away in the cloaked house where nobody could find them.

The second-to-the-last page had information on how Charles had found them. He had tracked down the bill of sale that Emmitt had signed for the cabin and land. It had been difficult to find, but with a little bribing and the right access to files he shouldn't have had access to, he deciphered the mystery.

In anger and greed, he took Emmitt and Mia and brought them to a bunker in New Mexico, leaving Ozzy for dead. He tried to force the two doctors to recreate their formula, but they refused. Charles didn't know how to handle defeat, and in a fit of rage, he ended their lives.

The ten pages contained a lot of words, but it was the line about Charles ending his parents' lives that stood out most to Ozzy. It read like a punch to his gut, a kick to his head, and a red-hot poker to his heart. The answer he had wanted for so many years had been given . . . and there was no giving that knowledge back.

"I am so sorry, Oz," Rin said.

"Me, too," Sigi echoed.

Clark scratched at his head affectionately.

"It's okay," Ozzy said, composing himself. "I've always wanted them to still be alive, but I've always known that was impossible. They would have tried everything to get back to me, but it never happened. It just isn't fair that the only family I've found happens to be the very person that has made my life so difficult and painful. Charles came to the cloaked house, stole my parents, and left me for dead. I was seven and he was my uncle. How could someone *do* something like that?"

"Power," Rin said. "What your parents created could make a person very wealthy and very powerful."

"Who cares?" Ozzy snapped. "What *is* power, anyway? How could humans care so much for something that ultimately destroys everything? He ruined my family and murdered my parents. And because of that, I'm alone in the world."

"Wait a second," Clark said defensively. "What am I?"

"Sorry. I know I have you."

"You have more than just Clark," Rin said. "But it must feel very empty finally putting the pieces together only to discover that the picture is grim. This is the worst kind of truth to discover."

"At least I know now. But what do we do?" Ozzy asked passionately. "I mean, are these papers enough proof? Can we use them to get Charles prosecuted? He killed my parents."

"No," Randall chimed in. "They're just papers. Now, if we had the testimony of this Eric fellow who dropped them off, you might have a chance."

"I know this is freshly festering within you," Rin said, trying to make his voice sound extra comforting. "But I don't think you should worry about revenge. Charles wants that tape and I have a feeling he won't stop until he gets it."

"Then don't you think that *now* might be a good time to cast a spell?" Ozzy said angrily. "Can't you just put an end to this by making his legs fall off or his head explode? What about your ad in the *ORVG*? Can you at least make him fall asleep? I hired you to make this better. You said two days and you'd have things in order. Well, things don't feel like they're in order."

"Things are just what they need to be. And remember, need is rarely comfortable."

"What does that even mean?" Ozzy asked, trying not to sound like a complete jerk in front of Sigi. "Should I not need *anything* anymore? Should I just destroy the tape? Will *that* make everything better? Will it bring my parents back? Will it punish Charles? I don't think so."

"You're right," Rin agreed. "But that tape gives us leverage and we should use it to our advantage."

"Really?" Ozzy said hopefully. "What kind of leverage?"

"First, we need to find a safe place to hide it. We'll let Charles stew tonight, and in the morning we'll call him and set up a meeting on our terms. Now that we know everything we do, he has no advantage. So we'll bring him a tape—a tape that will be secretly recording *him*. It's not beyond my powers to trick him into confessing what he did."

"You *are* pretty good at making people talk," Clark agreed.

"I was on the debate team in high school."

"You were?" Randall asked.

The old wizard looked at his much-older dad and sighed.

"Sorry, Brian . . . I mean Rin."

"It's fine, I got over that years ago."

"If it makes you feel any better, Grandpa, I didn't know he had been on debate either."

"Thanks, Sigi, it does."

Despite all of the dysfunction, Ozzy was a little jealous of the family relationship that Rin and his dad and Sigi sort of had.

"For now, let's—"

"Shhh," Ozzy said, cutting the wizard off. "Do you hear something?"

Randall looked around nervously.

"It sounds like someone's walking around in your backyard," Ozzy whispered.

Rin turned the lights off and Clark moved to the safety of Ozzy's hair. Everyone held their breath for a moment trying to hear.

The sound of rocks quietly crunching as something

moved around the back and the front of the house drifted through the room.

"Maybe it's Eric," Ozzy said in a hushed tone.

Clark flew to one of the blanket-covered windows and found a small hole in the corner near the top. He gripped onto the blanket with his talons and pressed his left eye up to the hole to look out into the dark night.

He flew back quickly and sat on Ozzy's left shoulder.

"Um . . . I don't know how to say this, but there are dozens of men in green closing in on the house. That's bad, right?"

"Horrible," Ozzy said.

"Get out of here," Randall said kindly. "Go before they catch you. Get in your car and get out of here."

"What about you?" Rin asked.

"I'm old and couldn't care less. Maybe I'll die tonight, maybe I won't. Either way, I'm okay with that. Now go."

Everyone looked at Rin.

"What do you say?" Ozzy asked while trying to breathe quietly. "Should we take one more car ride?"

"I think we should. I'll be back, Dad."

"Go be the wizard you were born to be," Rin's troll-looking father said.

It wasn't the most touching moment, but at least they weren't arguing.

"Oh, and son," Randall added. "If this is what it's like to be a wizard, then I have severely misjudged your path in life."

Rin smiled, looking more like a little boy than an old wizard.

"Come on, you guys," he said, leading the way out to the garage.

The three of them and their bird got into the car and buckled up.

"So how's this going down?" Ozzy asked.

"Well, Quarfelt taught me many things. I learned my first spells there. It was also the place I found my wand. But of all the lessons I learned, I think the one that sticks with me most is the advice a wizard named Umfuss gave me: 'Sometimes there is need for thought. Other times, a wizard is most powerful with action.'"

Rin turned on the car, threw it into reverse, and stomped on the gas. The car smashed through the closed garage door, sending it flying out and onto the ground. The little car rolled over the garage door and down the driveway as dark green figures dove out of the way. Once on the street, Rin slammed on the brakes and put the car into drive.

"Hold on! This could get crazy!"

"Like it already isn't?" Ozzy asked.

"I guess you're right. Oh, and Sigi—don't tell your mom."

CHAPTER FIFTY-EIGHT

STRUCK WITH WONDER

The three eccentrics and Sigi drove out of the neighborhood and onto the freeway without any sign of anyone chasing after them. Clark was in the back window keeping a lookout with Sigi by his side. A light rain began to spit on the windshield.

"Why aren't they coming after us?" Ozzy asked. "It makes no sense."

"We surprised them," Rin said. "They had to scramble just to get into their cars."

"Here they come," Clark cheeped. "And there's way more than one this time."

Ozzy looked out the back window and saw five black SUVs racing up from behind. The freeway was wide and filled with other vehicles, but the SUVs were flashing their lights and forcing everyone to pull over and let them through.

Rin had the small white car going as fast as possible.

He wove between other drivers and shot east on the I-40 freeway towards the mountains.

"Where are you going?" Ozzy yelled.

"I'm not sure, but a wizard would rather be confused in the mountains than concerned in the city."

"We're going to be confused either way," Ozzy shouted. "Do you think that formula my parents invented really worked?"

"It must have," Rin hollered. "It was enough to cause your parents to give up everything and hide in Oregon. It was also enough to cause your uncle to do the things he's done—and is doing."

The SUVs were getting closer. They took up all four lanes and made it look like a giant wall of black was rolling towards them.

The freeway began to head into the mountains as the rain picked up.

"There's too many of them," Sigi said. "I like not being bored, but I'm not crazy about this either."

"And we can't lose all of them," Ozzy pointed out needlessly. "This isn't going to end well, is it?"

"So now *you* can see the future?" Rin asked. "Stop witnessing things that aren't even there. Too many of you humans are scared by ghosts that haven't yet formed. The future is as much ours as it is Charles's. More so, actually, because you're in the company of a wizard."

Rin passed a small red truck and a yellow van.

"One of the SUVs is getting closer," Clark tweeted.

Rin looked into his side mirror and saw a single black vehicle break away from the pack and close in on them. It pulled alongside their car. The windows of the SUV were darker than the night they were driving though.

"What are they doing?" Ozzy yelled.

The passenger window rolled down to reveal a large man with a tight haircut and mean eyes. He motioned violently with his hand for Rin to pull over.

"I have an idea, "Clark said. "Roll down the back window just a bit."

"Why?" Ozzy asked.

"Just do it."

Ozzy found the button on his door and rolled the back window down two inches.

"Get ready for a beak-down!"

Instantly Clark shot through the window and into the open window of the SUV.

The bird bounced around inside the vehicle like a possessed pinball. He knocked the driver's glasses askew and broke a tooth of the large goon with the mean eyes. Ozzy and Sigi couldn't see everything, but they saw that the SUV was having a hard time trying to maintain control. As the driver batted at the mechanical assailant, he pulled at the steering wheel and the SUV twisted so sharply and at such a fast rate of speed that it flipped onto its side and went skidding across the freeway.

Rin kept his eyes on the road and his pedal to the floor.

Out of the rear window, Ozzy and Sigi watched as

the other SUVs slammed into the sliding one and a giant multicar pileup began to form, SUV after SUV running into each other. They plowed into the sides of the freeway, creating a dam of cars that blocked all four lanes and the shoulder.

Only one of the SUVs had managed to miss the mess that Clark had brought down. That vehicle didn't stop to check on all of its fellow thugs. Instead, it picked up the pace and continued to give chase.

"Wow!" Ozzy said. "Clark knocked out almost all of them with one blow. There's still one coming, though!"

"I can see that," Rin said, looking up at the rearview mirror.

"What about Clark?" Sigi hollered. "We can't just leave him!"

"That bird's resilient, and we can't stop now," the wizard insisted.

"I would have stopped for you," Clark said.

The bird had darted back into the window and landed on the top of Rin's headrest.

"You would have needed to come back for me," Rin yelled. "I'm nowhere near as capable as you."

"So you saw what I did?" the bird asked.

"Yes, and it was highly impressive." Sigi stroked the small wiry feathers on top of Clark's head while looking out the back window. "There's only one car left."

"It better hope it doesn't pull up next to us," Clark said, sounding tough.

The single SUV drew in closer.

"We can't outrun that thing."

"I'm not planning to. Here comes our exit."

Rin swerved right and took the Cedar Crest exit off the freeway. The SUV's tires screeched and whined as they followed suit. Rin drove down the off-ramp and right through the light at the end of the exit.

"Do you have any idea what you're doing?"

"Maybe," Rin said confidently.

The wizard followed a turn in the road that carted them north behind the Sandia Mountains and into heavier rain.

The SUV followed.

They were on a small highway driving towards the crest of the Sandia Mountains. Their vehicle passed a few stores, an old burnt building, and a couple of other cars, but otherwise it felt like a private racetrack that they and the SUV were racing on by themselves.

The black car tried a couple of times to come up alongside, but Rin's maneuvering of the poor little car kept them at bay.

"I don't know what to think!" Ozzy yelled.

"About what?" Rin replied.

"Sometimes it seems like you have all of this chaos planned out."

"Unfortunately, that means that sometimes I don't."

Rin turned sharply onto a road. Through the windshield wipers they saw a sign that read "Sandia Peak." It was dark and they were surrounded by trees as they headed into the forest and up the mountain.

"I feel better already," Rin said. "Trees make a wizard complete. Did you know that there isn't a single part of the Quarfelt landscape that doesn't have a tree within view?"

"*What?* Do you know we're being chased up a mountainside by maniacs in the rain?"

"Seriously, Dad, where are you going?"

Rin swerved to pass a single slow-moving car.

"We can't just drive and hope they run out of gas," Ozzy said. "Or hope that we flip onto a train, or that a bird makes it all better."

"Why not?" Rin asked.

"Yeah," Clark said, feeling personally slighted. "Why can't a bird make it all better?"

"I'm not saying you can't," Ozzy said, frustrated. "You already have, but at some point we are going to have to realize that we are out of options and should just . . . just—"

"Give up?" Clark asked.

"No!" Rin shouted kindly. "I think the word Ozzy is looking for is *hide*."

"Oh," the bird said, disappointed that his guess had been wrong.

"Listen, Ozzy, what happened to you as a child was horrific. But the time to run away is over. You were a child and you took that fear and used it to exist in the most amazing way. You're better today because of it. I'm not looking to drive into these trees and hide until the problem goes away. I'm looking to solve all of this right now."

It began to really rain. In the distance lightning flashed.

"Perfect," Rin said cheerfully.

The car screeched around a tight turn as the road climbed higher and higher.

"They're still right behind us," Clark reported.

Another tight turn was followed by more screeching tires.

"Before we get to the top, I feel like there are a couple of things I need to say," Rin hollered as he flew up the road. "First, my fee for all of this might be a bit higher than my initial estimate."

"I'm sure it will be."

"Second, nobody like you has ever answered my ad. Sure, I've found a few cats and removed a few warts, but you were the one person to dial my number who truly needed help. So thank you for that."

More screeching tires.

"Third, reality is important—don't let what you think will happen ever scare you. Instead, get into your ex-wife's car, drive thousands of miles, and make the future yours."

Lightning struck nearby and thunder followed. Each time, the lightning brilliantly showed off the lit-up forest.

"Fourth, Sigi, I'm sorry I haven't always been around. Being a wizard is important, but being your father means more."

"It's okay, Dad," Sigi said. "I know you were just doing what you had to."

"Well, you've turned out to be more impressive than I could have imagined. And as a wizard I have a great imagination."

"Thanks, Dad, but could you just watch the road!"

Rin swerved and the tires screamed and he drove higher up the mountain.

"This is good," Rin yelled. "There's something about immediate danger that makes a person honest and open."

Lightning flashed on both sides of the vehicle and all of them decided that now would be a good time to admit a few things.

"If we're being honest," Ozzy said, "I didn't want my parents to be dead."

"Well, I didn't want Patti to leave me."

"I'm getting a D in chemistry," Sigi admitted.

"And I'm running out of juice."

Ozzy turned Rin's phone flashlight on and held it up to Clark's back.

"Ahh. That's better."

The rain increased and the road became slicker. When the lightning flashed, Ozzy could see that there was mountain on the left side of the road and a steep dropoff on the other.

"They're still behind us," Clark said.

The report of the SUV's location wasn't necessary

because the vehicle was only a few feet away, their headlights shining directly into the back of the white car.

"I feel a little better now," Clark said. "I've got a charge. I could fly back and see if they have an open window I could squeeze through."

"No," Rin said. "Sit tight and keep charging."

The wizard turned a few more times and created some space between the little white car and the huge SUV. When he reached the top of the mountain, he pulled into a parking lot that belonged to a gift shop near the scenic overlook. It was late and wet so there were no other cars up at the peak.

"What do we do now?" Ozzy asked.

The wizard smiled. "Let's find out."

He slammed on the brakes and brought the car to a stop in the empty parking lot. He unbuckled his seat belt and got out. Ozzy and Sigi did the same on the other side. The moment they stepped out, a cold wind whipped up against their wet faces as the SUV came blazing into the parking lot.

"Come on!" Rin said.

Rin started to run up some stone stairs towards the closed gift shop.

"About a mile to the south of us is the highest restaurant in North America! And the top of the tram," he yelled.

"Why would you tell me that right now?" Ozzy yelled back.

"I find it interesting."

Two men climbed out of the SUV and began to give chase. Ozzy looked back. Lightning struck and he saw that one of the men was Charles.

Clark saw it too and made an exasperated noise. He jumped from Ozzy's shoulder and flew off to try to slow them down.

Ozzy, Sigi, and the wizard ran around the gift shop. They dashed up a long cement ramp to the top of the peak where the scenic overlook was. The overlook stuck out over the edge of the mountain and gave them a spectacular view of the lights of Albuquerque far, far below.

"Wow," Ozzy said.

"I know, right?" Rin said.

They had reached the end of the line. The overlook had a steel railing all the way around it. On the other side of the railing was a fall that no one could survive. Two lampposts glowed weakly on each end of the overlook.

"What are we doing here?" Ozzy asked. "They're going to find us."

"Yeah, Dad," Sigi said. "This seems like a bad idea."

"Of course they'll find us," Rin said. "That's the point."

"Shouldn't we run?" Ozzy suggested. "We could go over there to where the tram is. Maybe we can climb down the mountain."

"No. I like our odds right here."

"Unprotected, standing in the rain?" Sigi asked. "Standing on a deck hanging over the side of a mountain?"

"Yes."

"I might have to tell Mom about this, you know."

"Please don't."

"Also," Ozzy shouted, "one of those men in the car was Charles."

"Even better," Rin shouted back.

Lightning and thunder struck in the distance and Ozzy watched the dark sky fracture with light.

"Rin, this is not a good idea."

"Trust me, Oz, it's perfect."

Rin asking Ozzy to trust him struck a chord. His body buzzed and shivered under the cold rain. He had trusted this wizard to help him do some crazy things but now he wasn't so sure that had been a wise decision.

The rain began to let up; the lightning strikes were drifting farther and farther away. Ozzy looked back toward the closed gift shop. There, standing no more than ten feet from him, was Charles. He had gotten past Clark and around the building. Now he was wet, looking angry, and holding a gun.

Sigi screamed.

Rin spun around and saw what all the fuss was about.

"You made it," the wizard said calmly. His felt hat and hair were dripping wet. "Right where we wanted you to be."

Charles stepped closer.

"Sirius Knight and his kids, Salvin and Honi. I was wrong about you three. It takes a real eccentric to stand out in the rain on top of a mountain and think they have any advantage over me."

"Where's your other goon?" Rin asked.

"He's checking your car to make sure you didn't hide the tape in there. He's also contending with an annoying bird that won't go away. Now—is the tape in the car, or does one of you have it?"

Rin ignored Charles's question and asked one of his own.

"Do you know who this boy is?" he said, pointing at Ozzy.

"Why would I care?"

"You *should* know who he is," Rin said. "Because seven years ago, you kidnapped his parents and left him for dead in the woods."

Charles stood perfectly still, staring at Ozzy.

"His entire life he's wondered and hoped to find his family. And now he's discovered that the one half-uncle he does have killed his parents."

"I did no such thing."

"You had a beard back then," Ozzy spoke up. "You had a beard and you marched in with your men and took everything I had."

"Stop this!" Charles demanded. "You have no idea what you're talking about. The formula your parents came up with could have changed the world. No more idiots letting their free will ruin things for others. And those who don't know better could have been given guidance from us who do. So boo-hoo that you had a little pain in your life. You look fine. *I* was trying to *change the world!* Now, if you'll hand over that tape, I can finish doing so."

"What a stupid human," Rin said.

"I think I'm going to shoot you now," Charles said.

Ozzy felt something land on his right shoulder.

"I worked the other one over," Clark whispered into Ozzy's ear. "He's tangled up in some bushes that he was dumb enough to chase me through. Now I'll get *this* stooge."

Clark blasted off from Ozzy's shoulder and slammed into the right side of Charles's head. The evil half-uncle swore and waved his gun at the dark sky.

"Stupid bird! Where are you?"

Clark swooped in again and hit him from the left. Charles spun and shot into the air, hitting the bird and dropping him like a rock down onto the deck.

"No!" Ozzy yelled.

He and Sigi moved to run to the bird but Charles insisted they stay put.

"If he's dead, you'll pay," Ozzy said, seething.

"How could you do that?" Sigi yelled.

"He's a metal bird. What's death to an object?" Charles said cruelly. "He's obviously one of Emmitt's toys. Maybe I should examine it closer. Make a few of my own. Now, let's shoot somebody who's flesh and bone."

"Wait," Ozzy said. "Don't shoot anybody. I'll give you the tape."

Charles sighed. "That's more like it."

"First, let Sigi and Rin go."

"Who?"

"Honi and Sirius."

"Oh, well, if that's the condition then . . . no. How about you hand me the tape and then you three are free to do what you want. I couldn't care less if you live or die. But I guess you already know that, Ozzy."

The words hit Ozzy like a stone. He knew all too well what Charles's black heart was capable of. He had left him for dead years ago without a second thought.

Ozzy reached out his left hand and pointed. Under the weak lamplight, the contrast between his single finger and the rest of his hand was clear. He shook—and felt the universe drawing into him as if it meant to fill him with energy. He studied his finger as it pointed towards Charles. His mind began to buzz, and thoughts that weren't his own were visible to him. He could see what his half-uncle wanted. He could see how Charles still thirsted for the power and control he had eliminated Ozzy's parents for. He felt connected to the experiments and the possibilities his mother and father began years ago.

Ozzy closed his grey eyes and breathed in.

"Give me the tape." Charles's voice was like venom. "Let's finish the work your parents were too cowardly to complete."

Ozzy could see Charles's will clearly. Concentrating, he momentarily stole it away from him. Charles stood frozen as the boy sprang forward and barreled into him. He knocked him down against the deck. The gun flew from his hand and Charles's head slammed against the railing. Ozzy began to punch him as if he were the root of all his sorrow ever. And since he was, Rin let it go for a few moments before he pulled the boy off.

"That's enough," the wizard said. "Don't let your appetite for destruction consume your soul. There are better things in life to fill up on."

Sigi walked over to the gun and picked it up gingerly. She handed it to her father. The wizard racked a bullet from the chamber, ejected the magazine, and threw the gun and the magazine off the deck and down the mountain. Rin stepped back and stood by Ozzy and his daughter.

Charles slowly lifted himself onto his hands and knees and worked himself back upright. He looked at them all as they stood near the railing.

"You three aren't eccentric—you're mental. Now give me that tape."

Ozzy pulled the orange tape from his pocket and held it over the rail.

"Come any closer and I'll drop it. I don't know what's down there, but it's a long drop and you'd never see this again."

As Charles inched forward, Rin pulled out his wand and pointed it at him.

"Stay where you are."

"You're going to poke me with a stick?" Charles asked with disgust.

"It's a wand," Sigi said.

"Don't be foolish," Charles barked. "Ozzy, do you know how much that formula is *worth*? It could make us all wealthy beyond our dreams. Do you have *any* comprehension of its value?"

"I know it wasn't worth my parents' lives."

"It's worth more than all our lives combined."

"You and I have a different definition of value—it seems that my will is to let go."

Ozzy smiled and tossed the tape into the chasm. Charles lunged forward, screaming. He grabbed Rin's wand from his hand and tried to stab Ozzy with it. Rin moved quickly, pushing Ozzy out of the way and knocking both he and Sigi to the ground. Charles stood over them, holding the wand and sneering down.

"How stupid humans can be," he growled. "I'll find that tape. And I'll change the world." He lifted the wand above his head, laughing. "I don't need a gun to finish this. A wand can work just as well!"

Charles gripped the wand like a dagger and raised his fist, intending to thrust the wand into Ozzy's chest, but at that moment, the dark sky opened up and a terrific bolt of lightning snaked down and made contact with the wand. There was a tremendous crack mixed with the brightest light Ozzy had ever seen. Sigi, Rin, and Ozzy were blown backwards against the railing. Their ears rang and their eyes burned.

As their senses came back online they saw Charles lying there on the deck, his lifeless body smoldering. The metal core with an alder-wood covering might have been slow to work magic, but as a conduit for electricity . . . it was quite effective.

The rain picked up and the wind died.

Ozzy ran to where Clark had gone down and found the bird's body and his head lying a few feet away from each other. He showed the pieces to Rin and Sigi, trying hard to keep his composure.

The steady rain was soft but provided a comforting noise to a moment that felt more final than friendly. They all looked at Charles as he lay on the deck. Rin picked up his charred wand and slipped it back into his robe.

"I wish it could have ended differently," Ozzy said.

"It ended as it began," the wizard insisted. "With a boy being brave."

"Plus the magic of a wand," Ozzy added.

Rin smiled as he put his arm around his daughter. Under the soft light of the two lampposts he glanced at the bits of bird in Ozzy's hand.

"I wouldn't worry too much about Clark," Rin said. "You have your father's and mother's genius in you. Fixing him should be no problem."

Ozzy stood up and carefully put Clark's pieces into his hoodie pocket.

"What now?" he asked the wizard as rain washed down his face.

"Well, I don't know if you're aware of this, but Quarfelt is appearing. I can see it at the edges of my vision and in the shape of the landscape. It's here."

"We're going to Quarfelt?" Ozzy asked, looking around.

"No, I am."

"What?" Ozzy began to panic. "I don't believe it."

Rin smiled. "It doesn't matter if you do."

"Don't go," both Ozzy and Sigi pleaded.

Rin put one hand on Ozzy's shoulder and the other on Sigi's. "Sometimes our choices are not our own. Sometimes they're made by others. It might not be easy, but it's my responsibility to make things right."

"That makes no sense," Ozzy said, rubbing his temples.

"Let me put it in wompin lingo: Because you have made the brave decision to finish what was started long ago, you can now truly begin for yourself. I must move on and complete what *I* began."

"That makes even less sense," Sigi argued. "If you go, what are *we* supposed to do?"

Rin dug around in his front robe pocket and pulled out the car keys. He put them in the palm of Sigi's left hand as if they were a great token that had been forged in a fire of destiny.

"You should probably drive home," Rin told his daughter.

"I only have my permit."

"In Quarfelt, a person's permit is their bond."

"Dad, this is ridiculous," Sigi pleaded.

"I love you, Sigi. I'm sorry I haven't been there and sorry I must leave. But I need to make things right."

"Wait!" Ozzy shouted. "I didn't hire you to just abandon us."

"You don't *hire* a wizard—you value his time and pay him accordingly."

"Your ad said, 'Wizard for hire'!"

"Don't believe everything you read. And believe me, I wouldn't go if it wasn't what has to be."

The wizard gave Ozzy a short hug and Sigi a much longer one.

He then stepped back and looked at both of them.

"Sigi," he said solemnly, "tell your mom what happened."

A deafening crack of thunder sounded from out over Albuquerque. Ozzy and Sigi turned around to witness it and when they turned back, Labyrinth was gone.

CHAPTER FIFTY-NINE

AND IF MY MIND'S SOMEWHERE ELSE

The sunlight dropped down from high above the cloaked house, warming everything under its gaze.

Ozzy stood on the porch and closed the front door.

"Ready?" he asked.

"I think so," Clark said.

After Rin had disappeared, Ozzy and Sigi had left the mountain and anonymously called 911 to notify the police of Charles's condition. When the police arrived, they found no trace of a dead man and figured the call had been a hoax. What none of them knew was that Charles's body had been moved quickly by others who needed his death to go unnoticed. His demise was just one more secret that Harken Corporation had to keep.

The drive back from Albuquerque two weeks previous had been long and uneventful—no riding on trains or getting chased through cemeteries. Just a few stops and a few days of time spent with Sigi. By the end of it Ozzy no longer thought drive-thrus were magical.

Sigi had dropped Ozzy off at the train tracks and taken the car home to begin the long process of explaining to her mother.

Ozzy had considered going right to the authorities, but part of him wanted to be left alone for a while longer. He'd been relieved to find that the cloaked house had not been touched in his absence. Nobody had found it and not a thing had been toyed with. One of the stops he and Sigi had made on the way home had been to a Best Buy, where he bought a CD player, a couple of CDs, and another portable solar charger.

The first night home, Ozzy had walked around investigating every box and listening to Ben Folds Five.

I see that there is evil
And I know that there is good.
And the in-betweens I've never understood.

He loved being home, but he knew things were different now. He knew his life couldn't stay the way it always had. So after a couple of days alone, he had hiked to Sigi's house in hopes of working out his future.

Remaining hidden was no longer an option.

Ozzy met with Sigi and her mom. Together, they talked to the sheriff, who needed answers, so Ozzy filled him in on his life story. The sheriff was moved, but still wanted to know what had happened with Rin.

"Magic" was the only explanation Ozzy could offer.

Sheriff Wills eventually gave up that line of questioning. And since the only crime committed in his jurisdiction was Rin taking the cops on a high-speed chase, there was nothing he could do. Knowing he was beat, he backed down and even helped Ozzy find a lawyer to help him sort out what would come next.

With the court's help, it was resolved that the cloaked house and the land that surrounded it were legally Ozzy's. Contracts were being drawn up to make sure everything was proper and that it would all be his unconditionally when he turned eighteen. The only current stipulation was that Ozzy couldn't continue to live alone in the woods any longer.

"So this is it," Clark said as he looked out at the forest that surrounded the cloaked house. "We're doing this?"

It had been surprisingly easy to put Clark back together. His head had to be popped on and his wing patched up. But in the end, with a strong dose of sun, the bird had been raised from the dead so he could continue to pester Ozzy on a daily basis. Ozzy's relief at having him back was immeasurable.

"Yes," Ozzy answered.

"You're sure?"

"Positive."

"We could hide somewhere else until you turn eighteen. Then we could go wherever we want and do whatever we wish. You know—change the world."

Ozzy laughed.

"I don't want to wait. I'm going to start changing things today."

Clark hopped on Ozzy's head.

"Okay, but can we make sure those changes include a lot of metal staplers and finches?"

They stepped off the porch and walked away from the cloaked house and into the forest.

"You know we'll come back all the time," Ozzy said. "This still belongs to us. And you can fly here whenever you want."

"I guess."

Clark jumped down onto Ozzy's right shoulder and kept quiet.

So much had happened in the last little while. They both wanted it to mean something. Ozzy still experienced some painful thoughts, especially at night when darkness settled in and his mind would replay the incident on the mountain in his head. When this happened, his left hand would buzz, reminding him of the feeling he'd had seconds before he had tackled Charles. His brain had felt so strong at that moment, powerful. It would have been helpful to have his parents around to explain what had happened, but they were gone. The road trip had provided him with some answers, but it had also forced him to accept certain realities—his parents were not coming back. He missed them, but the deep darkness he used to feel was much shallower and easier to wade through now.

"Do you think you'll ever figure out what your ability is?" Clark asked as he scratched Ozzy's shoulder with his talons.

"I don't know." Ozzy stared at his birthmark. "I'm pretty sure my parents gave me something bigger than just this home and land. Now I need to find out what."

"You'd think hanging out with a wizard would have helped you discover it."

"You'd think."

"Rin used to say that we are all an extension of each other, that your experience is mine, just on a different frequency. If that's true, then we're all part wizard and part bird," Clark said. "What's a wizard bird called anyway? I bet it starts with a W. Warird? Wirdlock?"

"How about *bizard*?" Ozzy suggested.

"That does sound good," the bird chirped. "Of course, I wish Rin was here. He'd know the answer, or make something up, at least."

"I wish that too."

"Yeah. Instead he's in Quarfelt doing all kinds of amazing things."

Ozzy breathed in and out slowly as he walked.

"I never got to thank him—or even pay him, for that matter. All that magic for the price of some meals and gas money."

"Well, I'm glad to see you're still talking to yourself," a third voice said.

Ozzy stopped.

Standing directly in front of both the bird and boy was Sigi. She'd hiked halfway to meet him in the middle of the trees. Sigi's long, dark, curly hair was pulled back into a ponytail and her deep eyes were brighter than the shadows of the trees could hide. She was wearing a green tank top and white shorts.

"You didn't have to hike in," Ozzy said kindly.

"I wanted to make sure you weren't chickening out."

"No way. I think it's you and your mom that should be chickening out."

"It's a big house," Sigi said. "What's one more person living there?"

"One more person *and a bird*," Clark said, offended.

"Of course."

Ozzy stepped up to Sigi and they both continued walking towards Mule Pole Highway.

"So how are you?" Ozzy asked her.

"Meh." She shrugged. "Everything's kind of boring since our trip."

"Yeah, your dad knows how to make things interesting."

"It's weird," she said. "Over the last ten years I barely saw him, so I barely missed him. But now I just wish he would come home."

"Me too," Clark chirped.

"He'll be back," Ozzy said. "I have no doubt about that."

"Can you promise?"

"No, but I can predict."

"Fair enough," she said.

"I prefer 'More than fair.'"

Ozzy and the wizard's daughter walked quickly through the woods. The sun trickled in through the leaves above while squirrels and foxes dashed about. A soft breeze drifted around them as the sound of a distant train was heard.

Sigi held out her hand and Ozzy took it.

Clark chirped happily and all things pointed clearly to the fact that life, with its heartaches and complications, could never hide the fact that magic was very much alive.

DISCUSSION QUESTIONS

1. Have you ever had a friend like Clark? Who was it, and how did he or she show you devotion?
2. Do you think you would like living by yourself as long as Ozzy did? What would be the scariest thing about that?
3. Have you ever seen something like Rin's ad? What was it? Did you want to answer it?
4. Have you ever been served food like Rin's sister, Ann, served Ozzy? What did you do to get out of eating it?
5. Clark is quite remarkable. Do you ever wonder how things are made? Name something you've taken apart to figure out how it works. Were you able to get it back together afterward?
6. Have you ever listened to a cassette tape? What was on it?
7. What makes you different from everyone else? Why do you think diversity is good?
8. If you had a box full of money, what is the first thing you would buy and why?

9. Ozzy was devastated when the cloaked house was invaded. Has anything of yours ever been messed with or taken? How did you feel?
10. Rin says, "Ordinary things . . . might actually be magic. . . . There is magic in the force of gravity [just as there is] magic in the mail system." Name something ordinary that might actually feel magical to someone else.
11. Do you believe people are good until they prove otherwise, or do you doubt their intentions immediately? Why do you feel that way?
12. Ozzy's parents were working on some amazing things. Do you wish free will wasn't so hard at times? What decisions do you wish were made (or not made) for you?
13. If you could open your own fast food drive-thru, what kind of food would you serve?
14. Which breakfast food best describes you? (1) Eggs and tortillas and green chiles; (2) Biscuits and sausage gravy; or (3) Barbecue pork omelet (an "Eggy Oinker")? Why?
15. When Ozzy, Clark, and Sigi are driving with Rin to Albuquerque, Rin starts playing a driving game called "A wizard speaks." If you were playing that game, how would you fill in the blank? A wizard speaks and _____?
16. Do you believe that Rin is truly a wizard? Why? And if not, why not?

ACKNOWLEDGMENTS

This book was brought to life with the help of some talented and magical people. First, to Chris Schoebinger: I can't say enough. Chris has stood over this cauldron of words and story and conjured up the best of me: Thank you! To Derk Koldewyn, who has edited this with all the right incantations and punctuation: *Gracias!* To Richard Erickson, who is a wizard of design and has been a friend since my very first book: *Danke!* To Dave Brown, Jill Schaugaard, Rachael Ward, Ilise Levine, Heidi Taylor, and the entire Shadow Mountain team; you have each touched this story and made it glow. All of you seem way more talented than mere mortals: *Merci!* To John Rose, whose taste in music is second only to his spellbinding way of putting books in hands: *Takk!* To my agent, Laurie, who constantly brandishes her wand on my behalf: *Grazie!* And to Brandon Dorman, who created an amazing cover that is so good there must have been a powerful spell involved: *Samp!* (Which is *thanks* in Quarfelt.)

Because there is magic in everyday life, there are a couple

everyday people I must thank. Dan Gardiner: thanks for the long list of things you've done for me. Dad: thanks for the even longer list of things you've done for me. And Krista: thanks for always giving me lists of things to do. You make the task worthwhile.

Samp you. *Samp* you all!